'I must hide.' J[...] **large wardrob**[...] **stopped.**

She glanced back and forth between Jasper and the door.

'If Philip catches me in here he might force us to wed.'

Jasper stopped tucking in his shirt. She didn't know her brother very well if she thought he would force her into marriage, even after finding her in a compromising situation, but he couldn't take the chance.

He strode up to her, pulled the shirt over his head and flung it away. 'I think not.'

He took her by the arm and pulled her against him. She let out a startled squeak as she hit his chest.

'What are you doing?' Her fingertips pressed into his flesh, jarring him as much as her.

'Jane, open this door at once,' her brother demanded, and the brass knob began to turn.

'Making sure he sees me as an unsuitable suitor.' He pressed his lips to hers as the door swung open.

Author Note

When I wrote *A Debt Paid in Marriage* I had a lot of fun creating Jane. In many ways she is as serious and severe as her brother, Philip Rathbone, but with a naive confidence and a rebellious streak. They are wonderful characteristics that both help her and, at other times, create a number of difficulties. I enjoyed exploring how her old friend—and new husband— Jasper allows her to develop and overcome both these aspects of her personality.

Jane was a familiar character to me, but Jasper was a new surprise. This is the first friends-to-lovers marriage of convenience story that I have written. It was a treat to create Jasper and Jane's close childhood friendship, to explore the pain and troubles of their eight-year separation and how, despite the passing of time, they still remain close. Jasper sees Jane in a way she cannot view herself, and she does the same for him. Through their relationship they both get a second chance—not only at love but at life. I hope you enjoy this return to the characters from *A Debt Paid in Marriage*, and if you are new to the Rathbone family I hope you enjoy this story and get a chance to read where it all began.

THE SECRET MARRIAGE PACT

Georgie Lee

Published in Great Britain 2017
by Mills & Boon, an imprint of HarperCollins*Publishers*
1 London Bridge Street, London, SE1 9GF

© 2017 Georgie Reinstein

ISBN: 978-0-263-92576-0

Our policy is to use papers that are natural, renewable and
recyclable products and made from wood grown in sustainable
forests. The logging and manufacturing processes conform to the
legal environmental regulations of the country of origin.

Printed and bound in Spain
by CPI, Barcelona

A lifelong history buff, **Georgie Lee** hasn't given up hope that she will one day inherit a title and a manor house. Until then she fulfils her dreams of lords, ladies and a Season in London through her stories. When not writing, she can be found reading non-fiction history or watching any film with a costume and an accent. Please visit georgie-lee.com to learn more about Georgie and her books.

Books by Georgie Lee

Mills & Boon Historical Romance

The Business of Marriage

A Debt Paid in Marriage
A Too Convenient Marriage
The Secret Marriage Pact

The Governess Tales

The Cinderella Governess

Scandal and Disgrace

Rescued from Ruin
Miss Marianne's Disgrace

Stand-Alone Novels

Engagement of Convenience
The Courtesan's Book of Secrets
The Captain's Frozen Dream

Visit the Author Profile page at millsandboon.co.uk.

For Nicola Caws
in thanks for valuable guidance
and insight into my stories.

Chapter One

London—1825

The rat! What's he doing here? Jane Rathbone balled her hands into tight fists at her sides. She stared across the auction house at her one-time fiancé, Milton Charton. Camille, his plain and meek wife, was nowhere to be seen.

'The bidding for the Fleet Street building, a former tobacconist's shop and residence, will now commence,' the auctioneer announced. 'Do I have an opening bid?'

Milton raised his hand.

Revenge curled inside Jane. If he wanted the building, she'd make sure he didn't get it. She flung her hand in the air, upping the price and drawing the entire room's attention, including Milton's. The businessmen narrowed their eyes at her in disapproval, but Milton's eyes opened wide before his gaze shifted, she hoped guiltily, back to the auctioneer.

'What are you doing?' Justin Connor whispered from beside her, more amused than censorious. He was here with Jane's brother, Philip Rathbone, who intended to obtain a warehouse near the Thames. Jane had accompanied them because she'd had nothing better to do.

'I'm bidding on a building,' she answered as if she were purchasing a new bonnet. Thankfully, Philip had gone off to speak with an associate, preventing him from interfering with her spontaneous plan. Since she'd reached her majority last year, he no longer controlled her inheritance but it didn't mean he couldn't interfere in her management of it. With him occupied, she could spend her money how she pleased and she pleased to spend it on a building.

'I assume your sudden interest in acquiring property has nothing to do with Milton Charton,' Justin observed with a wry smile.

'It has everything to do with him.' She didn't care if she was buying a house of ill repute or what Philip thought about her little venture when he finally returned. Milton would not win the auction.

'Then by all means, don't let me stop you.' Justin waved toward the wiry man with the pince-nez perched on his nose who called for a higher price. Across the room, Milton raised his hand again and Jane was quick to follow, driving up the bid and making her old beau purse his lips in frustration. She'd once found the gesture endearing. It disgusted her today.

Milton's hand went up again and Jane responded in kind, pretending to be oblivious to the disapproving looks of the other male bidders. She ignored them, as she did their sons when they sneered at her bold opinions, or when their wives and daughters had whispered about her after Milton's surprise marriage to Camille Moseley.

The auctioneer continued to call for bids until the other interested parties dropped off, leaving only her and Milton. Except this time Milton hesitated before he raised his hand.

I almost have him. Jane suppressed a smile of triumph as she raised her hand without hesitation. Milton didn't have the means to compete with her, or his father's astute investment sense. Thanks to her inheritance, she possessed the money, and with her business acumen she'd find a way to profit from the building. It was a pity people were against the idea of a single young lady doing it. If they weren't, she might become a force to be reckoned with in the Fleet like her brother. As it was, she was simply a spinster aunt. Oh, how she despised Milton.

Jane raised the bid three more times as Milton became less sure about the price he was willing to pay to acquire it until he finally failed to counter her.

'Going once,' the auctioneer called.

Milton tugged at his limp cravat and shifted in his cheap boots, but he didn't answer.

I've won.

'Going twice.'

Milton frowned at her, but she held her head up high in triumph. He deserved to be embarrassed in front of his associates just as he'd humiliated her in front of all their friends.

'Sold, to Miss Rathbone.' The gavel came down, sending a shockwave of critical rumbles through the gentleman before they turned their attention to the next item on the block. They respected Philip too much to say anything openly to her, but it wouldn't stop them from thinking her odd. She no longer cared. With no husband or house of her own, the building would give her some much-needed purpose and a future.

Justin tipped his hat to her. 'Congratulations on your victory. Shall we go and collect your prize?' He motioned to the payment table. They would have to pass Milton to reach it.

'Yes, let's.'

She allowed her brother's old friend to escort her across the room, not only to rub Milton's nose in her victory, but to secure the property before Philip returned. She didn't want him to find a way to stop the purchase from going through. He wouldn't approve of an expenditure based solely on revenge. He preferred rationally motivated investments. So did Jane, except for today.

She fixed on Milton as she approached him, daring him to meet her gaze, and he didn't answer it until she was nearly on top of him. Better sense advised her to continue past him, but she wanted to dig the knife in a little deeper.

'Thank you for the rousing bidding war, Mr Charton.' She was determined he experience some of the humiliation she'd endured when he'd all but left her at the altar two years ago. 'I hadn't intended to buy a former tobacconist's shop today, but I'm quite delighted now I have it and you don't.'

Milton's dough-faced shock changed to one of gloating she wanted to smack from his full cheeks. 'The building wasn't for me. It was for Jasper.'

'Jasper?' Her heart began to race with an elation she hadn't experienced in years. 'But he's in America.'

He'd left, like so many other people in her life. He wasn't supposed to return.

'Not any more.'

'Did we get it?' The voice from her childhood drifted over her shoulder, bringing with it memories she'd long forgotten. She was gripped by the thrill of running with Jasper through the Fleet when they were children, of turning pennies into pounds with their schemes and eavesdropping on his older sisters at parties. With the memories came the hope in every wish she'd made for him to come back or to send her word he'd changed his mind about their future together. The letter had never come.

Jane fingered the beading on her reticule, ready to walk away instead of facing Jasper and having her cherished memories of him ruined the way Milton had crushed his. A long time ago, the three of them had been so close. Heaven knew what Jasper must think of her now, especially if Milton had been filling his ears with stories. She didn't want to see the same oily regard in Milton's eyes echoed in Jasper's.

No, Jasper is nothing like Milton, she tried to tell herself before the old fears blotted out her reason. *Then why did he never write to me? Because I scared him off the way I've scared off every other man since.*

Stop it, she commanded herself. She wouldn't allow either the Charton brothers or her own awkwardness to get the better of her; she would be sensible, as always. *It was only a childish infatuation anyway.*

Jane took a deep breath and turned, determined to face her past, all of it, except it wasn't the past smiling down at her, but the present. The lanky fifteen-year-old she'd parted from nine years ago was a man, and taller and sturdier than his brother Milton, who was one year older. During the time he'd spent in America learning the cotton trade from his uncle, his jaw had widened, carving out the angles of his cheeks and filling in the awkward gangliness she used to tease him about. He'd grown so tall she had to step back to see his face and the light brown hair mixed with blonde streaks. He wore a well-tailored coat of fine, dark wool with subtle black-velvet accents on the collar and cuffs. It was offset by the deep blue waistcoat hugging his trim middle. Savannah had added elegance to his masculine frame.

'Mr Charton, welcome home. I never thought you'd return.' She struggled to hold her voice steady despite the excitement making her want to bounce on her feet.

'Neither did I.' He took off his fine beaver hat to bow to her, revealing the slight wave of his hair across his forehead and the genuine delight illuminating his hazel eyes. Whatever Milton had told him, it hadn't poisoned Jasper against her. 'It's wonderful to see you. I've been looking forward to it. I didn't expect it to be here.'

He wanted to see me again. It was a far cry from the boy who'd told her not to wait for him after she'd finally summoned up the nerve to admit she craved more than friendship. She flicked a bead on her reticule before she eased her tight grip on the silk. Despite the awkwardness of their last meeting, he was here, as inviting as when he used to fetch her for another adventure. *Perhaps I did mean something to him.*

She moved to speak when Milton's bitter words interrupted them like clattering cutlery at a party.

'She bought the building.'

Jane struggled to hold her smile while Jasper's tightened about the edges. It sucked the thrill out of Jane's triumph and their unexpected reunion. She flicked the bead so hard it cracked, cursing Milton and her misguided impetuousness. It was Milton she'd wanted to hurt, not Jasper.

'Congratulations on your acquisition,' Jasper graciously conceded. 'You've always had your brother's talent for transactions. I'm sure you'll put the building to good use.'

'I'm sure I will.' She buttressed her confidence against the shame undermining her as powerfully now as the morning Mr and Mrs Charton had told her of Milton's elopement and apologised for their eldest son's behaviour. 'If you'll excuse me, I must settle my account.'

'Of course.' Jasper tipped his hat to her and stepped aside. 'I look forward to seeing you again, Jane.'

Her name on his lips sounded as natural as rain on a roof. She raised her eyes to his, catching the old mischief brightening the dark irises. It brought an impish smile to her lips. *This* was the Jasper she'd cherished, and he blotted out all memory of the one who'd forgotten her after he'd sailed away.

'I look forward to seeing you again too, Jasper.' When she did, it wouldn't involve scampering in the Rathbone garden, but she was sure, and she couldn't say why, it would be fun.

The heady scent of Jane's gardenia perfume continued to surround Jasper as she walked away with Mr Connor. Jasper had expected a great many things today, but seeing Jane hadn't been one of them. It was almost worth losing the building to hear her speak, the faint lisp she'd had as a child gone, her voice a tone closer to smooth velvet. Her posture had changed too, the stiffness of her movements having gained a more graceful and fluid charm. He'd caught the spark of pride lifting her chin when he'd complimented her on her business sense. In the brief exchange, it was as if nine years hadn't passed, but it had, turning her from a young lady into a woman who commanded his attention even from across the room.

'You lost the building to that arrogant chit because you weren't here,' Milton spat.

Jasper's elation snapped like dry hay. 'I was held up.' He'd slept later than intended, exhausted from another long night and the effort of maintaining the façade necessary to hide his nocturnal activities from his family. 'And watch how you speak of her. You were the one who betrayed her like a coward. No wonder she bid against you.'

'You always did side with her against me.' Milton curled his lip in irritation, not having the decency to be ashamed of what he'd done.

Jasper frowned. It wasn't only Jane who'd changed while he'd been gone. He'd looked forward to his reunion with Milton when he'd disembarked at Portsmouth, eager to unburden himself of the anguish and torment he'd experienced in Savannah during the yellow fever epidemic, but Milton wasn't fit to be a confidant. If he told his brother the truth about Savannah, and London, Milton would use it against him when it served his purposes, or simply out of spite. He wouldn't keep Jasper's secrets the way he had when they were young, the shared knowledge binding them together as much as the closeness of their ages. Jasper didn't know what he'd done to earn his elder brother's dislike and he barely recognised the one person he'd been closest to as a child, with the exception of Jane.

He spied her across the room where she bent over the payment table to sign the purchase register. He couldn't see her face, only the elegant curve of her hand on the pen and the fall of her red cotton dress over the roundness of her buttocks. For a moment he regretted never having written to her while he was away. He could have used her friendship, especially after Uncle Patrick had accused Jasper of driving him to his deathbed while Yellow Jack had stormed through Savannah.

Jasper studied the flimsy printed auction list, shoving the guilt aside as he searched for another available property to fit his needs. There was nothing. *Damn*. The building Milton had lost was perfectly situated on Fleet Street and would have been Jasper's best chance for creating a more respectable establishment than his current one.

'If she were a proper lady she wouldn't even

be here.' Milton flicked a piece of fluff off the arm of his poorly tailored wool coat. 'And if she'd acted more like a proper lady I might have married her.'

Jasper crushed the thin catalogue between his hands, wanting to thrash his brother with it. 'You're a fool, Milton, and growing older has only made it worse.'

'What's it done for you except bring you back with some tat you've been fortunate enough to sell despite the smell of plague clinging to it?'

Jasper stepped toe to toe with his brother. 'Shut your mouth before I knock your teeth out.'

Milton's smugness drooped like his backbone. Jasper threw the catalogue at his feet and strode off, done with him and the auction. His day and all his plans lay in tatters because of his brother and Jasper's own stupid mistakes.

He strode to the wide entrance door where men continued to stream in and out to examine the auction items. He paused on the threshold to take in the street, the stench of dust and filth making him cough. An open-topped caleche passed by filled with ladies smiling and laughing together, their lives like everyone else's carrying on in the bright sunlight illuminating the street. He should be glad for the activity after the deathly silence of Savannah and heartened to see not every world had collapsed, but after so much death it was difficult to do. Few here understood what he'd been through. Milton certainly didn't.

How dare he sneer at the epidemic. The pampered prat didn't know what it was like to be stalked by death, to have all his money mean nothing because no amount of it could buy food to stave off the gnawing hunger or save those you loved from being carried off. No one around him did, except those unlucky enough to have witnessed it in other places, or those poor souls confined to the deepest slums of St Giles and Seven Dials.

A dark mood threatened to consume him when a flash of red caught his eye. The Rathbone landau rolled past the auction house, the hood open to take advantage of the fine day. Jane sat across from her brother, her profile sharp as she spoke with him, hands moving with her agitation. The dark brown curls beneath the red ribbon that held the bonnet in place bounced in time to the carriage's pace. It mesmerised him as much as her full lips.

She didn't notice Jasper, but he couldn't pull his attention away from her. Seeing her again had been like stepping though the door of his parents' house after nine years in America and inhaling the familiar scent of cinnamon and brandy, the smell of his childhood.

He watched her until the vehicle rolled down the street and was finally lost in the crush of traffic. Isolation swathed him when she vanished from sight. Gone was the young girl who used to scamper with him and Milton, her surety in herself and her ideas eternally exasperating her brother and Jasper's parents. Gone, too, was the boy Jasper had been. An ocean of experience and deception separated him from everyone he'd ever known. Yet in his brief moment with Jane, he'd touched something of the innocent young man he'd once been. He wondered, if he sat with her a while, could he be carefree and blameless again? It wasn't possible. He couldn't weigh her down with the awfulness of his past or his present deceits.

He started down the auction-house steps and made for the jeweller across the street, ready to pay a pound or two for a fine walking stick or something equally expensive. His soul might be in the gutter. It didn't mean the rest of him needed to wallow there too. He'd escaped death. Now he'd make sure he enjoyed life again.

'Mrs Townsend and I trained you to handle your affairs better than this, Jane.' Philip chided from across the landau before he turned to Justin. 'You should've stopped her.'

'She's not my sister.' Justin threw up his hands in protest. 'Besides, she'd old enough to decide what to do with her money.'

'On that point, we disagree.'

'He's right. It's my inheritance and I'll spend it as I see fit,' Jane insisted.

Philip didn't answer, refusing to be baited into the fight Jane was aching for. Despite gaining control over her money there'd been little she'd been able to do with it except pay the milliner's bill. Seeing Jasper today had reminded her of the few clever transactions she and the Charton boys had hustled as children. The experiences had given her a taste for commerce, but as her dresses had become longer her world had reduced in size until it nearly choked her. Jasper's world had expanded and, judging by his fine clothes, he'd done well for himself in America. It made her wonder why he'd decided to return. 'You knew Jasper Charton was home, didn't you?'

Philip's jaw tightened, almost imperceptibly, but she caught it. It was one of his few tells. To her surprise, he didn't deny her accusation. 'Yes.'

'Why didn't you or the Chartons tell me?' It wasn't like the Chartons not to fête a family member, especially one who'd been gone for so long and endured so much.

'Mr Charton asked me not to. Jasper had a difficult time in Savannah and needed a chance to recover. He was very ill when he came home.'

'I'm sure he was.' Mrs Charton had shared news of the yellow fever which had ravaged the port city. Jane had worried along with her over Jasper, as eager as his mother was for the letter telling them things were all right. She might not have heard from Jasper for nine years, but it didn't mean she'd stopped caring about him. Waiting with Mrs Charton had felt too much like when she was six and her own mother had been stricken with the fever. The long days had passed as she'd prayed, hoped and bargained with the Almighty to make her mother better.

He hadn't listened and her mother had passed, and it'd been all her fault. 'Why did Jasper come back?'

'His cotton-trading business collapsed after the epidemic. He plans to use the money his uncle left him, and the capital he raised from the sale of his Savannah properties and goods, to establish a new business in London. Jasper needs the Fleet Street building you purchased and the opportunity it offers. Since you don't, we'll visit the Chartons tomorrow and you'll offer to sell it to him.'

'I'll do no such thing. I'll start my own endeavour with it.'

Philip flexed his fingers over the handle of his walking stick. 'Be sensible, Jane.'

'I am being sensible. I need something more to do than tend the rose garden and listen to my niece and nephews tear through the house.'

'And I've given you ample opportunities to do so.'

'Yes, always behind you and your reputation, never out in the open where everyone can see it's me successfully managing things.'

'As well as the merchants of the Fleet regard our family, they won't countenance a single young woman in trade. It would damage both your reputation and mine and hinder all our future dealings.'

She twisted her reticule between her hands, the deed to the building crinkling inside, before she let go. Philip was right. Customers and other merchants would recoil from her if she began openly to oversee some venture of her own. Jane dropped back against the squabs, cursing her unmarried state once again. 'I hate it when you're practical.'

'It's nothing but a headache when you aren't.'

The landau carried them past the building she now owned in the middle of Fleet Street. The staid façade with its small Ionic columns reaching up to the first floor sat squat between two taller ones. A round outline of dirt above the front door indicated where the sign from the now-defunct tobacconist's used to hang. She rested her arm on the landau's edge and tapped the wood. The building was hers and, despite what Philip said, she would not relinquish it; she would use it to make something of her life and escape from this limbo of being an adult while being treated like a mindless child. She needed activity, industry of her own, or she would run mad. Now she needed to decide what she'd do, and how she'd do it, without drawing attention to herself or needing Philip's help. Her brother might have her best interests at heart, but it didn't mean she wanted him or anyone else deciding her path.

She glanced across the landau at Justin who chatted with Philip. Perhaps he could be her secret front. He might help her, if only because he thought it a lark, but with his wine business and the demands of his wife and family, she doubted he had time to dabble in any endeavour of hers.

There must be some man willing to be the front for a business. She continued to trill her fingers on the trim, mulling through the people she knew and not finding one likely to support her admittedly odd idea. No one had ever gone along with her schemes except at one time Milton, and Jasper.

Jasper.

Jane stilled her fingers. She could become a silent partner with him in whatever plans he had for the building. It would be a perfect arrangement—except for her having to hide her involvement from everyone, including Philip. However, being a silent partner was better than nothing at all, and she would only have to be silent in public.

Unless I can find a husband, and quickly.

She rolled her eyes at her own ridiculousness, wondering if she was going mad from boredom and how long it would be until she began collecting small dogs and refusing to leave the house. If landing a gentleman was as simple as selecting a stock, she'd be a wife by now. Besides, all her friends and acquaintances had taken every man worth having in the Fleet, except for Jasper.

'Philip, did Jasper return with a wife?' Jane asked, interrupting his and Justin's conversation.

'No. Why?'

She shrugged. 'I was curious.'

Philip narrowed his eyes in scrutiny before Justin drew him back into conversation.

So Jasper isn't married. She rested her elbow on the landau's edge again and tapped her fingers against her chin. The vehicle vibrated beneath her arm as it crossed over the cobblestones. *And he needs money and a building, and I have both. I wonder if he'd like a wife in the bargain, too.*

She and Jasper had been friends once and

friendship was an excellent basis for a marriage. After all, she'd tried affection with Milton and look where it had landed her. There was no reason not to try something more practical with Jasper. He might have rebuffed her advances nine years ago, but this wasn't about romance. It was business. She could present her proposal in rational terms, appeal to his good sense and make him see how perfectly logical, reasonable and completely insane the idea was.

She dropped her forehead into her palm. *I should buy a dog and be done with all pretence to sanity.*

Even if she was foolhardy enough to approach Jasper with such an outlandish plan, he wasn't likely to go along with it this time any more than he had before. Nor was she thrilled by the prospect of leaving Philip's influence to surrender her fortune and all legal responsibility to a husband. However, she doubted Jasper would be difficult about it, especially if they came to an agreement beforehand on how she'd manage her affairs. She was certain they could, assuming their discussions even reached the negotiating stage and he didn't turn her down outright. He probably would and she didn't rel-

ish another Charton rejection. Two was quite
enough.

The landau turned off noisy Fleet Street and
on to quiet St Bride's Lane. The steeple from
St Bride's Church cast a thick shadow over
the houses facing it. Behind the high wall encircling the churchyard lay the graves of her
parents. Failure whipped around her like the
breeze. She'd failed her parents years ago, now
she was failing them, and herself, again.

I won't be a spinster.

Another rejection wasn't an appealing prospect, but neither was the future stretching out
in front of her like a dusty dirt road. With each
passing year her prospects for making her own
life were diminishing. Yes, Jasper might ridicule her for proposing this scheme, but if he
accepted…

She sat up straight and tried not to shift in
the seat. She'd have her freedom and a life,
home and business of her own at last. It might
not be the loving marriage like the one Philip
and Laura enjoyed, or the grand passion she
used to dream about while reading the scandalous books Mrs Townsend, her sister-in-
law's mother and Jane's old mentor, tutor and
confidant, used to slip her, but one could never

be disappointed by something one had never expected. Besides, she didn't need Jasper's heart, only his hand in marriage.

Chapter Two

'You're undressed! Why are you not up already? It's past noon!' Jane waved her hand from the top of Jasper's head to the rippled and exposed stomach, and the dark line of hair leading her gaze even lower. She was already out of breath from running up the Chartons' massive front stairs, but catching Jasper in his bedroom without his shirt was suffocating. His toned chest tinged with a honey hint of a tan nearly knocked her away from the closed door. She'd known Jasper Charton and his family her entire life. But she never thought she'd see quite this much of him.

'I wasn't expecting company.' Jasper wiped the last of the very musky and, if she was not mistaken by the scent, expensive shaving soap from his face and haphazardly hung the towel on the washstand bar. He made no move to take up the rumpled shirt sagging over the foot of the bed, and perched one fist on his hip as though it was every day an unmarried young lady burst into his bedroom unannounced. 'What are you doing up here?'

'We must speak about the building.' She fiddled with the key in the lock of the door but her shaking hand wouldn't co-operate and she gave up.

Concentrate! This was no time to be distracted. With her brother and Mr Charton downstairs, and Mrs Charton distracted by one of her grandchildren, Jane had precious little time alone with Jasper. 'I have a plan for it, but I need your help, as a friend. We're still friends, aren't we?'

His eyebrows rose in surprise. 'Even after what Milton did to you?'

'You had nothing to do with it, and he isn't pertinent to the matter I wish to discuss today.' Actually, proving to everyone, including herself, she could catch a husband was very much a part of this, but he didn't need to know it.

He cocked one eyebrow. 'You want to talk business, in my room, alone?'

She picked up one of the pair of diamond

cufflinks in the dish on the table beside her, then put it down. It did seem foolish when he pointed it out, but speaking here was better than trying to whisper downstairs and risking someone overhearing their negotiations. For this to work, everyone, including Philip, must believe they were marrying for the right reason. 'Of course. We have privacy.'

'Which makes me wonder if business is really all you want?' With a wicked smile he slipped the top button of his fall through its hole. He was teasing her as he used to do and the easy familiarity of their old friendship slid between them. It was more potent than the pulling of her pigtails and she adjusted the top of her spencer, breathless once more as she stared at his long fingers on the button, waiting to see what he might reveal. Offering him her innocence wasn't an unpleasant bargaining chip, especially since she was dying to finally experience the deed she'd heard Jasper's sister whispering about at so many parties. If she got with child it would certainly force the matter.

When the fall slightly opened she snapped out of her stupor. This wasn't how this was supposed to go. He wasn't supposed to undress or suggest more than business, even if what she was about to propose involved exactly that. 'Yes! Well, sort of.'

'Sort of?' He let go of the button, but failed to fasten the one he'd already undone. It revealed more of the dark hair leading from his navel to places unknown.

'I have a building and you need one for your new enterprise. We can become…partners in your endeavour.'

The word 'marriage' twisted her tongue. She still couldn't believe she was doing this. One would think she'd learned her lesson nine years ago. Apparently, she hadn't.

'Your brother won't be happy about you wading so openly into business. Or being up here.'

'I don't care what Philip thinks and I wouldn't be single when I share in the trade.' Jane took a deep breath, the portion of the negotiation she'd spent the better part of the night and this morning contemplating, and dreading at last upon her. 'I would be your wife.'

Jasper's smug amusement dropped like the towel off the rail of his washstand. 'My wife?'

'It's perfect, don't you see?' She hurried up to him, drawing close enough to feel the heat radiating off his skin. She took a cautious step back, acutely aware of how much taller and wider he'd grown since he'd left. She tried not to be distracted by the more intimate terms of marriage, but with the sunlight caressing the angles and sinew of his shoulders it was difficult. 'You want the building and I want my freedom. There's only one way for us to get both. We'll get married.'

'Married?'

'We'll work together to build up your whatever-it-is.'

'A club for merchants.'

'Excellent.' She had no idea what that meant, but they could discuss the details later. 'You've been gone from London for so long, you lack connections. My connections through Philip, combined with my keen managerial sense, the property I purchased—the one you wanted—along with your particular expertise in this kind of venture will make us quite a force. And you know how good I am with negotiation.'

He smothered a laugh. 'Yes, I remember.'

But he wasn't rushing to agree. The same tightness in the pit of her stomach as when she was thirteen and begging him to offer her some promise of a future together knotted her insides again. Anger began to creep along the edges of her confidence. 'You remember what good friends we were, though you never troubled to write me a single letter the entire time you were in Savannah. Do you know how much I could've used your friendship, even from across the ocean?' She winced at this slip. What in Heaven's name was she thinking saying such a thing?

'I do.' Regret flickered in his eyes and he raised his hand as if to graze her cheek, the ruby on his small finger glinting in the sun before he lowered it again. 'But marriage is different from children scampering through the Fleet in search of a shilling or eavesdropping on the adults.'

'You sound like my brother.' She crossed her arms in front of her. 'And I'm perfectly aware of the seriousness of a union, which is why I think one based on friendship is the best kind. Don't you agree?'

'No.' He didn't even hesitate in his answer. 'As much as I respect and admire you…'

'Don't.' She held up one hand, humiliation clipping her words. 'That's the drivel your brother tried to placate me with when he returned from Scotland with his simpering wife. I expect better from you, Jasper.'

'All right, you'll have it.' He dropped the lothario act and spoke to her as he had when he'd told her there could be nothing between them once he left for Georgia. 'There are extenuating circumstances preventing me from marrying anyone, even an old and valuable friend.'

'You're already married?' It wouldn't surprise her. Everyone appeared capable of finding someone except her.

'No.'

Well, this was a small relief. 'Betrothed?'

'No.'

'Keeping a mistress?'

'Of course not. Where did you get such an idea?'

She tilted her head in pride. 'I'm not a complete innocent. I read novels and the newspapers.'

He stroked his smooth chin with one large hand. 'And yet you are, aren't you?'

'If we married, I wouldn't be, now would I?'

His eyes flashed the same way they had when she'd turned around to greet him yesterday. 'No, I don't suppose you would be.'

'It'd be quite an honour for you.' She lowered her head and peered up through her lashes at him, imitating the young ladies she usually scoffed at during parties. She felt like a fool doing it, but she was willing to try anything to persuade him, even the promise of something more carnal.

'That's one way to put it,' he choked out through a laugh.

'Then why are you objecting?' She dropped the dewy-eyed pose, having expected him to respond with something other than humour. She was losing him as much now as when he'd set sail and she couldn't. She was tired of being a failure and she wouldn't fail at this. 'You need me and you know it.'

'Yes. I always have.' A loss greater than their mere time together, one she'd experienced the day her mother had died, and in the many years since, filled his words. Whatever had happened in Savannah, it'd scarred him like her parents' passing had damaged her. He did need her the way she needed him and for more than just a club.

'Then why are you refusing me?' she asked in a softer tone. It made no sense.

Voices from downstairs filtered up through the floorboards. He should insist she return to her brother, but he hesitated. She was offering him the building, her help in establishing a legitimate venture, and something his fifteen-year-old self would have sold his soul to acquire. But a wife? He was struggling to keep everyone out of his affairs, not searching for ways to draw someone deeper into them. Except this was Jane. If anyone could help him make a go of his club it was her, but he couldn't ask her to share his secret and to deceive her family the way he was deceiving his. Nor could he risk her realising the terrible man he'd become in Savannah, not when she viewed him as an old friend still worthy of her affection.

The time ticked by on the ornate dolphin clock perched on the excessively gilded bedside table while he racked his brain for a delicate path out of this indelicate situation. He needed a reason why he was refusing her, one she wouldn't try to logic her way around or hate him for saying.

'Be honest with me, the way you used to be,' she demanded.

I can't be, with you or anyone. Nor could he wilfully hurt her. She'd taken a risk by approaching him and he admired her too much to treat her as poorly as his brother had. Despite his not having written to her while he was gone, she'd still believed in him and their mutual past enough to ask him for his future. If he told her even one of the real reasons behind his refusal, it would put her off him and this idea, and he wasn't ready to pull himself down in her eyes.

There was a more subtle and less hurtful way to make her abandon this notion of marriage.

He stepped closer, affecting the smile he used to employ with agitated gamblers in Savannah, smooth, charming and convincing. 'Because I'm not sure you could handle the level of honesty I'm prepared to offer you.'

'What do you mean?' She didn't step back and he inhaled her flowery scent. It was lighter and more alluring than the cloying mixture she'd fancied at thirteen, the one which used to remind him of her whenever he inhaled it on a passing woman in Georgia. He might not have written to her after he'd sailed away, but she'd never really been far from his thoughts.

'Your brother wouldn't approve of the match.'

'I'm past the age of needing his permission to marry.' She waved her hand in dismissal, her fingertips grazing his chest before she pulled them back. Her faint touch raked him like a pitchfork. She must have felt it, too, because she clasped one hand in the other and nervousness softened the crease of irritation between her eyes.

'You shouldn't approve of me either.' He pressed his palm against the wall behind her, all the while ignoring the curves indicating her maturity. He must convince her to forget him by giving her a reason to run from him, no matter how much he wanted to slip his arm around her waist and pull her closer. 'You see, I don't want to marry. I want to enter into a less formal arrangement.'

Her gaze slid along the firmness of his bicep beside her ear, then traced the line of it to his face. She frowned at him. 'You want me for a mistress?'

Jasper swallowed hard to keep from laughing. Jane was nothing if not blunt and practical. She always had been, as well as headstrong and impetuous. It was a delightful combination of traits he still enjoyed and hated to drive away. 'You could say that.'

He allowed the suggestion to linger between them as if it had been hers and not his. Jane's lips parted in uncertainty, her full breasts hugged by the fitted yellow spencer rising as she drew in a long breath. He pressed his fingertip tighter into the wall, glad he hadn't removed his breeches for fear he might embarrass himself as he imagined her agreeing to his idea. It'd be a disappointment to them both if she did. He'd done a lot of dishonourable things, but he would never ruin Jane by following through on his suggestion. However, the temptation in her blue eyes, the faint brush of her breath across his naked chest almost made him relent. He could lean down and claim her lips and at last learn what they tasted like, after considering it so many times when they'd both been young, curious, and for the first time aware of one another as more than friends. He moved his head a touch lower, wondering if the old curiosity, as opposed to a desire for a business, had really brought her here. Whatever her motives, it was time for her to leave before someone discovered she was up here.

'Jane, are you in there?' Mr Rathbone's voice carried in from the hallway.

Jasper's fingers stiffened against the wall. *Too late.*

'How did Philip figure out I was in here?' Jane ducked under his arm and began to pace in the centre of the room, revealing how much she did care about her brother's opinion.

Jasper picked up his shirt and tugged it on. 'The new maid must have seen you. The woman is a busybody.'

Jasper had been forced to slip past her to leave the house late at night numerous times. What she was doing up at those hours he'd never discovered, but he suspected it had something to do with his father's brandy and if he could he would soon see the woman dismissed.

'Jane. Are you in there?' Mr Rathbone punctuated his question by pounding on the door.

'I must hide.' Jane rushed to the large wardrobe in the corner, then stopped. She glanced back and forth between Jasper and the door, the plotting narrowing of her eyes both familiar, and terrifying. 'If Philip catches me in here, he might insist we wed.'

Jasper stopped tucking in his shirt. She didn't know her brother very well if she thought he'd force her into a marriage, even after finding her in a compromising situation, but he couldn't take the chance. He strode up to her, tugged the shirt over his head and flung it away. 'I think not.'

He took her by the arm and pulled her against him. She let out a startled squeak as she hit his chest.

'What are you doing?' Her fingertips pressed into his flesh, jarring him as much as her.

'Jane, open this door at once,' Mr Rathbone demanded, and the brass knob began to turn.

'Making sure he sees me as an unsuitable suitor.' He pressed his lips to hers as the door swung open.

Jane barely heard her brother's angry breaths or Justin Connor's howl of laughter from the hallway. Jasper's warm mouth on hers consumed her entire attention. It made her knees weak and she shivered as Jasper slid his tongue out to tease hers, his large hand against her back pressing her firmly into his bare chest. There could be an entire crowd watching them and she wouldn't notice, all she wanted was for him to lay her on the bed, slide up her skirts and satisfy the ache making her almost moan. He didn't so much as move a hand down to grasp her bottom, but broke from the kiss and leaned back. A shock as powerful as the one he'd sent hurtling through her coloured his own hazel eyes.

This was definitely not how she'd imagined this plan unfolding.

'What the devil were you doing?' Philip's voice was so even it made Jane cringe. He hadn't said a word to her during the entire carriage ride home. Not even Justin, who leaned against the French doors of Philip's office watching them as if they were a theatrical performance, had dared to break the icy chill. Philip hadn't spoken until they were settled in his office with Laura and all their past quarrels and disagreements beside him. Jane preferred the silence. It was less lethal.

'I was trying to reach an agreement with Jasper about the building.' She straightened the tortoiseshell comb in her hair, attempting to remain calm and level-headed, but with Jasper's sandalwood scent still clinging to her spencer it was difficult. 'He didn't agree to my terms.'

'It didn't look like it when we stumbled in on you,' Justin observed through a restrained laugh.

'Don't you have a wine shop to see to?'

'This is much more fascinating.'

'Justin, please.' Philip rubbed his temples with his fingers, addressing Jane once again. 'You decided to discuss the matter with Mr Charton alone, in his room, while he was undressed?'

'It wasn't my intention when I first went upstairs, at least not the portion where he was undressed.'

'You shouldn't have been up there at all.' Philip dug his fingers harder into his temples while Laura and Justin exchanged amused looks. Not so Philip. He dropped his hands to the blotter and pinned her with a seriousness to still her heart. 'You risked ruining your reputation and our relationship with the Chartons, and for what?'

My freedom, she wanted to cry, but she bit it back. He was right, again. With her ridiculous plan, she'd risked more than minor humiliation or the disapproving tsking of merchants and their wives. The Chartons were good enough friends to be discreet about the matter, but they weren't a family renowned for keeping secrets. There were too many of them. It would only be a matter of time before someone heard of this and it would end whatever slim chance remained of her some day finding a husband.

'Ever since Mrs Townsend married Dr Hale, you've been stubborn and wilful,' Philip stated.

'She hasn't been so bad since my mother left,' Laura said, trying to soothe him. Given Laura and Philip's past, and the way she'd snared Philip by surprising him in his bath with a pistol when she and her mother had been on the verge of ruin nine years ago, she was the last to pass judgement on Jane's behaviour.

'No, she's been worse than usual.' Justin chortled.

Philip glanced at Justin who took the none-too-subtle hint for him to leave.

He winked encouragingly at Jane as he passed, but she couldn't muster so much as a tight smile to reward his optimism. He would go home to his wife and children. When this was over, Jane would still be alone.

Laura remained behind, the pity in her eyes adding to Jane's disquiet. She didn't want to be pitied by anyone, for any reason. There'd been enough of that in the weeks after Milton's betrayal and years ago after she'd lost her parents.

Philip rose and came around the desk to face her, his anger fading to brotherly concern. 'What's wrong, Jane? Tell me the truth and we'll find a way to deal with it.'

She stared at the portrait of their parents hanging behind Philip's desk, too ashamed to look at him. He'd guessed her plan today had involved more than a desire to be wilful, but she couldn't explain to him the guilt and aching loneliness carving out her insides, and how it always grew stronger around the anniversary of their parents' deaths. He would try to banish it with logic and reason. Jane had learned long ago certain notions couldn't be dislodged with either. 'I told you, I want industry of my own.'

'But that's not all of it, is it?'

In his tender voice there lingered the memory of him holding her the morning their mother had died only a week after their father had passed. She'd cried against his chest and followed him around for the next month, clinging to him because she'd been afraid he'd die, too. He'd never pushed her away, but had kept her by his side until the day she'd finally been brave enough to let him out of her sight and go play with Jasper. Even when she'd been thirteen and doing all she could to disobey him, he'd never failed to love her. He was the only one, and she was at last succeeding in driving him away, too.

She screwed her eyes shut and forced back

the tears. Everyone she'd ever cared for—her father, her mother, Jasper, Milton, even Mrs Townsend—had all abandoned her and it was her fault. She hadn't done enough to keep their affection, like she hadn't behaved well enough to keep her mother from going away.

'Perhaps we can discuss it,' Laura offered.

Jane opened her eyes and took in the two of them standing side by side. It was meant to be a show of compassion, an attempt to reach out to her, but it only pushed Jane further inside herself. Their happy union drove home her growing isolation and how far down in importance she was to everyone.

'There's nothing to discuss.' It would sound childish spoken aloud. There were many people who loved her, but each of them had their own lives while she hovered on the periphery, watching theirs unfold while hers was stuck like a coach in the mud. 'I'd like to be alone now.'

If they didn't leave, then all sorts of immature things might tumble out of her, along with tears.

Philip nodded, took Laura's arm and escorted her from the room.

Jane stared out the French doors to the

blooming roses in the garden, her mother's roses. She struggled hard to remember her mother tending them, her old dress dusted with dark soil, oversized gloves covering her hands. If Jane closed her eyes she could just catch the faint scent of her mother's lilac perfume above the wet earth, hear her melodious voice calling for Jane to bring her the spade. It was the only clear memory she had of her mother and she wasn't sure if it was real or something she'd created, like the image of a happy life with Milton.

How much enjoyment will he derive from this little incident? It'd taken her ages to face everyone again after he'd eloped with Camille Moseley two weeks before their wedding. She didn't relish having to endure more ridicule or proving to everyone he'd been smart to do it because she was nothing more than an obstinate hoyden. Philip was right—instead of making things better for herself, she'd once again made them worse.

Jane marched to the doors, threw them open and stepped outside. She stopped on the shaded portico to take in the sun-drenched garden. At the back was a high wall broken by a metal gate, separating the Rathbone garden from the alley and mews behind it. There'd been many family gatherings here, parties and celebrations, quiet moments, and one or two daring ones. It wasn't a comforting sight, but a confining one.

No, this won't be the extent of my life.

She stepped into the sunlight and allowed its warmth to spread across her face. Today might have been a disaster, but it was one of the first times in nine years that she'd been adventurous, and alive, and it was all due to Jasper. She craved more of what she'd experienced today, not the guilt and humiliation in Philip's office, but the heady delight in Jasper's embrace and the pleasure it'd ignited inside her. She stared at the pink rose bobbing on a bush in front of her. This was dangerous. Emotions weren't supposed to play any part in this plan, yet they'd slipped in between them the way his tongue had between her lips.

She touched her mouth, remembering his wide-eyed amazement when they'd parted from the kiss, and his more pressing reaction lower down. Perhaps it was good he'd tried to dissuade her from the union by acting the rake. It'd stopped her from making more of a fool of herself with him, as she had at thirteen.

She flung her hands down to her side. No, this wasn't about some silly girlish infatuation; it was about seizing a future and she must make him see it. Hurrying in to her brother's desk, she snatched up the pen and set a blank sheet on the blotter. In swift strokes she told Jasper Philip was considering forcing him to make her an honourable woman and they must discuss it before he took action. She didn't like lying to him, but it was the only way she could think of to tempt him here so she could overcome his objections. After all, he'd said he needed her and he did, as much as she needed him.

'What the hell were you two doing?' Jasper's father blustered while his mother sat embroidering, as sensible and calm as her husband was agitated.

'Discussing business,' Jasper answered in all seriousness. He slipped his hand inside his coat pocket and fingered the letter which had been delivered a short time ago. He had to admire Jane's tenacity; she was determined when she set her mind to something and she'd set her mind on him. With the firm imprint of Jane's breasts against his chest sharper than a shot of brandy, the thought of allowing things to play out as Jane had written held a certain appeal. After the kiss, she could have asked him to rob a mail coach with her and he would have gone along. It had taken him hours to come to his senses.

His father dropped the crystal stopper of the decanter on the table beside it. 'In your room?'

'I didn't invite her there. She appeared all on her own.'

'Preposterous. It's not something a lady of her breeding would even consider.' His father shook his head. 'Next you'll tell me she gambles and I detest gambling. Men default on my loans because they're throwing their money away at the tables while leaving their children to starve and their businesses to founder. Why, I had a cheesemonger's son in here the other day trying to beg money from me because he's wasting everything while his father slaves away. The man made me sick.'

This wasn't the first time Jasper had heard this sort of thing. He'd grown up having the evils of gambling drilled into him. He should have listened to his father.

'I think this little incident sounds exactly like something Jane would do. She's always been a bit wild.' His mother drew a long thread through her embroidery hoop, amused rather than disgusted by Jane's more than usually outlandish behaviour. 'You remember the time she dressed up as a boy to visit the coaching inn with you and Milton.'

'Or the time she went with us to buy tobacco at the auction, thinking she could sell it at a higher price by the docks.' It was one of Jasper's fondest memories of Jane.

'She made quite a profit from that little endeavour, didn't she?'

'So did I. It was Milton who lost money because he wouldn't listen to her and buy a pouch.'

'Well, there's your brother for you.' His mother loved her children, but wasn't blind to their faults, not even Jasper's. If she ever learned the true extent of them, she'd throw Jasper out of the house. She was a patient and tolerant lady, but even she had her limits. If his father ever found out where Jasper's money really came from he'd exile him from the family for good.

Jasper took a deep breath, pushing back his worries. He'd make sure his father never discovered the true source of his income or his inheritance.

'What the devil has got into the two of you?' His father frowned. Mr Rathbone had informed Jasper's parents of the incident, to his surprise leaving out the part about the kiss. It was a good thing he had. With so many Charton siblings, there were few secrets anyone in the family could keep. At times, Jasper was amazed he'd been able to hold on to his for so long. 'Miss Rathbone isn't a child any more, but a grown woman who should know better than to act like a wh—'

'Henry, mind your tongue,' Jasper's mother warned.

'Don't get me wrong, I love the girl like she was my own and she has an admirable head for investments, but all this nonsense today does make one wonder.' He took a hearty drink.

'She's stubborn, like her mother, God rest her soul.' Jane's mother had been Jasper's mother's best friend.

'You're lucky Philip didn't march you two up the aisle.' His father poured himself more brandy, stopped by a stern look from his wife from filling up the glass. 'Maybe I should. Man like you establishing himself in London after being gone so long doesn't need Philip

Rathbone working against you. You need him with you.'

Being so intimately connected to Mr Rathbone was the last thing Jasper needed. If anyone could ferret out Jasper's secret it was Philip. Jasper had caught the scrutiny her brother had lodged at him the moment he'd broken from Jane in his bedroom. It was the look he remembered from when they were kids and the man could guess at once exactly where they'd been and what they'd been up to. He had the elder Mr Rathbone's gift for sizing people up in an instant.

Jasper fingered the letter again, wondering if her note was to be believed and if Philip was indeed planning to haul Jasper and Jane to the altar. If so, he'd have to find a way to turn Philip down and it wouldn't be any easier than refusing Jane. He admired him and his father was right, he couldn't afford to make an enemy of the man. The best he could hope for was Philip turning his attention elsewhere and having no reason to pry into Jasper's affairs by insisting on a wedding.

'Whatever happens, you can't let it distract you from establishing your club. The money from the sale of your American goods won't support you for ever,' Jasper's father continued. 'I'm still amazed what you brought back from Savannah garnered as much as it did.'

'It appears there's a better market here for old Louis XIV than in America. So much for superior English taste.' Jasper forced himself to laugh, pretending like always to be lighthearted. It was the only way to hide the lies weighing him down.

'You'll run through the money if you keep spending it like a drunk earl,' his father blustered and Jasper pressed his lips tight together to hold back a retort. Like the rest of his family, his father failed to understand why Jasper indulged in a few fine things. Death had brushed up against him in Savannah and he was determined to embrace life in London. Besides, it wasn't only himself he spent money on, but on the footmen and dealers who needed it more than he did.

'I don't know what you learned about managing your affairs from your Uncle Patrick. Heaven knows he…' A warning look from Jasper's mother made his father abandon whatever line of reasoning he'd embarked on concerning his mother's favourite brother. 'Either way, you're here now, not in America. You must be

swift and decisive and stop missing out on opportunities like the Fleet Street building.'

Jasper nodded as his father continued to lecture him about how to handle his affairs, but
Jasper's thoughts wandered from his future
and his past to fix instead on Jane. He touched
the letter again, the paper smooth like her lips
beneath his. He'd meant for the kiss to put her
off him. Instead of dissuading her, he'd given
her even more reason to pursue him and for
him to accept. In her soft sigh he'd heard her
whispering for him to follow her out of the
shadows of his lies and into respectability.

He wondered if he could.

He plucked a glass paperweight with a
wasp suspended inside it off the table beside
his mother, the glass cool and smooth against
his palm. At one time he would have followed
Jane's intuition and believed, like she did, in
everything working out as planned. After the
things he'd seen in Georgia he no longer could,
and he couldn't corrupt her the way his uncle
had corrupted him.

However, if anyone could help him establish his club, it was Jane. She'd always had a
knack for making money.

He rolled the glass between his palms,

amazed to find himself considering her offer. A partnership with Jane might have advantages, but it held so many risks. Living as one man during the day and another at night was wearing on him, and not having complete privacy in his parents' house while his Gough Square town house was being repaired further complicated things. He'd inherited the residence from Uncle Patrick and had intended to move there in the weeks after he'd came home. Then he'd got a good look at the place. It hadn't been well maintained in the thirty years since Uncle Patrick had left it. Jasper had been forced to employ a builder to see to the much-needed repairs before he could hope to move in. They were almost finished and he would at last have complete privacy, one he didn't wish to impede with a marriage.

He couldn't continue the deceit inside the intimate bonds of a marriage, but as a friend, she might understand. He could confide in her the way he hadn't been able to do with Milton or anyone else, and trust her to keep his secret the way she'd trusted him enough to be alone in his room and take his nakedness in her stride, confident he'd do nothing against her will. He was certain of it, even if it risked making her recoil from him.

His hand stilled, trapping the paperweight between his palms before he set it down. He hated to lose her regard so soon after he'd returned, but he must reveal a little of the ugliness ruling him in order to make her understand why they could not marry.

Chapter Three

Jane trudged upstairs after a tense and uncomfortable dinner. Philip's anger had vanished, but there'd been no mistaking his weariness over her behaviour and his constant need to correct it. If her niece and nephews hadn't chattered throughout the entire meal, masking the adults' silence, she would have been able to hear herself chew.

The lively conversation she used to enjoy at meals before Mrs Townsend had left to marry Dr Hale no longer existed. Instead, all discussion seemed to focus on Thomas, Natalie and William's lessons or antics. Jane loved her niece and nephews, but she missed Laura's mother and the long hours they used to spend discussing the latest gossip or news. Mrs Townsend, or Mrs Hale as she was now, might not be far away, but Dr Hale's busy medical practice commanded her time, leaving her little freedom to linger over tea with Jane.

She stopped at the top of the stairs, wishing she could speak with Mrs Townsend the way she used to, especially to discuss Jasper's unexpected kiss. She had no idea what to make of it, or how to stop thinking about it. With one finger she traced the curve of the polished wood banister. The potent memory of his tongue caressing hers made her heart skip a beat and his silence all the more irritating. He hadn't rushed to answer her note.

I should've listened to Philip and simply sold Jasper the building. Her plan had only succeeded in making her appear like a desperate fool. How many times did Jasper have to tell her he wanted nothing more from her than friendship before she'd listen?

Friendship was the only thing I was offering. He was the one who wanted more. And she should have pushed him away and upbraided him for his forwardness and salvaged something of her pride. If she hadn't enjoyed the kiss so much she would have.

I can't believe I was so weak. She slapped the top of the rail and strode down the hall to her room. Inside, with the door closed, she undid the front flap of her dress and shrugged out of the garment. Laying it aside, she breathed deeply against the soft boning of her stays and made her way to the washstand. She poured some water into the bowl, dipped her hands in and was about to splash her face when her eyes met Jasper's.

'Good evening, Jane.'

She jumped back with a stifled yelp, sending the water in her hands spilling down over her neck and chest, and rolling under her stays. The cold liquid made the fabric of her garments stick to her skin. 'How did you get in here?'

Jasper stepped out of the shadow between the washstand and the armoire, took the towel from the rail and handed it to her. 'The way you taught me to when we were children.'

Except Jasper was no longer a boy; he was a man, as his semi-nakedness had proven today. She snatched the linen out of his outstretched hand, careful not to brush against him. He dropped down on the bench at the foot of her bed and watched her dry her face. Together with Milton, they had spent many nights huddled there, whispering their plots for surprising the housekeeper with frogs and getting a peek at the shops, at least until the day the adults had made it clear there were to be no more night-time games between them.

'Is there some reason you decided to sneak past Philip's men to come see me?' She should speak to Philip about his men failing to guard the house, but she was more flattered than perturbed. Milton had never been so bold.

'Yes, I received your note.'

Jane twisted the towel between her hands. 'And?'

He shook his head. 'You have to give up on the idea of us, Jane.'

She tossed the damp towel on the washstand. 'As you did when I was thirteen and I told you I'd wait for you?'

'This isn't a child's game.'

'Then why bother with all these theatrics? Send a note and be done with the matter.'

'I can't.' Jasper came to stand over her. He smelled of night-air-dampened wool with a hint of spicy snuff. It was a heady mixture which enticed her to draw up on her toes and inhale, but she kept her feet firmly on the floor. If she was going to be rejected, again, it wouldn't be while sniffing him. 'I know you,

Jane. Once you decide on something it's difficult to talk you out of it, but I must.'

She took a step back, ready to tease him with some of the same heat he'd tried to singe her with today. He wasn't the only one who could play the game of wiles. 'Are you sure that's the only reason you're here?'

He slid his gaze down to her chemise and the tight breasts beneath it. She wasn't sure what he could see through the wet cotton, but she hoped it was a great deal and made him at least regret his rejecting her. He took his time admiring her and she shifted on her feet, trying to ease the tension creeping through her. She was seized by the desire to fall on him and do all the things she'd imagined while she'd stared at his half-naked body in his room. There was no Philip to stop her. If Jasper took her in his arms and fulfilled the offer in the press of his lips against hers this afternoon, she wouldn't put up much of a resistance.

The low rumble of a suppressed laugh rippled out of his throat. 'You think you know something of the world and men, but you don't.'

She raised her chin in defiance. 'I know enough.'

He leaned back against the bedpost and pinned her with the same wicked smile as he had right before he'd kissed her, his confidence as annoying as it was seductive. 'You don't know anything. Not about me or about life.'

He was right and it chafed as much as the wet chemise sticking to her stomach. She'd seen nothing of the world and, except for this afternoon and a rather dull few minutes in the dark part of the garden with Milton, she had very little experience with men. 'You think you're the one to teach me?'

'Yes, and I'll prove it.' He slid her dress off the chair where she'd tossed it and held it out to her. 'I'm going to show you something no one else in London knows about me.'

She tilted her head at him, puzzled by his sudden seriousness. Whatever he had planned clearly didn't involve more of his naked body against hers. Too bad. 'You have the French pox?'

He jerked back. 'No!'

Well, at least this finally struck a blow. 'Then simply have out with it and save us both the bother.'

He shook the dress at her. 'It's better if you see it.'

'I can't. If I sneak out with you and Philip discovers me gone, he'll commit me to a convent.' She'd wounded her brother enough today with her silly scheme. She didn't want to worry him if he came in and found her gone.

'You have to be Catholic to become a nun.'

'Not with Philip's contacts.' Her brother knew someone everywhere and could always get exactly what he wanted when he wanted it. She wished she were so abundantly influential.

'Well, before you're cloistered, come with me. You'll understand why we can't marry after you see it and how the fault is with me, not you.'

The pain edging his entreaty made her heart ache. She wanted to pull him out of his darkness, not because she was plotting to ensnare his hand, but because she didn't want her old friend to suffer alone the way she did. 'I don't care about your faults.'

He lowered the dress, his expression filled with the same anguish as the night he'd told her about his parents' plans to send him to apprentice with his uncle. She held her breath, silently urging him to confide in her once more, but as fast as the old Jasper appeared he was gone, covered by the smooth gallant who'd embraced her this afternoon. 'Come on, the Jane I used to know wouldn't have shied away from an adventure.'

He was right. She'd always been the one to drag the Charton brothers into mischief. How things had changed. Milton had turned out to be a bigger rat than the ones shuffling along the garden wall, Jasper had gone off to find his life and Jane was still waiting for hers. Tonight she would have it. 'All right, I'll go with you.'

She took the garment, her fingers brushing his before she pulled back. It was as fleeting a touch as a raindrop, but it doused any remaining reservations she might have about going with him. This was dangerous, not in a get-with-child way, but in a lose-your-head-and-be-hurt-again sort of way. However, while they were together tonight there was still a chance to change his mind.

She snapped out the dress then lowered it to step inside, very aware of how bending over revealed the tops of her full breasts above the stays and how keenly he watched her. She hid her sly smile by focusing on doing up the tapes. Let him be tempted and then try to tell her he wanted none of it. She didn't believe him or the salaciousness of his secret. They were rarely as interesting or as awful as people painted them.

When she was done dressing and had donned a sturdy pelisse, he held out his hand to her, his fingers long and his palm wide. 'Are you ready?'

Her heart raced as the old memories collided with the coming thrill of a new adventure. She hadn't felt this excited or daring in ages. She slipped her hand in his, drawing in a sharp breath as his fingers closed around hers. 'Yes.'

'You can't marry me because of a warehouse?' Jane stared up at the squat building, the mouldy stench of the nearby Thames River making her wrinkle her nose. 'These don't frighten me. Philip owns a few.'

'It's not the warehouse, it's what's inside.' He fiddled with a small iron ring, making the keys hanging off it clatter together.

'Unless you have bodies for the anatomists stacked in there, I very much doubt it. Even then, I could probably do something with them.'

'I don't doubt you could.' He shot her an appreciative smile as he unlocked the door and pushed it open. 'But I'm not a resurrectionist.'

'Good, it's a rather smelly business.' She strode through the small door set beside the larger one used to load and unload freight.

He joined her in the darkness of the warehouse, drawing the door closed behind them. Slivers of moonlight fell in through the high windows at the top and the few cracks in the wooden walls, illuminating the dust kicked up by their entrance. The warehouse was nearly empty except for a few paintings in large, gilded frames leaning against a far wall. They were kept company by an overly ornate set of bergère chairs, a few crates and a wide but dismantled four-poster bed. 'Shouldn't there be more here? It seems a waste to pay rent to store so little.'

'They're the last of what I brought back from America. I sold the rest. Besides, storage isn't the only thing I use this building for, as you're about to see. Come along.' He led her through a narrow door at the far end, past empty crates without their lids and bits of straw littering the floor around them.

Beneath the steady cadence of his boots, Jane caught the dim sound of laughter and footsteps from somewhere overhead. She thought she was imagining it until Jasper opened another door to reveal a narrow staircase. More laughter and voices drifted down from upstairs. 'Are you having a gathering in a warehouse?'

'You could say that.' He avoided her eyes as he slid the keys back in his pocket.

'Jasper Charton, are you running a house of ill repute?'

His head jerked up. 'No, at least not the kind you're imagining. Even if I was, don't appear so excited. It isn't right for you to be so thrilled at the idea.'

'It isn't right for me to be in a warehouse with a single man in the middle of the night either...' she threw open her arms '...and yet here I am.'

'Yes, here you are.' He pulled his lips to one side in displeasure, as if his plan wasn't unfolding quite as he'd imagined. Good. It'd be a welcome change to have someone else's plans go awry instead of hers.

'Well, are you going to show me?'

'I'm debating it.'

'The time for that has passed.'

'I suppose it has. Come on then.' Jasper took her hand, his fingers tight around hers as he started up the stairs. She held on to him, the pressure of his skin against hers making her a touch dizzy as they climbed to the first floor. Her curiosity increased with each step as she tried to guess what he'd brought her here to see. She hoped it wasn't just warehousemen relaxing over cards after a long day. She was tired of disappointments. There'd been too many of them lately.

They stepped into the hall and stopped before a closed door. Light slipped out from under it along with muffled conversation and the faint aroma of pipe smoke. She studied the light beneath the wood, noting how it dimmed and brightened as someone on the other side passed between the source and the door. She waited anxiously for him to open it and reveal what was on the other side, but instead he led her past it to the far end of the hall. She could see the dark recess of an opening and the top of another, much wider, staircase leading back down to the ground floor and the front of the building. It was quiet here, the sounds drifting out of the other room muffled more than they should be in an old place like this. There was also nothing here except a lantern on a metal hook breaking up the endless line of knotted planked wall. She wondered if he meant to lead her back into the warehouse when he reached up and pushed aside the wide plate connecting the metal base to the lamp. It exposed a brass ring hidden behind it.

Now he really had her attention.

He pulled the ring and a portion of the planked wall popped open, revealing a door concealed by the wood and the darkness.

'Impressive,' Jane conceded, jealous. As children, they'd dreamed of having a secret room of their own. The empty space beneath the stairs in the Charton house was the closest they'd come, but every adult had known about it, along with every servant who used to check there first whenever they couldn't find them.

'Don't compliment me yet.' He unlocked the door and led her into an office far more opulent than Philip's. Gilt-framed paintings adorned the far wall and an elaborate peacock inkwell punctuated the lustrous blotter. Sumptuous leather furniture complemented the narrow-legged burled-wood desk and added to the gaudy wealth of the decor.

'Are you sure you're not running a house of ill repute because your office is decorated like one.'

'This came from my uncle's house in Savannah. He had a penchant for gaudy furniture. I sold the worst of it a while back.'

She hated to think what the rest of it looked like if this was the most conservative. She was about to say so when he faced her, as serious as a bailiff. 'Promise me, no matter what happens between us, you won't reveal to anyone what I'm about to show you.'

She didn't share his sense of gravitas. 'Your accounting books?'

He ignored her humour and took her hands. His eyes bored into hers with a severity she'd only seen the morning they'd laid her parents to rest. It turned her as serious as him. 'I brought you here because I can trust you, I always could, and I need someone to confide in. I thought I could do it with Milton, but he's proven himself unworthy.' A stricken look crossed his face, reminiscent of the one Philip had worn the morning Arabella, his first wife, had died after giving birth to their son Thomas. 'Promise me.'

She imagined the loss of his closeness with Milton might be to blame for the darkness colouring his eyes, yet deep down she suspected it wasn't. 'I promise.'

He let go of her and went to a painting of a

large house with tall columns hanging on the wall. He swung it aside to reveal a peephole. 'Come look.'

Jasper held his breath as Jane rose on her tiptoes and pressed her face to the hole. The light spilling out of the room beyond spread over her fine nose and high cheeks, and he caught something of the mischievous imp he'd begun to love before his parents had sent him to America. Except it wasn't their past captivating him tonight, it was the present. She was so stunning and innocent and he longed to draw her close instead of pushing her away. He couldn't because she deserved better than a damaged and deceitful man, and it was already too late. There was no stopping Jane from being disgusted by what he was showing her and no way of preventing her from telling everyone if she decided to betray him.

She won't. It was the old bond they'd shared in childhood when they used to sneak away from lessons with the bird-like tutor to go and play. It continued to connect them, despite the years they'd spent apart. 'This is how I make my living.'

'You're running a gambling hell.' She

pressed her hands against the wall and leaned in closer to the hole.

He rested her painting on a small hook, then slid aside the portrait of a dog beside hers to view the tables full of men playing cards across the green baize. The cut-crystal lamps hanging over each table cast circles of light to surround them. Men recruited from the nearby slums who'd demonstrated even a modicum of manners moved between the guests to re-fill brandy glasses and light cigars, and, most importantly, extend credit. 'Not only do I own the Company Gaming Room, I'm the house bank. The players bet against me and most of the time they lose.'

A loud cheer went up from across the room as Mr Portland, a rotund man with a long face, threw up his hands in victory. 'Sometimes, they win.'

Mr Bronson, a lanky gentleman in a fine suit and a bright red waistcoat, Jasper's partner in this affair, approached the winner to offer congratulations and payment.

Jane studied him, but he continued to ob-serve the room, bracing himself for the sneer of disgust he was sure was coming. They'd both been raised to detest gambling as man after man had approached their fathers and brothers for money to cover their debts and save the businesses they were throwing away with the dice. Jasper was contributing to the very thing which had ruined so many, including him.

'Why, Jasper Charton, I never thought you had it in you to be a rogue.' He turned to face her, stunned to discover her blue eyes, illuminated by the candlelight concentrated through the hole, open wide in amazement.

'You're not supposed to be impressed.' He set the dog painting over the hole and then reached past her face to return the house painting back to its original position.

'I admit it's a bit shady, but it doesn't mean I can't appreciate what you've done and how much you've accomplished in a matter of months.'

'It's a gambling hell, not a cotton-import business.' He pressed his knuckles into his hips. This wasn't the reaction he'd expected and yet he couldn't help but smile. This was exactly like something she would do. 'I thought your brother raised you to detest gambling?'

'I thought your father did the same. It seems it didn't stick for either of us.' She cocked her thumb at the wall. 'I assume he doesn't know about this.'

'No one in the family does. Can I trust you not to tell them or use this against me in your matrimonial pursuit?'

'Of course. I'm not low enough to black-mail a person.' Jane crossed her arms beneath her round breasts. 'But I don't see how you'll keep it from them for ever. Isn't this illegal?'

'No, but it's not entirely legal either, rather a grey area, which is why I don't draw much attention to it.'

'And no one around here has noticed so much coming and going at night?'

'Drunks are the only people in this area after dark and a dram here and there keeps them quiet. It, and the front and back en-trances, are why I chose this building.'

'Impressive.' Despite himself, he basked in her compliment before her next questions dis-solved it. 'Did you do this in Savannah?'

Guilt struck him as hard as shame. 'I did.'

'What did your uncle think of it?'

He strode to the fireplace, debating whether or not to take her deeper into his confidence, but the freedom to finally speak about this part of his life muted his usual caution. He'd brought Jane this far, there was little harm in taking her a touch further. 'He's the one who taught me to do it.'

'He was a gambler, too?' She rushed to join him at the ornately carved marble mantel.

'He never gambled and neither do I. It isn't wise.'

'Well, he certainly wasn't a cotton merchant, was he?'

'Maybe when he first went to America, but he couldn't tell the difference between Egyptian cotton and South Carolina cotton by the time I joined him. I was as stunned as you are when I learned of his true trade.' Stunned and in awe. To a young man of fifteen who'd thought he'd been banished from his family and consigned to a colonial backwater, the vice-filled rooms and the income they gave him had been a scintillating temptation. He'd embraced the life, even when its darkness had shown itself in the haggard faces of losers at the Hazard table. 'Pretending to my mother to be a cotton merchant was Uncle Patrick's way of explaining the source of his wealth without offending anyone's sensibilities.'

'And your mother never suspected the truth?'

'She's quick, but Savannah is a long way

from London.' The distance was the most enticing aspect of coming home, but not even an entire ocean could separate him from his past failures. 'She loved her brother, but my father wasn't as enamoured of him. Father would've despised him if he'd known the real source of his income.'

'And he wouldn't have sent you to him.'

A sense of lost days flitted between them. He wished he'd never left, then all the horror he'd witnessed, and all the sins he'd committed, might not have happened and he'd be worthy of accepting Jane's hand. 'Uncle Patrick built a fortune on merchants, sea captains with prize money, cotton traders and tobacco planters looking for more respectable entertainment than the seedy dives by the docks, a way to fill the time between when they saw their wares off and when they returned to their rural homes or ruined themselves at our tables.'

'If they were stupid enough to gamble, then they got what they deserved,' Jane pronounced.

'I used to think so, too.' *Until Mr Robillard.* He stared into the fire, watching the flames dance the way they had in the biers scattered throughout Savannah to try to drive off the miasma sickening the city. It hadn't worked. 'I've learned a little more compassion since then and I have rules about limits. The men who play here know I won't allow them to end up drunk and broke in the gutter.'

It was a lesson he'd learned the hard way, one his uncle certainly hadn't taught him. If he'd learned it sooner, many men and their families might have been saved from destitution. Try as Jasper might to atone for his sins in London, he couldn't make up for the many he'd committed in Georgia.

'How do you keep this a secret? I recognise most of the men in there from their dealings with Philip. They must recognise you.'

'They've never seen me in there. The man in the red waistcoat who spoke to the winner is Mr Bronson. He was Uncle Patrick's long-time employee in Savannah. After my uncle died…' Jasper took a deep breath, forcing back the memories '…I offered him the chance to be more than a servant and to share in a good amount of the profits. He's the face of the Company Gaming Room, the one clients approach with troubles and concerns, then he comes to me. It hides my involvement in the club.' It was one of the many façades he'd adopted since coming home. 'My clients are merchants, businessmen, or foreigners with a taste for English gambling who'd never be admitted to one of the more fashionable clubs.'

'You don't cater to toffs? They'd be more lucrative.'

'And troublesome. Their titled fathers would wreak havoc if their progeny lost the family estate to a mere merchant. The toffs also find my wager limits repugnant. They can afford to throw away their fortunes. Most merchants can't.'

'Then why is Captain Christiansen in there?' She pointed to the wall, beyond which sat a lanky gentleman with his long fingers tight on a fan of cards, who Jasper knew sat at his usual table with more empty drink glasses than chips in front of him.

'He's a second son and he's losing the money he earns from captured ships, not his father's wealth, otherwise Lord Fenton would be in here putting a stop to it at once.' Jasper motioned for her to sit on the leather sofa behind her. He took a box of fine sweets off the corner of his desk and held them out to her. 'I also allow him to play here because he offers the other patrons information about oversees interests and ports they can't obtain elsewhere.'

'A wise decision.' She selected one round confection dusted with sugar, pausing to look up at him through her thick lashes. 'If this is the source of your income, then why did you want a building in the heart of the Fleet? It'd be hard for you to hide your activities there.'

She bit into the treat, as perceptive and tempting as ever. He tossed the box on his desk, then sat on the leather chair across from hers. 'Many men come here for more than cards; they want to discuss contracts, stocks and markets in a space more conducive to sensitive deals than a coffee house. It's the edge my establishment offers, the one I wish to cultivate and turn into a respectable business. The building would've been the perfect place for it.'

'You could have the Fleet Street building if you agree to my terms.' Her tongue slid over her bottom lip to lick off a bit of confectioner's sugar clinging there. The gesture almost made Jasper slide across the gap and take care of the sweetness for her. Instead, he threw his hands up over the back of the leather's curving edge. Not only should she not be here, but he shouldn't be reacting to her like this. It wasn't right and still he couldn't dampen the heat rising inside him.

'You know I can't.' It was time to think with his mind and not parts lower down. 'I'm not an honest merchant like Milton or my sisters' husbands.'

'Good, I'm glad.'

'Don't be.' He'd been naive about the dangers and temptations which could rob a man of his worth. He was too familiar with them now and didn't want to visit them on her. 'It isn't easy being up all night, sleeping in the day, and lying to everyone about everything.'

She leaned forward with the same determination she'd used to approach him this afternoon. 'Then let me help you become respectable again. We can establish the club together, secure more patrons and devise many means of making money off them, either through wine and cigars or expensive baubles for their wives sold at inflated prices.'

Jasper rubbed his eyes with his fingers. 'Jane, be sensible.'

'I am being sensible. A busy man must placate his wife and jewellery is an excellent way to do it. By selling ready-made pieces at the club we can save merchants a trip to the jewellers.'

Jasper peered at her through his fingers. 'I hadn't thought of that.'

'Fine stationary for their contracts would also be good and the services of a private solicitor to keep things confidential.'

Jasper rubbed his chin. 'Property agents might not be a bad idea, either, and we could take a cut of their sales.'

She laid her hands smugly on her knees. 'See, I can help you.'

He snapped out of his interest. He was supposed to be putting her off him, not being drawn into a potential partnership. 'No, you can't.'

'I can and you'll see it and change your mind.'

He leaned forward, one elbow on his knee. 'I promise you, I won't.'

She matched his position, bringing her face close to his. 'I promise you, you will.'

They stared at one another in challenge, so close together he could see each curling lash rimming her eyes. The temptation to kiss her again gripped him and he was certain she would allow it, but he held firm against the desire to lean in and claim her lips. He was here to discourage her, not trifle with her. The rattle of dice and conversation from the adjacent room drifted in despite the thick padding he'd paid builders to add to the walls. Her small breaths glided over the back of his hand where it hung between his knees, the need to resist her beginning to lose its urgency. He'd expected her to loathe him, not go along with him as if he'd invited her to a box at Drury Lane Theatre. Maybe allying himself with her wouldn't be as dangerous as he'd first believed. She could help him and in deeper ways than mere negotiations and sales.

He sat back, putting distance between her and temptation. Revealing his involvement in a gambling hell was one thing, but he wouldn't entice her into this life the way his uncle had enticed him. 'I think it's time to get you home.'

'But we haven't resolved anything.'

'We'll discuss the rest in the carriage.' He checked the glass peephole hidden in a knot in the door to make sure the hallway was clear, then tugged it open. 'We don't want your brother to discover you missing and make you Sister Mary Saint Jane.'

She wagged one finger at him. 'Don't think you'll put me off so easily.'

She strode past him and into the hallway, her confidence as alluring as her perfume.

* * *

Jane allowed Jasper to lead her out the way they'd come in and to hand her into the waiting carriage. The night chill made her shiver as she settled against the fine leather seats. She could pull the rug up over her knees, but the bracing air kept her on guard to continue her fight. Warmth might lull her into cosiness and make her forget what she needed to do on the ride home, her last real chance to change Jasper's mind. She'd seen his determination waver when she'd made the suggestion about the jewellery and the solicitor, and again when they'd faced one another. He might outwardly protest, but inside he was weakening.

He settled across from her and with a knock on the roof set the conveyance in motion. They rode in silence as the carriage came around the building and passed the front entrance of the hell where a few vehicles waited for their riders while another pulled up to the front door to let off a new arrival. Then the building faded into the distance and the warehouses gave way to narrow streets and dark, ramshackle buildings. After a street or two, Jasper covered a large yawn with the back of his hand.

'If you allowed me to handle things, you'd

hardly have to do any work,' she offered. 'You could sleep in until noon as much as you like. Unlike some wives, I wouldn't mind.'

'I appreciate your offer, but I won't have you lying to your family the way I've had to lie to mine.'

'It wouldn't be a lie, just an omission of certain details, which I have no issue with. After all, Philip and Laura don't consult me on their affairs and decisions. There's no reason why I should worry about their thoughts on mine.'

'It isn't so easy. It's been hard misleading my mother about my exhaustion or lying to my father about why I can't make morning appointments. If taking up residence in other lodgings while my town house is being repaired wouldn't invite more questions from them I would. As it is, they think I'm tired all the time because I'm still recovering from Savannah and the crossing. Do you know how many times my mother has threatened to summon Dr Hale? They trust me and I'm deceiving them and it eats at me.'

'What eats at me is continued failure and disappointment.' She took a deep breath, working to settle herself. He was flustering her and she would lose the debate if she allowed her emotions to run roughshod over her reason. 'I've managed the weight of those for the last few years, I think I can manage the bother of a few harmless fibs.'

'I don't doubt you can,' he explained softly, 'but I won't let you.'

Her chest constricted. Those were the same words he'd used the night of his farewell party when they'd stood in his father's study and said goodbye. She'd blurted out how she'd grown to care for him as more than a friend and would wait for him to come back. He'd been touched by her offer, but had refused to allow it, sure he wouldn't return.

Except he had.

She stared out the window misted with dew. A few fat drops slid down the glass, catching others as they went before dripping off. This wasn't about an old infatuation she'd put behind her ages ago, this was about establishing her future with him. Despite all his protestations against her, he was here with her alone in his carriage with enough faith in her to reveal his greatest secret. It was a more honest response than all his excuses against their marriage and it gave her hope she could still win his co-operation, if not tonight, then perhaps in the near future.

'I'm sorry I didn't keep in touch with you after I left,' he offered. 'More than once I wondered what you were up to here in London.'

'Not very much.' She smoothed her skirt with her hands, touched by his apology. It eased a great number of old disappointments. 'There were dances and picnics, shopping and dinners, and the weddings of all my friends. No one took a fancy to me, at least no one who didn't bolt.'

'I'm sorry for what Milton did.'

'Don't be. I wasn't in love with him as much as I was in love with the idea of my old friend being my husband.' The possibility still held more appeal to her than waiting for some future romance. She didn't need love, not if she had Jasper, her friend, for a husband.

'I'm surprised Philip allowed the engagement. He of all people should have recognised Milton's weakness.'

'He did, but I didn't listen.' She'd ignored every warning thrown in her path until the morning Milton had left her. 'I wish I had. It would've spared me a great deal of embarrassment.'

'You're better off without him.'

'I am and his eloping spared me from having to wear the thin little ring he purchased. His poor wife has it now.'

'Milton always was miserly.' Jasper grinned and so did she, glad to find some humour in her misfortune.

'What about you? Did you impress the ladies in Savannah?'

He reached up to grab the strap above the window. 'I had my share of amusements.'

'Did you now?' She was as curious as she was jealous.

A spark of mirth lit up his eyes. 'There was one tobacco merchant's daughter I tried to court, but she rebuffed me the moment she discovered I wasn't a lord but from the same solid merchant stock as her father.'

'Did she ever get her title?'

'No, she died in the epidemic.' The mischievous Jasper faded into one much older than his twenty-four years. He turned to stare out the coach window at the dimly lit streets, a darkness coming into his eyes which made her shiver. 'You have no idea the things I lived through in Savannah.'

He spoke with a weariness she understood.

It was the one she'd experienced during the two weeks of her parents' illness and which swathed her around this time every year. Jane leaned across the carriage and clasped his fingers tight. 'It's over now.'

The pressure of her touch seemed to startle Jasper, but he didn't recoil from her. Instead he turned his hand over to hold hers. 'No, it's not. It's still with me and sometimes as real as you sitting there.'

He let go of her and sat back, rubbing his thumb across the tops of his knuckles as he fisted his hand and brought it to his lips. A long moment passed and the clatter of the equipage settled in the quiet. Then he lowered his fist to his knee, tapping it in time to the rocking of the coach. 'When the epidemic first began no one really thought anything of it. Every summer there were incidents of yellow fever—even I had a mild bout of it the summer before. It'd claim a few people and then disappear when the weather turned cold. It was clear something was different that year.'

'But you didn't know what.'

'Not until it was upon us.' He continued to stare out the window, his attention fixed on something not outside, but in the past and across an ocean. 'Those who could fled to their plantations, but death followed them. I was one of the thousands caught in the city after the quarantine.'

'How awful it must have been.' She longed to embrace him and drive away the sadness in his eyes, to comfort him the way he'd done for her so many times around the anniversary of her parents' death, but she didn't move. It was clear by the stoic set of his jaw he didn't want her pity any more than she ever wanted anyone else's.

'It wasn't so bad at first, with people flocking to our hell to enjoy themselves before death snatched them away. I enjoyed life with them; you see, once you've had Yellow Jack, you can't catch it again, but it doesn't mean you can't suffer or be afraid. We stayed open until the authorities closed all the public places. By then everything was falling apart, and even if you weren't sick, you were starving. No amount of money or influence could buy you food. It was the first time I've ever experienced what it was like to be without and unable to provide for those I care for.'

'Your uncle?'

He nodded. 'There was nothing I could do

to save him and I could barely feed him either. It's the reason I started the hell when I came home. Yellow Jack may not be here, but I've seen what happens to people who fall into poverty. I don't ever want to be unable to provide for those I care about again.' He offered her a sad and apologetic smile. 'Unfortunately, gambling is the only trade I know.'

'I understand. I'm not supposed to want a business, but without a husband, in the end, it might be the only thing to keep me should something ever happen to my inheritance. I don't want to be spinster, but I certainly don't wish to be a poor one.'

'You won't be. You're too clever.'

She wished she shared his high opinion, but she didn't. He had his hell and would some day have his club. She would still be alone and growing older. However, nothing she had suffered or endured compared to what Jasper had gone through. She admired his strength and vowed to be more like him. He hadn't given up in the face of death and sickness. She couldn't crumble beneath a few setbacks.

The carriage rocked to a halt at the entry-way to the alley behind the Rathbone house, the one which led to the garden. The mist had

thickened during their ride, but the faint outline of the garden gate was visible. It'd been
a lifetime since Jane had last viewed it from
this angle, when she and Jasper and Milton
had returned from an outing, with her dressed
in Philip's old clothes and a soft hat covering
her hair. Back then, she used to creep through
the shadows and in the garden gate, steal past
Philip's room and slide into bed as if she'd
been there the entire night. Tonight, she'd do
it again once more.

Jasper stepped out of the coach and held out
his hand to help her down. She gripped it as
she joined him on the pavement, reluctant to let
go. She didn't want to leave him to ride home
alone with the memories of all the awful things
he'd seen accompanying him. To her surprise
he didn't release her hand, but covered it with
the other one. 'Thank you for not judging me
too harshly for what I do.'

'I could never judge you harshly, not even
for refusing me.'

'It's why I trusted you.'

She wrapped her arms around his neck and
pulled him close. 'If you need someone to talk
to, don't be afraid to come to me. I'll listen and
keep anything else you want to tell me a secret.'

She squeezed him tight and then, before he could refuse this offer, hurried across the short distance to the garden gate, conscious of him watching her the way he used to do to make sure she was home safe. At the gate she stopped. The moisture collecting on the wrought iron wet her fingers while she slowly pulled it open to keep the old hinges from squeaking.

Jane threw Jasper one last look. He touched his hat to her, the faint grey of it just visible in the silver light of the half-obscured moon. She slipped into the garden, past the fragrant flowers and the dew-moistened stepping stones, her regret at having to leave him as strong as the scent of the roses.

The mist grew thicker and colder the moment Jane disappeared from sight. It wasn't like the air in Savannah which could drown a man with its heat, but lighter and more mysterious, like Jane. He opened and closed his hand at his side, the warm pressure of Jane's fingers against his still lingering, along with her concern.

He took hold of the carriage-door handle to keep from chasing after her and changing his mind. It'd been a relief to speak with her instead of trying to hold back his memories, and the truth of his income, as he did with his family. When they'd spoken of Savannah, she hadn't hugged him in pity like his mother had when he'd first come home, the spaces under his jaws hollowed out, the depths of his suffering hidden like the banknotes tucked inside his trunks. Instead, Jane had merely listened, her presence stopping the spectre of the past from rising up from the shadows to consume him.

He stepped inside the carriage and rapped his knuckles against the top to tell the driver to move on. Each turn of the wheels carrying him away from St Bride's Lane, and Jane, made him more agitated. So many mornings he rode home from the hell before dawn, yearning for someone to speak with about the night's challenges or simply to view him in a better light than he viewed himself. With his family, he had to pretend his troubles were not what they really were and allow lies and falsehoods to separate and isolate him from the people who'd welcomed him home.

The carriage made the turn towards the warehouse and rolled past the cluttered windows of the shops locked tight for the evening. Soon, the shops gave way to the square, shapeless buildings lining the river. Weariness began to smother him the closer they drew to the hell. He was exhausted by the deceit and the walls it created around him, except there wasn't one between him and Jane. Tonight, she'd listened. The concern in her blue eyes calling to him, the hints of yellow near the irises reminding him of the sky during the many sunrises he'd been glad to meet during the awful weeks of the epidemic. The flicker of her pulse against his fingertips had been a potent reminder of how alive and good the world could still be and how he might be a part of it again.

The warehouse came into view and the carriage slowed to a stop. He hopped down, his determination not to marry Jane weakening with each step as he approached the rear door. It would be risky having someone so close, but she might be the one person who could keep him from sliding further into the darkness. He'd seen what years of loneliness and dissipation had done to Uncle Patrick. Uncle Patrick had spent his life surrounded by others, fêted and admired, and in the end all his money couldn't buy their loyalty or their help when he'd been at his weakest. Jasper didn't want to become like him. He'd thought to pull himself out of his old life by his own bootstraps. Maybe it was a more feminine hand he needed for the final steps.

He took the key ring out of his pocket and swung it on one finger, imagining the two of them working together and rising in prominence like her brother, or wielding the kind of influence his father enjoyed. It would be like his first few years in Savannah when he used to mingle with influential men or host parties in his Franklin Square house. For a time tonight, with her, he'd been free to be his old self and not have to lie. It was the life he'd imagined when he'd gone to the auction, the one he'd thought he'd lost until Jane had appeared and made him realise it could still be his.

He clutched the keys in his palm, stilling their spinning. It was one thing for Jane to know about his hell, it was another for her to be involved in it. He couldn't corrupt her the way his uncle had corrupted him or risk leaving her to wrestle with even a small measure of the guilt and blame he endured because of the affair with Mr Robillard. Except it wasn't a part of the hell she wanted, it was a part of him and his club. He could give her the club, and himself, and keep back the hell and the ugliness of Savannah. She needn't be involved in the tempting of players, but she could share in the freedom it offered to enjoy the finer aspects of London, the ones denied to her by her current situation. She'd come to him with a proposal for a partnership, to help him build a reputable professional life with the added benefit of more enticing nocturnal pursuits. It was an opportunity he could no longer resist. His time with her had always been an adventure. It would be again.

Chapter Four

'Miss Rathbone, good morning,' young Chester Stilton greeted Jane as she came downstairs for breakfast. Despite having been up most of the night, she'd awakened at her usual time just after sunrise. Force of habit was stronger than fatigue.

'Mr Stilton, it's a pleasure to see you here so early.' It wasn't, but she had to be polite to Philip's clients. After the last day and night, she'd had her fill of young men and was in no mood to entertain any more. All she wanted was to continue on to the dining room and the large pot of coffee sure to be waiting there.

'I certainly didn't ask to come at this ungodly hour, but my father insisted.' Mr Stilton's thin upper lip pulled back in displeasure, revealing teeth as yellow as a wheel of cheese.

Rumour was he rarely rose before noon, long after his industrious, and poorly named, cheesemonger of a father had gone to work to support his family and pay off his wastrel son's large tailor bill. She wondered how long it would be until Chester Stilton began to seek loans to support his spending habits, assuming he hadn't already done so to maintain his supply of the gaudily striped waistcoats, white hats and bright blue coats. 'My father is here to pay off the loan your brother extended him last year. He wanted me to join in the discussion and learn a little something about money, as if I should take lesson like that from a man like your brother.'

Jane stiffened. 'With all the credit the tailor extends you, one would think you possessed ample experience handling money, and debts. How proud your father must be of your ability to spend his hard-earned money on your clothes.'

'As proud as your brother must be of paying his spinster sister's milliner bills. You couldn't even land staid Milton Charton of all people.'

'I'm holding out for better prospects than the limited ones before me.' How dare a man whose waistcoats were of more use to his father than he was pass judgement on her or Philip's worth. She made a motion to leave, but he stepped in front of her.

'As much as I don't care for your brother or his moneylending ilk, for the right price I'd gladly take you off his hands.' He swept her with a lascivious gaze which would have made a lesser woman blush.

She didn't so much as twitch, but stared him down the way she would a slug crawling on one of the rose bushes. 'What an honour to be added to the long list of other wealthy women in the Fleet who've spurned you.'

His lip dropped down to cover his yellow teeth. Before he could answer with what she imagined would be a less than witty response, the door to Philip's office opened and the elder Mr Stilton, sharing his son's long face and displaced front tooth, emerged smiling from inside. 'Thankfully the better sort are hungering for my particular brand of cheddar, otherwise I don't know where we'd be. Thank you again for your assistance, Mr Rathbone.'

Mr Stilton grabbed Philip's hand and shook it vigorously before coming down the hallway to stand beside his son. 'Miss Rathbone, how wonderful to see you this morning. I hope my son wasn't being too cheeky with you, although if he was I wouldn't mind. Chester, you couldn't do better than to have an interest in Miss Rathbone. The girl is as sensible as she is pretty. What do you say, Miss Rathbone, any interest in my boy?' He clapped Chester on the back, failing to notice the chill between Jane and his son.

From over the elder Mr Stilton's shoulder Philip shook his head ever so slightly. Jane hardly needed the warning. Chester might feel he'd finally hit the bottom of the matrimonial barrel, but she wasn't so desperate, yet.

'Thank you for your kind offer, Mr Stilton, but I'm afraid my interests lie elsewhere.'

'More's the pity.' Mr Stilton shook his head, then turned to Philip.

Jane didn't hear what he said as she strode off to the dining room, doing her best to appear dignified. Once out of view, she stormed inside and up to the sideboard, immediately garnering Laura's attention.

'Jane, what's wrong?'

'Nothing, except for the yellow-toothed wastrel of a cheesemonger who decided to insult me this morning.' She scooped out a hearty helping of eggs and smacked them down on her plate, wishing the china was Chester's face and the spoon something more substantial. Jane marched to her place at the table beside Laura and tossed down her plate, causing some of the egg to spill over the side and on to the polished surface. She dropped into the chair the footman held out, her one comfort being the cup of black coffee he set beside her plate. She stared at the dark liquid, wondering if she could slip some brandy into it without anyone noticing. It would take the edge off her anger and the disappointment in herself.

There'd been a grain of truth in Chester's insult. She was a spinster and time was not improving her situation or her prospects. When she'd held Jasper's hand last night, she'd wondered if her fate was about to change, but it hadn't. Despite his insistence, and her gut feeling, a morning like this one made it hard for her to believe the fault was with Jasper and not her.

'Don't let him get to you.' Laura laid a calming hand on Jane's arm. 'You're a wonderful young lady and some day the right man will come for you. You'll see.'

'When?' Jane demanded, poking the eggs with her fork.

'I don't know, but we'll put our minds to it and find you someone, or at the very least, something to entertain you. Perhaps you could stay with my mother for a while? She might introduce you to some of the new surgeons Dr Hale is training.'

'You mean men who haven't heard about my being thrown over?' She shouldn't be sulky with Laura. It wasn't her sister-in-law's fault she was on the shelf. If she weren't so bold with her opinions and insistent on having her way, she might not be in this situation. She could only imagine how many young men who'd been trounced by her during debates on stocks must be gloating at this comeuppance.

'That's not what I mean,' Laura clarified, more understanding than annoyed. 'But you could help her. It might take your mind off—'

Thomas, William and Natalie came barrelling into the room, talking at the tops of their voices. Judging by the dirt on Natalie's dress and the dust on the boys' shoes they'd been playing in the garden.

'Mama, Mama, Thomas pulled Natalie's pigtails,' William, the youngest boy, lisped over the noise of his brother and sister trying to get their mother's attention. The bedraggled young governess sagged against the doorjamb to the dining room before she recovered herself and entered, keeping to the rear, knowing Laura preferred to be involved in most of the children's issues. Unlike many mothers, Laura didn't relegate the children to the second-floor nursery not to be heard from until it was time to be presented to their parents. Instead, they ran openly through the house like whirlwinds, as Jane, Milton and Jasper used to do.

'No, I didn't,' Thomas insisted, with all the seriousness of Philip and Jane. His hair was lighter like his mother's, while his younger half-sister and -brother had the darkness of Laura's.

'William started it,' Natalie accused.

'No, I didn't.' The little boy took a swing at his sister and the two of them were back to squabbling.

Jane tried not to sigh while she waited for the row to die down, but the children were insistent in their quarrel. Laura threw Jane an apologetic look which begged her to be patient, but Jane was tired of waiting. With a half-understanding smile, she left her coffee behind and fled the chaos of the dining room for the quiet of the hallway. In the past she and

Mrs Hale would have crept off to the garden to discuss the matter. There was no one to speak with now. She wandered past her brother's office to the back door leading to the garden. The Stiltons were gone and Philip sat behind his desk, speaking with his warehouse manager about some goods he'd been forced to seize from a client who'd defaulted on a loan. If Philip had been alone, she might have at last talked to him. She needed to speak with someone, to believe there might be one person who'd listen and give some attention and priority to her concerns. The truth was, there was no one.

Jane wandered out into the garden. She stopped at the edge of the portico and took in the sun falling across the white and red roses bouncing on their stems in the light spring breeze. The sight of the flowers didn't calm her as it usually did, it only added to her frustration. If her mother were here, she would listen and make Jane a priority as she had when she was six. But her mother and father were gone and it was her fault they'd left.

Stop it. She sat on a bench in the centre of the garden. Frustration, anger and loneliness welled inside her until she wanted to walk through the gardens and knock each bright rose from its stem. She closed her eyes until it passed, but the disquiet accompanying it failed to ease. She wanted a place and life of her own and she had no idea how to find one.

'Good morning, Jane.' Jasper's voice carried over the birds and the distant noise of the streets.

She rose and turned so fast, the garden swam, but Jasper remained stable in the centre of it. 'What are you doing here?' She wasn't sure if she was delighted or distressed by his unexpected arrival.

'I came to see you.'

'Well, I'm not sure I wish to see you.' She crossed her arms over her chest, flattered and irritated all at once. 'I've had enough of condescending gentlemen this morning.' *No matter how impeccably dressed they might be.* Jasper, like young Mr Stilton, was no stranger to his tailor, but there was a muted elegance to his dress the gaudy young cheesemonger lacked.

'Tell me who's ruffled your feathers and I'll pummel him for you.' He said it with a smile, but she caught a hint of seriousness in the slight narrowing of his eyes. If only she could set him on Mr Stilton. The cheesemonger's son deserved a beating.

'He isn't worth bruising your knuckles.' A little hope fluttered in her chest. He'd risen rather early this morning to seek her out and she suspected it had something to do with last night. 'I assume you're here to discuss more than my morning's conversations.'

'I am.' He motioned to the bench.

She dropped down on the stone, the coolness of it seeping through her morning dress. He sat down beside her, the heat of his body noticeable against the chill of the spring morning. 'Well? What brought you here?'

Unlike most people, he didn't flinch or scowl at her directness.

'I've given a great deal of thought to what we discussed last night and I've realised you're right.' He stretched out his legs. His boots covered his calves before stopping just below his knees and the polish reflected the grey of the house. 'I need your skills and talents, your knowledge of the Fleet and business. And what more could a man ask for then a friend for a wife?'

Her heart raced so fast she thought she might have to run around the garden to calm it. *He wants to marry me, to have me help him with his club.*

She smoothed the front of her dress with the air of aloof uninterest Philip had taught her to assume when haggling with difficult merchants. She might have proposed first, but she wasn't going to jump at his offer like some desperate spinster, or allow her desire to prove people like Chester Stilton wrong lead her into another mistake. 'So you now believe we'd be good partners?'

'Yes.' He clutched the edge of the bench with his gloved hands and flexed his fingers over the stone. 'When I told you my secret, you didn't hate me for it or threaten to reveal it. Instead, you understood and wanted to help. You have no idea what that means to me.'

'Yes, I do.' She'd held back from telling Philip and Laura so many truths because she didn't want them to laugh or scoff at her. Jasper wouldn't laugh. He never had, not even when she'd blurted out how much she'd cared for him nine years ago. He could have been cruel and taunting, but instead he'd been tender and honest, saying he didn't feel the same way. She was glad for that now. It meant he couldn't play on her emotions as his brother had. But his honesty didn't extend to everyone—Jasper was willing to deceive his family about who he really was and what he did for a living. He could easily deceive her, too, about the depths of his affinity for her and his reasons for changing his mind.

'With your brother's connections we can secure a common licence and be married by the end of the week and you could start work on the Fleet Street club at once.' He leaned closer to her and lowered his voice. It flowed over her like a warm breeze. 'Besides, I got a little taste of you the other day and I liked what I sampled. Marry me and there will be more of that, much more.'

A chill raced along her arm and it sparked her curiosity about the more intimate aspects of a union. The idea this *could* become something deeper than two friends making a bargain hovered between them. It almost made her forget about her objections. Almost. 'Be serious.'

'I am serious.' Jasper didn't sit back, but rested one elbow on his knee, remaining tantalisingly close. 'I thought you were, too, after your outlandish proposal which, if I know your brother, got you nothing except some bother.'

'I was serious.' She was also scared.

'Then why resist now?'

She took a deep breath, not wanting to be so vulnerable, but this was no time to hold back. Her entire future rested on this one proposal, and her getting it right this time. 'I don't want you to marry me out of some temporary convenience or because I'm an easy solution to your present problems. I don't want to be forgotten or overlooked the moment you no longer need me and I don't want you to conceal things from me the way you've concealed them from your family. I was embarrassed enough by your brother's secret when it came out. I don't want to be surprised by any of yours. I want you to be my friend, my true, real and forthright friend, like you used to be.'

He stared down at the ground, his mirth fading.

'You can't do it, can you?' she challenged, the prickliness she'd first greeted him with returning.

'No, I can't talk about everything I experienced in Savannah. Surely you understand.'

She studied him and how the sun and the shadow from his hat darkened the circles under his eyes. Philip had taught her long ago to read people, but she'd never been as talented at it as he was. However, there was no mistaking the depth of Jasper's pain, one she understood all too well. Like her, there were things he couldn't talk about either. 'I do.'

She glanced over her shoulder at the spire of St Bride's Church rising up over the house and the churchyard where her parents lay.

'The anniversary was last week, wasn't it?' he asked, following her gaze.

She turned back to him, her grief softening. 'I'm surprised you remember.'

'How could I forget?' He had accompanied her every year to lay flowers on her parents' graves and sat beside her in the churchyard while she'd grieved.

Jasper studied Jane, wanting to drive away the strife clouding her eyes. He'd never seen her so weak or vulnerable but, like him, their time apart had changed her. She'd been cast aside by his brother, humiliated in front of everyone, then left to linger as a spinster. He wouldn't treat her so shabbily, but she'd asked for an openness he couldn't bestow, all the while having no idea what she was asking for. He couldn't tell her about Mr and Mrs Robillard and risk her recoiling from him. Nor could he embroil her in the business of the hell and make her as dirty as him.

'Well, Jasper?' she prodded.

He might not be able to tell her everything about the hell or his past, but he could share his current situation with her—if not the worst parts of it, then certainly the best. He could help her to enjoy life the way he intended to after so much death and find a way to make sure the darkness never touched either of them again. He took her hand and met her steady gaze. 'I don't want you for mere convenience. I want you because you are my closest friend. I promise I will respect you as you deserve and be as open and honest with you as I can be.'

A hope he hadn't seen in anyone, including himself, since well before the epidemic brightened her face. It lightened some of Jasper's strain. In her innocence, she believed all would be well. With her beside him, perhaps it would be. 'We must speak to Philip at once so he can make arrangements. I'm sure he won't object.'

'I do not give my consent.'

Jane stared at her brother, dumbfounded. Laura peered back and forth between the couple and her husband, as shocked as Jane. Jasper stood casually beside her, hands crossed in front of him, hat dangling from his fingers as if their future together wasn't at risk. It irritated her more than it comforted her, adding to her annoyance at Philip's answer.

'What do you mean you don't consent?'

Philip folded his hands over the blotter. 'I have reason to doubt the veracity of Mr Charton's interest in you.'

'The veracity of his interest?' She forced herself not to shift on her feet and to face him as she would a difficult butcher trying to overcharge her for poor-quality meat. She recognised this look; it was the one he used to give her whenever she'd ask to go to the milliner's for a new dress. He'd always suspected her of choosing something much too adult for her young years, and he'd been right. At thirteen, almost everything she'd done had been to test him, to prove to everyone she was no longer a child but a young woman capable of making her own decisions. It had taken Mrs Hale's gentle guidance to make her realise she was not yet an adult and there was no reason to look older simply to spite the world. However, she was an adult now and she wouldn't cave under his scrutiny.

'He did his best to dissuade you from a union yesterday and now he wishes for your hand. I want to know why,' Philip explained to her, not Jasper.

'He wasn't against it. He was merely surprised by the way I went about discussing the matter. Even you said it was ill-advised.' Her conceding the point didn't ease the stern set of her brother's jaw. 'Since he's had some time to consider it, he's come to realise, as I have, we're still good friends and it would be a perfect union. Don't you agree?' She took Jasper's hand, demonstrating some affection, but careful not to overdo it. If she told Philip the two of them were madly in love, it would make him even more sceptical.

'I do.' The lightness in Jasper's answer made her wonder if he realised how in danger of having their plans thwarted they stood. She might be over the legal age to marry, but they needed Philip to obtain a common licence and arrange the church, and anyway, she wanted his consent. She was going to have to lie about the true source of Jasper's income, she didn't wish also to sneak behind her brother's back to the altar.

Philip eyed Jasper with hard scrutiny. 'I'd like to speak with Mr Charton, alone.'

Jane threw Jasper a wary look, but he didn't appear ruffled by the requested interview. Instead, he nodded to let her know all would be well. She hoped so. The idea of having yet another one of her plans fail irked her.

'I can't believe Philip is being so difficult,' Jane complained to a sympathetic Laura when they were alone together in the front sitting room.

'He's doing what he believes best for you,' Laura explained, despite the perplexed crease between her brows. Evidently, Philip's behaviour baffled her, too. 'He always has.'

'I've decided what's best for me and it's Jasper.' Jane dropped on to the sofa near the window.

Laura didn't argue with her and Jane was almost disappointed. She craved a little vigorous debate. It wasn't just Laura and Philip who were sceptical. She had her own doubts and they'd been nagging at her since they'd left the garden to speak with her brother. She wondered if there was anything about Jasper she should be concerned with. If there was, Philip was sure to sniff it out. Oh, how he irritated her; she wanted to rely on her own intuition and judgement and stop being dependent on his.

'Mr Charton strikes me as a very charming and persuasive gentleman. I'm sure he'll bring your brother around.' Laura sat down beside her. 'Though I do wonder how you two arranged all this in so short an amount of time.'

Jane stopped fiddling with the tassel on a pillow and stared at her sister-in-law. *Do she and Philip know I slipped out with Jasper last night?* No, it wasn't possible. Philip's men might be very astute and loyal to him, but they weren't infallible, as Laura had proven when she'd crept in here. She hadn't even had the advantage of Jane telling her the best way to do it. Since then, she'd won Philip's heart and had helped him to move past the grief which had left him distant and closed off from everyone including, at times, her.

She wondered if she and Jasper might ever come to have a relationship like Philip and Laura's. Love hadn't been a part of their negotiations. Good. It was better if she never expected it as then she'd never be disappointed. Besides, she was too old to fantasise about romantic nonsense. Compatibility was more valuable than a passion, even if it dampened instead of ignited her heart. She'd believed in love once and maybe some small part of her still did. It didn't matter. This was an excellent arrangement. She hoped Philip realised it, too. In the meantime, there was Laura's scrutiny to address.

'I chanced to meet Jasper while leaving Mrs Fairley's yesterday afternoon. We had a very long discussion on the matter.' It was a shady version of the truth, omitting the more scandalous details of his having slipped into her bedroom to spirit her away to a gambling hell in the middle of the night. She wondered if she should mention at least the leaving with him in the middle of the night part to force Philip's hand. However, if he hadn't marched her and Jasper up the aisle after the incident at the Chartons', she doubted he'd insist on a marriage because of some late-night escapade. Philip was much too level-headed to act out of emotion, which further worried her about his conversation with Jasper. She hoped Jasper was managing well.

'And what did you discuss with Mr Charton?' Laura leaned forward in the same manner Mrs Hale used to do when she and Jane shared gossip. It was almost enough for Jane to drop her voice and tell her the truth, the way she used to with Laura's mother. She missed the old intimacy, connection and friendship. It'd never come easy to Jane except with Mrs Hale, and Jasper, but not even they knew the darkest guilt she carried about her parents' death, nor could she tell them about the hell. Jasper had sworn her to silence and she would be worthy of his faith in her.

'We discussed his business and how I could help him with it.' If Jasper was working to win Philip over, then Jane must do the same with Laura.

'You two discussed business?' Laura tilted her head in disbelief.

'Your mother and Philip went to a great deal of time and trouble to teach me accounts, contracts and negotiations so I could some day help a husband manage his affairs. It's time I finally put those skills to use instead of trimming roses and telling the housekeeper how to make sure the grocer doesn't short-change us. I'm tired of being useless.'

This was as close to the truth of her and Jasper's discussion as Jane was willing to venture.

'I understand.' Laura took Jane's hand. 'When my uncle sold my father's draper shop and I was left with nothing to do every day, I almost went crazy. I was so accustomed to working, I couldn't sit idle. I can only imagine how it's been for you. I'm sorry I didn't see it before or do more to help you.'

'It isn't your fault, it's no one's, except perhaps mine.' Jane unclenched her fingers, wondering if she should have made an effort to speak with Laura sooner, but there were some things Jane couldn't share with anyone. 'Somehow, I've managed to drive good gentlemen, and one very bad one, away.'

Laura squeezed her hand. 'Not at all. You're simply discerning, like your brother, and you've been waiting for the right one. I think Mr Charton is perfect for you and I believe Philip will see it, too.'

Jane wasn't as convinced of her desirability as Laura, nor of having been waiting for the right gentleman. If she had, it hadn't been out of choice.

Footsteps in the hallway made them both rise and face the door. Philip entered first and

Jane studied his face, searching for signs of an answer. The lines at the sides of his mouth were softer and the suspicious scrutiny previously hardening his blue eyes was gone.

Jasper convinced him!

Jasper strode in behind him as if his gambling house had received a massive win. He winked at her and Jane had to resist throwing her arms around his neck in congratulations. Instead, she returned the wink, blaming the racing of her heart on the thrill of them having succeeded. Though he would be her husband, she refused to view him as anything but a friend with more intimate benefits.

'I give you both my consent to marry.' Philip kissed her forehead in congratulation, as he used to when she was young and did well at her maths lessons, before she'd grown older and begun to rebel against him for reasons she still didn't entirely understand. When he straightened, he took her hand and gave it to Jasper. 'Mr Charton and I will speak tomorrow about drawing up the marriage contract and securing the common licence. You can wed as soon as the required seven days are past.'

Jane wondered what Jasper had said to convince Philip of the need for a quick marriage.

With Milton, he'd insisted on a long engagement, giving Milton time to live up to Philip's low expectations. Perhaps Philip now allowed the wedding to hurry because he was tired of looking after her and exhausted at having to talk sense into her. He was giving her to another man and relieving himself of the burden.

No, I shouldn't be so uncharitable. Whatever her brother's motives, there was no mistaking his tender expression, much like the one the elder Mr Charton sported whenever he mentioned his grandchildren. It eased a measure of her fears, as did Laura's excitement.

'Wonderful!' Laura embraced Jane in congratulations. 'You two will be very happy.'

Jane returned the hug and over Laura's shoulder she caught Jasper's eye. A strange awkwardness stiffened his movements as he shook Philip's hand. She stepped away from Laura and Jasper let go of Philip. Jane and Jasper faced each other but his attention darted around the room with a tinge of uncertainty before he fixed on her. It was then the reason for his unease struck her. He might trust her with the secret of his gambling house, but there was another, darker one directly behind it, something to do with the things he couldn't tell her about Savannah. It reminded her too much of Milton and how he'd managed to conceal his relationship with Miss Moseley. Worry dampened her enthusiasm. Once the parson's mousetrap was sprung, they'd be stuck with one another for better or for worse. In her haste to change her situation, she wondered if she'd inadvertently made it worse.

Jasper sat at his desk in the warehouse office, dealing with an order for wine, but the memory of Jane continued to dominate his thoughts. Perceptive as always, she'd realised at once that they were going to be man and wife. She'd also caught his momentary doubt while he'd shaken Mr Rathbone's hand. It had caused her to retreat into a reserve making her resemble her brother. He'd wanted to tell her his concerns had nothing to do with her and everything to do with him, but there hadn't been a chance.

He slipped the ruby ring off his finger and turned it over and over. In Savannah, he'd spent years collecting money, property and influence, and in the end it had been worthless. In London it was different and yet it wasn't. Money made the difference between having a proper life or doing without. All he needed to do was look at his footmen and dealers to see how wages had lifted them out of poverty and given them and their families the chance to thrive instead of merely subsist. Once Jasper had wed Jane, she would become his responsibility. If Jasper lost everything to some extremely lucky gambler, or if their families learned of the hell and turned their backs on them, it would be like Savannah all over again. Except, this time, there'd be no family or inheritance or collected goods to help him start over. They'd be ruined and he'd be the cause of it.

'A right lucrative night last night, Mr Charton,' Mr Bronson greeted Jasper as he entered the secret warehouse office. The older man drew out his vowels in the lazy way people from Savannah did. Jasper had found it amusing during his first year in the bustling port city, the easy manner of speech slipping into his own so that a few years into his apprenticeship his accent had become too garbled for anyone to guess where he was really from. It'd given him an air of mystery in Savannah, charming the ladies during garden parties at the big plantations. It had made him stand out here, too, as his seventeen-year-old twin brothers Giles and Jacob enjoyed teasing him about during family dinners. He'd struggled to lose the languid manner of speaking, but now he was snapping his vowels in place as day by day he left his time in the southern state behind. He wished his past and his concerns were so easily set aside. 'What about Captain Christiansen. How did he do?'

'Lost another five hundred pounds before we sent him home.' Mr Bronson handed over the man's signed debt, then dabbed his forehead with his red handkerchief, the warm room making him perspire.

Jasper slipped the ruby ring back on his finger as he examined Captain Christiansen's name scrawled at the bottom of the paper. 'Seems like more than a man who hasn't taken a prize ship in a while can afford to lose.'

Mr Bronson strode to the window and slid up the sash. The cooler air laced with warmth from the coming summer spilled into the room. 'Didn't go quietly this time either, complained loudly about having a right to spend what he wants.'

'Not in my establishment, especially if he's going to make a scene. Scenes aren't good for business.' Jasper stared out the open window and the early morning sky dotted with thick clouds. The fresh air wasn't refreshing so much as unsettling. 'If he returns tonight, keep an eye on him. Hopefully, his current losses will encourage him to be more cautious with his play.'

'And if they don't?'

'We may have to find a discreet way to bar him from the club. We don't need Lord Fenton coming in here trying to redeem his son.'

Mr Bronson hooked his thumbs in his waistcoat pockets. 'Don't get y'all scraping to those sallow-faced men. Be better if you'd chucked them out like we Americans did.'

'Some days I agree with you, but old habits are difficult to break.' Jasper dusted his signature, then blew it off and handed Mr Bronson the papers.

'Yes, they are.' Mr Bronson rolled the debts in his hands. 'How many old habits are you going to give up when you have a wife nosing about?'

'None. She'll simply accompany me to the jeweller's and the theatre and help me enjoy my fine wine and food while working with me to establish the club.' Jasper leaned back in his chair, far less cavalier than he appeared. Jasper had told his partner about his plans before he'd approached Jane and now silently agreed with him. Once Jasper and Jane were living together as man and wife, he'd have to balance what he told her about the hell with what he held back, giving her just enough to satisfy her interest while keeping her ignorant of all the goings on. It would mean more deception, but it was necessary. He couldn't stand to have Jane spit on him like Mrs Robillard had when Jasper had approached her with his condolences. 'Better to be a married man than risk becoming a recluse.'

'You don't need a wife to avoid that.' Mr Bronson chuckled. 'You have a cook and a housekeeper and more willing company in other corners to see after your needs.'

'True, but how many of those paid people stayed around to help Uncle Patrick after he fell ill?'

'We don't have to worry about that here in London.'

Jasper touched the edge of the bills of mortality tucked beneath his blotter. 'I hope not, but there are other tragedies capable of befalling a man and leaving him in need of someone with more interest in his affairs than payment to step in and handle them.'

'I thought that's what you had me for.' Mr Bronson laughed. He removed a pouch of tobacco from his waistcoat pocket along with a clay pipe and began to pack the bowl with the fragrant weed.

'I do, but relations are sometimes more reliable.' Jasper wouldn't fail Jane the way Mr Robillard had failed his wife. 'I also know you Yanks. You'll want your own establishment sooner rather than later, to make something of yourself, to be your own man.'

'You are right, Mr Charton.' Mr Bronson pointed the stem of the pipe at him before setting it between his teeth. 'I'll have to strike out before you expect me to take a missus.'

'I wouldn't dare temper your excursions into the West End by suggesting such a thing.' Jasper waved his hand in the air to indicate the future. 'At least not yet.'

Mr Bronson took a deep drag on his pipe, then let the smoke out of the side of his mouth. 'Have you told her about Mrs Robillard?'

'No.' A breeze rustled the curtain, carrying into the room the faint scent of summer. Jasper rounded the desk and slammed the sash closed. 'You're not to tell her.'

'You can trust me to keep silent. I've been where you are, what with my father, God rest him, being a preacher and railing on about the ills of drink and cards. He'd have starved before taking my money if he'd learned how I really earned it.' Mr Bronson fingered the watch chain hanging in an arch from his pocket to where his father's timepiece hung from a button. 'No reason a lady has to hear about such ugliness.'

Mr Bronson touched the rolled debts to his forehead in a kind of salute, then turned on the heels of his fancy boots, the best his money could buy in London, and strode out of the room.

Jasper rested his hands on the back of one of the pair of shield-backed chairs near the window and took in the room. He should return to work. There was a great deal to be done now the Fleet Street building would be available, and Jane had given him new ideas, but he couldn't. He stared at the fire burning in the grate. Summer was slowly descending on the city, bringing with it unknown threats. His hands were tight on the carved wood and the edge of the fancy decoration bit into his palms. Yellow Jack couldn't touch him or anyone here, but it didn't mean some other pestilence might not come in with the summer wind and snatch away what remained of his peace of mind. Except it wasn't really disease he feared here as much as his own failings.

He left his office and entered the quiet of the gaming room. The smell of tobacco smoke, stale wine, sweat, hope and desperation hung thick in the air along with the dust motes. Everything had been set to rights, the chips stacked neatly at the tables, the packs of cards beside them fresh and ready to be opened by the dealers tonight. The Hazard wheel sat silent, too, the white balls lined up and waiting to click into place as men cheered and spent their money.

Jasper picked up a Hazard ball and rolled it between his fingers. He pitied many of the players, especially those like Captain Christiansen who rushed into forgetfulness through the cards. Jasper wondered what horrors Captain Christiansen had seen during his time at sea and if those memories drove him to recklessness the way they'd driven Jasper to return to this life.

He gripped the Hazard ball tight, his sins pressing down on him. There'd been many times before the epidemic when he'd begun to question this profession, but he'd ignored his doubts. Wealth, influence, standing, his uncle's pride and his own had drowned out the voice of his conscience. Mr Robillard's pistol shot had silenced the gaiety and left his conscience screaming. It still did and yet he'd come crawling back to this life the moment he'd set foot in England.

He set the ball down beside the others and, winding his way through the tables, left the gaming room, avoiding his reflection in the gilded mirror across the room. He didn't have the stomach to face the real Jasper, the one he hid from Jane and everyone, the ugly crooked thing his uncle had made him and he'd willingly become.

He locked up the upstairs rooms and left through the main warehouse. In the cavernous space, employees he paid well to keep quiet among their dockworker brethren unloaded shipments of wines, cards, food and other goods for tonight. The activity made his establishment appear like all the others crawling with carts and horses, with drivers and men calling to one another to shift about the various merchandise coming and going. Outside, the rising sun just touched the peaked tops of the buildings. Soon it would be higher and cast light into the deep shadows between the warehouses, further tanning the already ruddy faces of the men streaming in and out of the district as they went about their morning work.

Usually the bustling activity invigorated Jasper, but not this morning. He was pulling Jane into the mire by asking her to keep this secret the way Uncle Patrick had asked him to keep his. How long until he corrupted her the way he'd been corrupted?

No, I won't let that happen. They'd work hard on the club during the day, and he'd see to it they enjoyed themselves at night, both in town and in bed. She would remain ignorant of the true business of the hell until he could finally part with it.

'You there, you scoundrel,' a woman's voice rang out, silencing a few of the workmen stomping past Jasper, their backs bent under the weight of the casks they carried. 'I'll have a word with you.'

Jasper faced the woman barrelling down on

him the way Mrs Robillard had approached
him once. Her clothes were too worn to make
her a merchant's wife, but the reticule weighed
down by something heavy swinging by her
thick hips set him on edge.

'If you think I'm going to allow you to ruin
my son the way my husband ruined himself,
you are wrong.' She jerked up the reticule and
stuffed her hand inside. The memory of Mrs
Sullivan pulling a gun on him the night she'd
lost her prized diamond at a dice game rocked
him. Mrs Sullivan had missed.

He didn't wait to see if this woman's aim
was any better, but closed the distance between
them. 'How can I help you, madam?'

He offered her a hearty smile, the one he
once employed with planters and their wives
as he placed his hand on her wrist to stop her
from removing whatever weighed down her
reticule.

'Let go of me, you wicked man.' She jerked
free of him and her hand came out of the bag
empty. She was oblivious to the many workers
taking an interest in the conversation. Jasper
needed to quiet her and quickly. He didn't possess enough money to silence them all.

'Please, step inside my warehouse and we can speak.'

'We can speak here. You think I don't know what you're getting up to in this place?' she screeched. 'I've seen the money Adam comes home with and I know there's only one way he be can be earning it.'

At last he understood who the woman was and how to deal with her. He stepped closer and dropped his voice, painfully aware of the men around him leaning against crates while they pretended not to listen. 'Adam is my employee, not a client, and a very well-paid one because I trust him to remain quiet about my business, as I'm sure I can trust you, too.'

He reached into his pocket and plucked out a banknote. He didn't look to see the value before he took her hand and pressed it into her palm. She closed her fingers on the note and tugged it out of his grip. Then she opened the crumpled paper and her light eyebrows rose with surprise. Everything about her demeanour changed as she shoved the money inside her bodice.

'I understand completely, sir. I'm so sorry if I misunderstood, only his father was a gambler, and a drinker, and all but ruined us, forcing us from our home and into the filth of St Giles.' Tears filled her eyes and she wiped them away with the sleeve of her faded dress. 'When Adam started going out at night and coming home with money, I worried he was turning out like his father. I followed him here last night, heard the men talking about their wagers and I thought for sure I'd lost him.'

'Your son is one of my best footmen.' Jasper wrapped his arm around her thin shoulders. 'But if the wrong people find out about this place and shut it down, he'll lose his good wages.'

She peered up at him with round and worried eyes before her gaze darted to the watching men as she realised her mistake. 'I won't tell anyone. You can count on me. His wages keep me and his sisters from starving and allowed us to move out of St Giles. I assure you, I wouldn't knowingly do anything to jeopardise this place, Mr…?'

'Patrick,' he lied. She knew too much already.

'Mr Patrick. Thank you for all you've done for him. I'm so sorry for thinking so little of you.' She kissed the back of his hand, grateful in a way he didn't deserve. He smiled and accepted it despite the urge to climb in the carriage and be alone with his shame. When at last she took her leave, hurrying off even faster than she'd approached, Jasper strolled to his carriage to appear to all as if nothing was amiss and give no one a reason to consider the matter.

The men went back to their work and Jasper stepped into his carriage. Once inside, the vehicle set off and he sagged against the squabs, breathing for what seemed like the first time in days. 'It's all right.'

Except it wasn't. There'd been a moment when he'd feared her accusations would rise and the woman would announce to the entire wharf what took place above stairs at night. If too many people learned of it, then it would only be a matter of time before word spread and he could no longer keep this place a secret from his family. They'd already put him on a ship once and sent him off believing they'd never see him again. To be in London and banished from their circle would be worse, especially if he dragged Jane down with him.

The carriage rocked to a stop in front of the Charton house. Jasper climbed out and jogged up to the front door, hoping no one was about.

He needed peace to think and cursed again the repairs to the town house. When he'd first arrived home, the noise of his nieces and nephews, the talk of his parents and the continued comings and goings of his sibling had been a welcome relief after the deathly still of Savannah. Today, they would be an annoyance.

'Is everything all right, sir?' Alton, the butler, asked when he pulled open the front door. The thin man with the wide nose had been with the family since Jasper was a little boy. He knew Jasper as well as his old nurse, forcing Jasper to lie to him the way he lied to everyone else.

'Yes, thank you.' He made for the stairs, eager to reach the solitude of his room before anyone else noticed he was home. He didn't make it.

His mother came out of the front sitting room, concern furrowing her brow at the sight of him. 'Jasper, you seem troubled. Is anything wrong? Perhaps something you'd like to discuss with me about your evenings?'

She studied him the way she had when he was a boy and she used to summon him to her dressing room to interrogate him about what he'd been up to in the street. The vague notion she might know about the hell drifted through his mind before he dismissed it. If she had learned of it, she'd never be this coy in approaching him about it.

'No, nothing.' Jasper flashed the widest smile he could muster, feeling like a fool and a charlatan. But they were the ones who'd sent him away to learn his uncle's trade, even if they'd been ignorant of what it'd really involved. With all the subtlety and finesse of a fifteen-year-old, he'd railed at them for their decision and done everything he could to make them change their minds. They'd remained firm in spite of their own doubts and love for him, believing Uncle Patrick would provide their second son with the best opportunity to make something of himself.

His tension softened as he took in his mother's concerned face. They hadn't known the truth and they still didn't. If they ever learned about it, their guilt would be as great as his. They'd done what they'd thought best for him. Now, he would do what he thought best for them by allowing them to remain ignorant of the real consequences of their decisions and his. 'I'm fine. I had trouble sleeping again last night.'

'The dreams again?'

'Yes.' It was the reason he'd been giving for weeks to explain his long nights out. There had truly been nightmares when he'd first come home, but now they'd faded. Sadly, his need to use the excuse had not. 'After I woke up, I went to the theatre, and then to Mr Bronson's. I needed to be around people and I didn't want to disturb anyone here.'

'Of course,' his mother agreed with some hesitation. Then she reached up and took him by the chin, turning his face side to side to examine him. 'You look like you did when you first came home.'

He knew exactly what she meant. It was the reason they'd given him three months of peace before announcing his return. 'I haven't been sleeping well.'

His mother removed her hands from his face and clasped them in front of her. 'I think Jane will be good for you. She'll help you to deal with many things and perhaps forget some of your old experiences.'

Jane. He glanced at the side table in the entrance hall and the blue German glass pitcher the same deep azure as her eyes. It wasn't only the risk of discovery he'd faced today, but the very real threat of violence. If Adam's mother had had the chance to remove the pistol weighing down her bag, and Jasper and Jane had already wed, Jane might be a widow and left to deal with the revelations about Jasper and his club. He had too much honour to foist his embarrassments and troubles off on someone else the way Mr Robillard had done. 'I must see her this morning. There are matters we need to discuss.'

'Of course.' His mother patted his hand. 'Be good to her, Jasper. She deserves it and you deserve her care.'

'Yes, she deserves the best.' Sadly, it wasn't him.

Jasper removed his hand from hers and made for outside, refusing to hail a hack or summon the carriage again. He needed the brisk walk as he made for St Bride's Lane.

The surety with which he'd pledged himself to Jane began to dim in the bright daylight. He'd had doubts once about what he did in Savannah and he'd ignored them, blithely carrying on until they had destroyed people. *That* had garnered his attention. He'd had reservations about bringing Jane into this sphere, but he'd ignored them, too, insisting the best course of action was to link her life with his. This morning's encounter made him doubt his decision. It was one thing to burden her conscience with a few of his secrets. It was another to place her in real danger or set her up for potential embarrassment the way Milton had done. He couldn't allow Jane to be hurt.

It wasn't long before Jasper reached the junction of St Bride's Lane and Fleet Street. He stopped at the opening of the lane. It was calm compared to the bustle of the main thoroughfare. He should keep walking, go to his town house and make sure all was on course with the repair work to welcome them after the wedding, but his feet wouldn't move. With the practised skill of a man always betting against others, he weighed his risks against the odds. Leaving her now would certainly hurt her and turn her against him for good. The risks of his lifestyle were less clear, but potentially more deadly. He didn't want to deliberately hurt her, but he didn't want to see her wounded because of his more illicit life. Perhaps, if she understood something of the danger, at least as much as he was capable of telling her, she might help him decide. It was a

gamble he didn't wish to take, but he couldn't
ignore his intuition this time.

A sick feeling swam in the pit of Jane's
stomach as she faced Jasper. Until this moment, his unexpected appearance had been a
welcome distraction from drawing up guest
lists, breakfast menus and packing her things.
He hadn't smiled once since he'd arrived, nor
cracked a joke or made light of anything. It
was eerily similar to the way Milton had approached her the morning before he'd eloped.

'What exactly are you trying to say?' Fear
tightened her throat. *He's going to call it off.
No, if he'd changed his mind he would have
sent a note instead of coming here himself.* It
was slim comfort. There was a reason he was
standing here viewing her as if he'd already
lost her.

'I want to make sure you understand fully
what we're about to do, including the potential dangers. It's something we may have overlooked in our rush to wed.' He glanced past
her to make sure no one was eavesdropping.
Then he shifted closer and dropped his voice.
'Not every player loses. There's a very real
chance someone could win and bankrupt us,

or a cheater I unmask might lash out at me or you. You must be sure this is the kind of life you want.'

He's trying to get me to cry off. She certainly would not. If she had to club him over the head and drag him up the aisle to ensure he said his vows, she would. She wouldn't be humiliated in front of the Fleet Street community again. 'After a lifetime of living here, having been in the house the night Laura's uncle tried to kill her, I'm well aware of the risks involved in dealing with money and people.'

'I don't doubt you can handle any challenge our life together might create.' His words were light, but there was no missing the deep furrow marring his brow, or his insistence in pressing on. She might not be willing to end things, but it didn't mean he wouldn't. 'But we can't be so lax about it or the realities of our situations.'

'Which are?'

He hesitated before he answered. 'The danger aligning yourself with me might put you in.'

She waited, bracing herself in anticipation of the words she expected to follow and end everything. Outside, her niece's and nephews' high voices rang out, tensing Jane's already tight nerves, but still Jasper didn't speak.

Don't do it, please, don't turn away from me. Her cheeks burned with her silent shame until she was sure they were the same red as her velvet dress. She didn't want to beg or to be this weak in front of him, but his pulling back cut deeper than when Mrs Hale had moved away. He'd promised to create a life, home and business with her. They weren't even married and he was already reneging on his word.

'What's really wrong, Jasper, please tell me?'

Jane studied Jasper with the same pleading look as the men who approached Mr Bronson in search of more credit. Her desperation cut him because he'd caused it. Instead of waiting and better thinking things through, he'd come here in a panic and created a doubt which hadn't existed before and it had hurt her.

Down the hall, the back door leading from the garden squeaked opened. The Rathbone children's footsteps rang through the house, accompanied by their high voices as they called to one another. It echoed with the sound of his childhood when he and Milton used to tear through the same door and race upstairs to find Jane and bring her out to play. He especially remembered the months after her parents' deaths when he'd come here to fetch her, eager to see his heartbroken friend smile again. Those days were gone, but Jane was here with him, as beautiful and trusting as back then. He couldn't throw her over the way his brother had. If she'd set her mind to facing all challenges with him—and Heaven knew after living with Philip Rathbone she was the best woman to do it—he couldn't push her away. He would find a way to keep her safe.

He pulled her to him and clutched her tight against his chest. Resting his chin on her smooth hair, he inhaled her gardenia scent and allowed it to soothe his concerns. 'Forgive me. I didn't mean to startle you with my visit. I just wanted to make sure you were completely aware of what marrying me means.'

She relaxed against him with a sigh of relief and slid her arms around his waist. 'Of course I'm aware of it. Despite it all, I still want to be your wife and work with you.'

'And you will.'

She leaned back but didn't pull away, her

usual exuberance colouring her cheeks with a pink more alluring than the shameful red he'd brought to them a few minutes before, the weight of her as natural in his arms as his coat on his shoulders. 'Philip spoke to Reverend Claire this morning. It's all set for Friday at eleven o'clock, the soonest we could do it given the seven-day wait. The Reverend was stunned when he found out I'm marrying you. I'm surprised he didn't look up the rules of consanguinity to make sure it's all right for a woman to marry her former fiancé's brother.'

Jasper laughed, the first genuine one he'd enjoyed in ages. This was how it had always been between them and this was how it would continue. He'd make sure of it. 'I don't think he's so medieval.'

'I hope not for I have no desire to appeal to the Archbishop for a dispensation.'

He softly cuffed her under her chin. 'We could always elope and stun a few more people.'

'And deny everyone in the Fleet the chance to come and gawk? Heavens, no. I want them to be there when we see this betrothal through. And we will.' Her warning was clear. She would make him live up to his promise.

'Yes, we will.' He took her hand and brought it to rest over his heart. Her pulse flickered in each fingertip against his as he drank in her wide blue eyes and the full lips which were parted in anticipation. She wasn't just his greatest friend; she was about to be his wife. At fifteen, he'd longed for this, but he'd hesitated to tell her for fear she'd laugh at him. Then the night of his farewell party, with the single candle in the study making her eyes sparkle, she'd vowed to wait for his return. The missed opportunity had crushed him. It wasn't only his family he'd been exiled from, but a future with her. It was why he'd denied any feelings other than friendship and why he hadn't written despite dreaming of her. He'd been too angry over the chances stolen from him.

But they hadn't been stolen, only delayed.

The old bitterness faded under the soft pressure of her fingertips on the back of his neck and her stomach against his as he leaned down to press his lips to hers. A charge of passion arched between them, driving away his exhaustion and worry, and invigorating him like nothing since before the dreaded summer in Savannah. In her arms, the future surrounded him and he wanted to embrace it as he did her. With her help, he'd build a new life and at last bury the old one. He'd finally leave Savannah behind and Jane would be there to help him do it.

Chapter Five

'Are you sure you want to wear this dress?' Mrs Fairley, the blonde modiste, asked as she laid the silk creation across the back of the *chaise* in her fitting room. The modiste had sewn this dress for Jane's wedding to Milton, making it the only one she could have ready before Friday. Jane had insisted Mrs Fairley keep it, determined to wear it to the next Charton party and give Milton a taste of what he'd rejected. When the opportunity had finally arisen, Mrs Fairley had talked her out of her revenge, making Jane realise she'd only embarrass herself.

'Yes, I'm going to wear it.' After Jasper's visit this morning, Jane didn't want to waste money on a new gown she might not use. If this one didn't make it to the altar she'd sell it in Petticoat Lane herself instead of allowing it to moulder here like some shed skin. Then she'd use the money to buy a dog.

'Let's see it on you.' Mrs Fairley helped her pull on the dress, then ushered her up on to the stool. The cream-silk skirt brushed the tops of Jane's stocking-clad feet, the intricate embroidery of the interlaced diamonds decorating the hem and weighing it down. Blue-and-silver embroidered flowers coloured the bodice and set off her blue eyes. The dress was stunning, despite its past, and she craved the chance to wear it, at last to be a bride instead of a cast-off spinster—assuming Jasper intended to go through with the wedding.

'Are you excited about the marriage?' Mrs Fairley asked as she knelt to examine the hem.

'Yes.'

'But?'

Jane fingered a bit of lace. After this morning, she needed to speak with someone, and Mrs Fairley had always been discreet, even back when Philip had been the one paying her bills. 'I'm worried about Jasper. He was acting strange this morning.'

She explained about Jasper's visit and how sure she'd been that he would break the betrothal. What she didn't say was how, while she'd waited for him to do it, it had reminded her of sitting beside her mother's bed when she was six and begging for her to forgive her for being naughty, begging her not to leave. Jane bit her tongue, refusing to cry. She'd made so many promises during her parents' illnesses, vowing never again to disobey them and apologising over and over for slipping off to the fair against their wishes and bringing the fever into the house. In the end, her promises hadn't made a difference, neither had Milton's. There was nothing to make Jasper honour his.

'Do you think there is another woman?' Mrs Fairley asked as she slipped a pin in the hem.

Jane took a deep breath, the silk sliding up and over her chest before settling back into place. 'I don't think so, but it seems I'm the last to realise when a man takes a paramour. Besides, he hasn't been back in London long enough and there's nothing stopping him from marrying whoever he wants.'

'He wants to marry you.'

Jane touched her lips with the tips of her fingers. His kiss this morning had surprised her as much as the one in his bedroom. Despite having seen it coming, she hadn't expected the force of it. She'd leaned in to Jasper, savouring the tender pressure of his mouth against hers. In the salty taste of him there had lingered more than a deal or mere friendship and convenience; there had been the tantalising hint of a deeper connection. When he'd pulled back, she thought she'd seen the same realisation in his eyes but his smile and quick wit had covered it, making her wonder if she'd imagined it. Jane took another deep breath, almost afraid to say the next words aloud but they'd been boiling inside her since he'd left. 'I'm no longer sure he does.'

'I assume your brother approved the marriage?' Mrs Fairley knew Philip well. He'd loaned her the money to establish her shop after her husband had been wounded in France. She'd done a great deal of business with his family and friends ever since.

'He did.'

'Then take his consent as proof of your good judgement.'

'What if he's wrong this time?' Buying a building on a whim was one thing, but a marriage was entirely different. Once they were wed, Jasper, as her husband, would control her money, property and everything else. She doubted he'd act like a tyrant, but the darkness in his eyes when he'd first arrived at her house made her uneasy. She didn't want to marry him only to find out he wasn't the carefree friend she adored but someone else, a stranger she knew nothing about. 'What if I'm rushing into something I can't undo?'

'You wouldn't be the first Rathbone to do so, would you?' Mrs Fairley teased.

Philip and Laura had hurried to the altar and in the end found love. Jane wasn't convinced her haste would be rewarded nor was she willing to hope for such a happy outcome. Love had not been a part of their negotiations. 'Maybe Philip approved the match because he thinks it's his last chance to get rid of me?' The idea Philip had finally lost faith in her made her tremble.

Mrs Fairley stood. 'Mr Rathbone would never do anything not in your best interest. He loves you too much.'

Jane tried to believe it, but after having so many people leave her it was difficult to think her brother wouldn't do it, too, some day.

Mrs Fairley laid her hands on Jane's shoulders, squeezing them to ease the tension. 'Maybe it's not you Mr Charton doubts, but himself. Maybe he doesn't believe he's worthy of you.'

If so, he'd certainly be the first. 'Not Jasper. He's always been so sure of himself.'

'You think you know him, but I imagine, given your time apart, there's still a great deal for you to learn.' Mrs Fairley said it as though the discovery would be a grand adventure.

Jane wasn't so sure. Mrs Fairley was right, she didn't know Jasper as well as she believed, and she was making decisions based on nostalgia and desperation instead of reality. She didn't want another engagement to end, but marriage was the most binding of contracts. If she got it wrong, it might ruin her life more than it helped it. She twisted her hands in front of her, hating this uncertainty. There was only one way to face it. She must see Jasper again and put her doubts and his to rest.

'I hear you had a bit of an odd encounter with Adam's mother today,' Mr Bronson observed as he touched a burning reed to the bowl of his pipe and inhaled.

Jasper signed a paper, then set it aside to study his partner. 'Who told you about it?'

'He did, apologising the entire time. Thought

I'd talk to you about what you want to do about it. Can't have her getting hysterical in public again.'

'There's nothing to be done. Tell him we spoke and make it clear he needs to ensure her silence. Then we forget the matter.' He wouldn't see Adam's siblings suffer from the loss of their brother's wages because of his mother any more than he could have abandoned Jane this morning. He set his pen in the elaborate holder, still cursing his foolishness. In the future, he'd have to be more careful about keeping his concerns regarding the hell to himself. 'Is Captain Christiansen here?'

'He is, but he isn't playing too deep, at least not yet. He's only had one or two drinks and the night is still young. However, there's the son of a cheesemonger in there with a fever to his play I don't like.'

'Yes, I saw the man's debts from last night. Cut him off when you go back inside and tell him he's banned from the club. Let him ruin himself elsewhere.' The Captain he would tolerate, but not the cheesemonger's son. The man didn't possess enough business knowledge to make his presence here of any value.

'You really going to give this up?' Mr Bronson waved at the office.

'When it's feasible. I'll turn ownership over to you and retain a percentage of the profits.' He picked up the wine order and added a few bottles of Spanish wine to it. Mr Portland, who owned a good many stocks, was more willing to speak to others about them after a few glasses of the tart liquor.

'Ah, so the answer is yes, and no.' Mr Bronson circled his pipe stem in the air.

'I can't afford to lose the income, not with a wife to support.' And the money he needed to send to Mrs Robillard and pay for his workers' wages.

'Probably children, too, they have a way of coming along.'

'I won't see them go without if the club isn't as lucrative as I hoped.' Rapacious hunger, and the filth and horror of disease had seized him once. He'd vowed never to become poor and end up in Seven Dials with the twin evils plaguing him or those he cared for again.

'Does your wife-to-be know this?' He set the pipe between his teeth.

'Not yet.' With her accounting skills, he knew he couldn't keep this detail from her or hide the transactions regarding Mrs Robillard for ever.

'Don't see why you need to tell her at all. A woman shouldn't be involved in a man's business.'

'I don't agree.' Except he did. Jane would have as large a hand as she wanted in the club and his life, but he would not allow her to be entangled in the business of the hell, or his past.

'For a man with so much to do you certainly sleep late.' The melodious female voice carried over the quiet of Jasper's bedroom, drawing him out of a deep sleep.

He opened his eyes, straining to see through the darkness cast by the heavy curtains covering the windows.

A little light sparked and then met the wick of a candle. It illuminated Jane's round face while she carried it from the hearth and set it on the table beside his bed.

'What are you doing in here?' He picked up the ornate dolphin clock next to the candle and peered at the hands. One-thirty. He didn't usually sleep this late. It explained the fatigue sticking to him like mud.

'I came to fetch you to visit the building on Fleet Street. I didn't expect to find you still in bed.' She stood over him like his mother used to do, more tempting than scolding with the glint of mischief in her azure eyes.

Jasper pushed himself up and leaned back against the stuffed pillows, trying to shake off his weariness. 'How did you sneak past my parents?'

'I didn't sneak. I came in through the front door. Your mother was the one who sent me up. Since we're betrothed and a date is set it seems she is no longer scandalised by the idea of my seeing you déshabillé.'

'So I see.' His mother possessed a practical sense of things.

'Even if she hadn't told me to come in here, your father's security is so lax it's a wonder the thieves of London aren't parading through the sitting room every day helping themselves to their things, and yours, though I'm not sure who'd want *your* things.' She picked up the clock, wrinkling her nose at the overly ornate gilding on the case before she set it back down. 'Your decor will have to change once we're married.'

'I look forward to it.' And to more intimate

time in the bedroom with her. The memory of
her lips beneath his made him trill his fingers
on the cool sheets, eager to touch her silken
hair and a few other soft and enticing places.
He crossed his hands on his stomach. Temptation was dangerous, as he'd discovered in Savannah, but he'd be a liar if he said he'd never
been tempted by Jane. At fifteen, despite their
long friendship, salacious thoughts of her had
cost him many a goodnight's sleep. He could
imagine what his fifteen-year-old self would
say if he knew he was days away from experiencing one of the many fantasies he'd con-
cocted about her in the middle of the night.

'So, what, or should I say who, kept you up
so late last night?' she asked in a crisp voice.
There was no missing the jealousy flavouring
her question or the true intention of this visit.
*She's here to make sure I uphold my end of
the contract.* Her brother had taught her well.

'I was quite free of female company if
that's what you're getting at.' He ran his hands
through his hair, determined to prove himself and make her forget yesterday's misstep.
'But if you'd like to keep me awake tonight, I
wouldn't protest.'

Her eyes dropped to his chest, then lower

down to another muscle hidden beneath the coverlet. 'I'm keeping you awake right now.'

'Indeed, you are.' He laced his fingers behind his head. 'Anything in particular you'd like to do about it?'

'Not this morning.' The faint hint of pink colouring her cheeks undermined her courage. It increased his desire to pull her into bed and teach her something, but he didn't. He doubted his mother was so open-minded when it came to their betrothal.

It was time to get down to less pleasurable business. 'What about the Fleet Street building do you wish to discuss?'

She rose, plucked his discarded Jermyn Street shirt off the foot of the bed and flung it at him. 'Get up and we will visit it together and I'll tell you.'

'I've given a great deal of thought to the food we'll offer here,' Jane announced while they stood in the entry hall of the musty building. It had been closed up for weeks and the remnants of tobacco and shattered clay pipes lay scattered across the unpolished floor.

'Shouldn't we consider the condition first?' He wiped a line of dust off the dull banister.

In the midst of their dirty surroundings, Jane dazzled in her fitted blue pelisse with the stiff collar brushing the slant of her delicate chin. The hint of the cream dress beneath, and the smooth skin of her chest visible at the open V, made concentrating on work a challenge.

'I did, right after I purchased it. My builder assures me it's sound and, with little more than some cleaning and paint, we can open as soon as everything else is in place. Tell me which rooms you intend to use for what activities and I'll start gathering the necessary items.'

He motioned with his hat to the front window overlooking Fleet Street, determined to think about the club and not the subtle hint of her curving hips beneath her long skirt. 'We'll offer cigars and wine in there. The back room will be a lounge.'

'And upstairs?'

'Private rooms for men to conduct confidential business.'

She crossed her arms under her full breasts. 'What kind of confidential business?'

'The business kind of business.' He took her hand and slid his other around her waist. Her eyes widened when he snapped her close, her chest catching like his before his wink drew out her smile. Then he waltzed her into the dining room before spinning her out so her skirts flared around her ankles. He let go of her, sending her whirling gracefully across the empty room. 'Do you think we should offer dancing?'

'Certainly not. We don't want to distract men from spending money.' She pressed one hand to her chest and struggled to speak through her giggles. The collusion making her eyes flash reminded him of when they used to sneak out to Club Row Market to feed the puppies for sale before their owners caught them. 'But we'll serve better fare than what they're used to and give them a reason to bring clients here instead of dining at home.'

'Good idea. I'll leave it to you to choose the chef and the menu since you're more acquainted with London tastes than I am.' He spun his hat between his hands, picturing the room full of tables covered with white linen and fine port and beef with men discussing contracts and trade. Jasper would stand proud among them instead of skulking in the shadows of night. His only ties to the hell would be the money which would continue to come in and protect them from the prospect of poverty.

'I already have an idea for a special cheese,

a delicacy to tempt them. We must also choose the decor. This must look like a respectable place of business, not a colonial bordello.' She slid him a teasing look before turning her attention to the dining room. 'You can close the hell at once and sell its contents to pay for what we need here.'

Jasper tightened his grip on his hat, denting the brim before he released it. 'I can't.'

She whirled to face him, shoulders set for a fight. 'Why not? I thought you wanted to leave it behind.'

'I do, but I owe it to Mr Bronson to offer it to him before I depart. I can't do it as a gutted shell.'

She narrowed her eyes at him as if wanting to say she didn't entirely believe his intention to give it to a friend instead of closing it outright. 'Have you spoken to him to see if he even wants it?'

'I have and he does.' At least this was the truth.

'And will you be keeping a share of its profits?'

Damn, she was too intuitive. He wasn't ready to have this conversation, but there was no avoiding it now. 'Yes.'

'You can't expect to clear your conscience with a toe in each world.'

'I can't risk us going broke if the club fails either.' He wouldn't have them burning through his money and hers in an effort to stay out of debtors' prison.

'It won't fail. We won't let it, especially if our livelihoods depend on it.'

He didn't share her confidence, not after all the times he'd seen men go from wealthy to broke with one turn of the cards. His silence dimmed her optimism.

'We will be able to attract enough patrons to support the club and us, won't we?' Jane picked at the button on her glove in a rare moment of self-doubt and it struck Jasper hard. It wasn't like her to question her plans.

'We will. Mr Bronson will spread the word among our guests, especially the more influential ones. We'll offer them a special membership, entice them into joining and others will follow. It always worked in Savannah.'

'Did it now?'

'Attracting patrons is the one other skill Uncle Patrick taught me that I excelled at. How do you think I drew men to the Company Gaming Room so fast?' The sense of accomplishment he used to experience on nights when every chair at every table was filled and a crowd two or three deep stood behind them gripped him. He should be ashamed, not proud. The one consolation was realising he'd soon put some of what he'd learned to reputable use.

'Then I have no doubt we'll be successful in London.'

Her faith in him was touching if not disconcerting. His uncle had believed in him and he'd let him down. He wondered how long it would be until she and all the others, both here and in America, who relied on him, suffered the same disappointment.

'Hello?' Mr Bronson called out, breaking the quiet between Jasper and Jane. 'Anyone here?'

'In the dining room.' Jasper turned as his associate strolled into the dining room. 'We were just talking about you. I was telling Miss Rathbone what an excellent partner you are.'

'So exceptional, I brought you last night's take.' He handed Jasper a leather folder full of banknotes.

'Thank you, but how did you find me here?'

'I went by your house and they told me you were here.' This wasn't the first time Mr Bronson had gone searching for him at the Charton house. He'd met Jasper's family shortly after their return and during the many times he'd collected Jasper on the pretext of other business while they'd been establishing the Company Gaming Rooms.

Jasper tucked the folio under his arm and drew Jane to his side. 'Miss Rathbone, allow me to introduce my associate, Mr Gabriel Bronson.'

'A pleasure to meet you.' Mr Bronson swept off his hat and folded into a deep bow.

Jane curtsied, then rose with an impish smile. 'Quite an angelic name for a gambler?'

'My father was a preacher.' Mr Bronson set his hat on his head and hooked his thumbs in his waistcoat pocket. 'Tried to redeem me before I was even a man. Didn't realise I was already lost.'

'And what about Jasper, how lost was he in Savannah? He's told me so little of it. I want to know what he was like there.'

Mr Bronson exchanged a wary glance with Jasper. 'There isn't really much to tell. It's not so different here than it was there. He still enjoyed the finer things like clothes, and wines, but he had to come to London to find the finest fiancée.'

To Jasper's amazement, Jane blushed. 'I don't believe you. There must have been something different about him there.'

Mr Bronson took his tobacco pouch out of his pocket and swung it in a small circle in front of him. 'Well, Jasper did attend the theatre more and of course there was the gaming room.' He described to Jane the gaming room in all its glittering and gaudy splendour and Jasper's and Uncle Patrick's place in it, trips to the theatre and parties at the finest Savannah homes with the mayor and other influential men. Jasper could barely recall the lively and carefree man he used to be before the epidemic, the one he could be again with Jane by his side.

'I didn't realise Jasper was so influential in Savannah, or how wide a swathe he cut through high society,' Jane remarked with amusement when Mr Bronson finished his tale.

Jasper shook his head. 'It wasn't as impressive as he's making it sound.'

'Or you're being modest.'

'He's right Miss Rathbone, I might have embellished a little, but I want you to think well of your husband-to-be.'

'Will you be at the wedding, Mr Bronson?' Jane asked.

'No. I don't fancy formal events, but I wish you all the best, Miss Rathbone. You've found a fine man in Jasper.' He slapped Jasper on the back. 'Now, if you'll excuse me, my bed is calling.'

With another imperial bow he took his leave.

'For a rake he's a charming man. I see why you chose him to be the face of your gaming room,' Jane observed once he was gone. 'And you're right. It wouldn't be fair to sell it out from under him. I'll use my money to purchase the necessary furniture and accoutrements.'

'No, I have ample funds for it. I'll advance them to you and you can purchase what you need with them. I'll also give you free rein on contracts and spending once we're married, sooner if you'd like. We can visit my solicitor, Mr Steed, tomorrow and make all the necessary arrangements.'

'Yes, I want everything to be in place so I can begin at once and, while the hell is still yours, make sure the two of you promote the benefits of our club,' Jane added.

'We've already begun. I can also sell what's still in the warehouse since I'm sure you have no desire to see it installed in our house.' He came up to her and placed his arms around her waist, holding her as naturally as he breathed.

'You're right. I have no desire to decorate like the Sun King.'

'Too bad, the bed in the warehouse is quite sturdy.' He pulled her tighter against him.

She laid her hands on his shoulder and playfully peered up at him. 'Is it, now?'

He brought his mouth so close to her ear, his lips brushed the lobe as he whispered, 'Very.'

She shivered and he closed his eyes, nearly groaning at the sweetness of her response.

'Then perhaps we can keep the one piece.' She ran her finger along the lapel of his coat, the gesture as tempting as it was subtle.

He was about to accept the silent invitation in her eyes and touch his lips to hers when the bells of St Bride's Church rang out and Jane jerked back. 'Oh, we have another appointment.'

He brushed her neck with his lips. 'Are you sure you want to go?'

She pushed him out to arm's length, the businesswoman in her winning out over the vixen. 'We aren't married yet and there's a cheesemonger expecting us.'

* * *

A half-hour later they stood in Mr Stilton's shop, sampling a variety of cheddar like none they'd ever tasted before. It was difficult for Jane to concentrate on the tang of the cheese with the taste of Jasper still so sharp. He wore a fawn-coloured coat over a dark waistcoat. Both were tailored to fit his firm chest and offer a hint of what she'd seen the other morning. In the carriage on the way here, she'd considered tempting him into another peek, but had refrained. She'd been audacious enough in her proposal, she didn't wish to appear like a harlot or ruin the delights of the wedding night with her impatience.

'What do you think?' She licked a crumb off her lip, subtle in her teasing, aware of Mr Stilton watching them.

'It's a true temptation to the palate.' The potency in Jasper's eyes stole any suggestive responses from her tongue. Flirting didn't come naturally to her, except when she was with him.

'I sell this variety to some of the most important men in London.' Mr Stilton rocked on his heels in pride, his soft chin raised.

'An excellent angle for marketing it to our

clients, at a mark-up, of course,' Jane suggested to Jasper.

'Of course.'

Jane fell silent while Jasper spoke to Mr Stilton about how much they would need and a possible date for delivery. She calculated the price, as she had with everything else connected with establishing the club, and it was substantial. If Jasper harboured doubts about the solvency of their venture then she couldn't fault or chide him for hanging on to part of the hell. Not even her inheritance would be enough to save them if the losses proved too large. She'd seen enough men come to Philip for loans for shops and ventures only to have a fire, flood or sunken ship send them spiralling into insolvency. Even Philip had once come close to losing everything. In the months after they'd lost their parents, while he was caring for her and taking over their father's business, he'd extended a sizeable loan to a silversmith who'd defaulted. It had almost ruined his entire business. Mr Charton, having been a good friend of their father's, had stepped in to help stop Philip from being ruined. She'd been a child then, but in her grief she'd caught the strain in Philip's face and overheard enough conversations to realise the severity of what was going on. Philip had worried with Mr Charton over not being able to provide for Jane or being forced by his losses to leave her with the Chartons and it had terrified her. She'd been a burden he hadn't needed at a time when everything had been falling on his shoulders and there'd been nothing she could do to help him. She wondered what burden she now placed on Jasper and if this was why he'd hesitated about the wedding yesterday.

Jane stepped a touch closer to Jasper. She'd wrangled him into marrying her. It made her wonder whether he offered wanton kisses, suggestions and compliments because he really wanted to or because, having made his decision after yesterday's doubts, he must now convince them both it was the right one.

'Thank you, Mr Stilton, for everything.' Jasper shook the cheesemonger's hand, then guided Jane towards the entrance of the shop, his arm solid on hers.

She placed her hand over his as they stepped outside on to the pavement. She was no longer a helpless child, she was a grown woman who would not be a burden to him; she would be a partner in their success. It was how much of a partner he intended to be that she still worried about.

They left the shop and were not three feet from the entrance when Chester Stilton staggered out of a hack, his usually pristine clothes as rumpled as the skin beneath his eyes. With her doubts trailing her, he was one of the last people she wished to encounter and she tugged on Jasper's arm, hoping to hurry past before he noticed them. They were not fast enough.

'Miss Rathbone, here to change your mind about my offer?' Chester called out, forcing her and Jasper to face the man.

'I see your credit with your tailor has run out.' She motioned to the patched tear on his lapel.

He reddened with shame at being caught looking less than impeccable. Then he leaned in close to her, his eyes as bloodshot as his breath was foul. 'Come to sneer at me, spinster?'

'Mind how you address her,' Jasper warned from beside her.

Mr Stilton curled one lip at him, revealing his yellow teeth. 'Who are you?'

'Jasper Charton.' Jasper took Jane's hand. 'Her fiancé.'

'Picking up your brother's leftovers, I see,'

Mr Stilton sneered before turning to Jane. 'What did you do to get him? Purchase him like you couldn't purchase his brother?'

Jasper slid in between Jane and the cheesemonger's son. He stood a good head taller than Chester and leaned so close to him, he was forced to bend back to avoid being nose to nose with Jasper. 'Speak to her like that again and I'll see to it your debts are called in. I don't mean your debt at the tailor, I mean the gambling ones you've run up at the Company Gaming Room.'

Jane stifled a squeak of surprise while struggling to hold her look of disdain. *Mr Stilton gambles at Jasper's hell.*

Mr Stilton's lips dropped down over his teeth and the blood drained out of his flushed face. 'How do you know about those? I've never seen you there.'

'I'm a well-connected man. If you don't wish to be strung up by your debts, or have your father inadvertently learn of them, you'll keep your opinions about Miss Rathbone to yourself. Do I make myself clear?'

Mr Stilton flicked a nervous glance at Jane before nodding in agreement.

'Good, then we've settled the matter.' Jasper

straightened, turned to Jane and offered her his arm. She took it, jutting her chin out in defiance of Mr Stilton when they stepped around him. 'Good day, Mr Stilton.'

Jane didn't dare speak until they were down the street and well away from the cheesemonger. 'Why did you threaten him with his club debts?'

His arm beneath her hand stiffened. 'Because he deserved it for insulting you.'

'But you risked him finding out about your involvement in the hell. If he had, he's weasel enough to have used it against you.'

'I've seen him gamble. He isn't smart enough to make the connection.' Jasper stopped and faced her. 'Besides, you're worth the risk.'

Jane's back stiffened. She'd waited years for someone to value her like this, someone not related to her by blood or marriage. The fact it was Jasper seemed right, but the old doubts refused to be silenced. 'No, I'm not.'

He brushed her cheek with his fingers. 'Despite what you believe, you're an exceptional woman worthy of respect and admiration. I'm the one who doesn't deserve you.'

'Of course you do.' People shuffled by on the narrow pavement, silently scolding them for blocking traffic. Jane was barely conscious of their censure as Jasper caressed her cheek with his thumb. He'd been willing to risk having his respectability challenged to defend her, and it was obvious he didn't regret it. This more than his words—his offer to turn over his affairs at once, or his kisses, spoke to how much he valued her and their coming union.

Mrs Fairley was right. Jane hadn't made a mistake.

Chapter Six

'In case you're unfamiliar with what will take place tonight, allow me to explain,' Mrs Hale offered while Laura did up the buttons on the back of Jane's wedding dress. With her straight nose and auburn hair tinged with grey, Mrs Hale resembled Laura, except her eyes were pale brown while Laura's were hazel. 'When a gentleman and a lady are alone together...'

'Yes, I'm well aware of what will transpire.' Jane had eavesdropped on Jasper's sister enough times when she was younger to learn the full extent of things. However, having an understanding of how the deed worked and experiencing it were two very different things. Jane took such a deep breath, she feared the buttons might pop off their threads. If what was to come with Jasper was anything like his kisses, she wasn't sure how she'd make it through tonight without melting into a puddle.

'Too bad, I was looking forward to describing it in more flowery language than I usually hear in Dr Hale's practice.' Mrs Hale laughed from her place on the sofa. It was the first time the three women had been together in months and her presence helped calm Jane. She'd been like a mother to her, helping her grow from a young girl to a woman and calming her on more than one occasion when Jane had been fuming over some slight or one of Philip's decisions. In Mrs Hale's smile and the delighted way she spun her cane as she held it in front of her, Jane could almost imagine her own mother here.

She would be here if it hadn't been for me. Jane tried to smile while the other ladies continued to joke and tease, but her lips were as tight as her nerves.

'If you have any questions after the deed, you know where to find me.' Mrs Hale clapped with the same restrained exuberance she'd shown when Laura had made her a grandmother. Then she rose and came to stand beside her, fingering the fine embroidered lace cascading from the shoulders of the dress to brush the hem of the skirt. 'I'm glad you'll finally be able to attach a good memory to this bit of silk. You deserve to be happy.'

Her eyes misted with tears as she took Jane by the shoulders and turned her to face the mirror. Any reservations Jane might have had about the dress vanished as the thirteen-year-old girl who'd spent days in this room mourning the departure of her friend, and praying he might some day return, rose up inside her. He had come back to her. He was the first.

Philip rapped on the door and then entered. He wore his best morning suit, as handsome today as when he'd married Laura. He stopped at the sight of his sister, and his eyes shone with pride. 'You're lovely.'

He came forward and pressed a tender kiss to her forehead. Tears blurred her vision, but she brushed them off with her gloved fingertips, not wanting to meet Jasper with red eyes. Philip was almost the only parent she'd ever known, and for all her wanting to have a home of her own, she was at last leaving his. Every argument they'd ever had and each disagreement meant nothing compared to the affection in his smile.

'Thank you.' *For everything.* He'd always

been a loving brother, doing his best to raise her. She'd miss his steady presence, despite all of their butting heads.

'Are you ready?'

The day she never thought would come was here at last. She would finally be a bride. It was time to go and claim her life with Jasper. 'I am.'

Jasper stood at the altar, Reverend Claire beside him, his younger brother Giles serving as Jasper's best man while Jacob sulked in the pew at not having been chosen. A few years ago it would have been Milton beside him, but he was the only Charton not in attendance. He and his wife had elected to stay away from the church, but at his father's insistence he'd grudgingly agreed to bring his wife to the wedding breakfast at the Rathbones'.

Jasper's three elder sisters and their husbands and children sat in the first few pews. While his numerous nieces and nephews whispered and giggled with the Rathbone children, his sisters and his mother sniffed into their handkerchiefs. A few months ago they'd been worried he'd die in Savannah. They were overjoyed to see him now on his wedding day.

He rubbed the back of his neck and the slight perspiration beneath his collar. They cared for him and he was deceiving them all. They'd despise him if they ever found out about the hell and shun him just as surely as they embraced him today. He'd have no one to blame but himself if they did. If the day ever came, he hoped they showed Jane as much tolerance as they'd extended to Milton. He couldn't bear to have her cast out of her family for his mistakes.

'You're not nervous, are you?' Giles ribbed, pulling Jasper out of his worries.

'No.' He exchanged a hearty smile with his younger brother. 'Just eager.'

And he was. The day he'd left London with Jane's willingness to wait for him still fresh in his mind, he'd believed every hope he'd ever harboured of being with his closest friend was finished. He'd make sure she never suffered because of him, or viewed him with the same disgust he'd come to see his uncle with. She would remain innocent where he'd been corrupted and he would do everything he could to make sure she never wanted for anything.

The organ struck up, drawing Jasper and the entire church's attention to the back. Jane appeared at the top of the aisle, resplendent in an ivory-silk dress with a train of lace, walking with dignity beside her brother in time to the organ music. Her cobalt-coloured eyes fixed on his, so alight with joy it took his breath away. He'd thought luck had deserted him in Savannah, then he'd come home and met her again. She knew more about him than anyone in this church and still she was willing to bind her life to his. He didn't deserve her admiration, but he'd find a way to be worthy of her.

At last, Jane reached him and, after a few words from the Reverend Claire, Philip offered Jasper his sister's hand and her future. Jasper couldn't stop the smile from spreading across his lips and Jane answered it with a playful one of her own. It echoed with the memories of them laughing together at his eldest sister Olivia's wedding. At the reception, they'd played the game of what if, taking turns imagining who their future partner would be. Secretly, he'd hoped it would be her. Today, it was. It wasn't desperation that had guided her up the aisle to him, but a connection they'd shared for years, one which hadn't been broken by time or distance or all his sins.

At Reverend Claire's instruction, they faced him. While the Reverend spoke, Jasper was aware of nothing but Jane beside him, her fingers solid against his and her light perfume brushing his senses. She was as gorgeous, trusting and innocent as he was dark, experienced and dishonest, but if she believed in him then it was time to start believing in himself.

When Reverend Claire asked if there was anyone who objected to the marriage, Jasper didn't flinch or peer over his shoulder to see if someone came forward. No one, not even his previous doubts, spoke up.

Reverend Claire drew out the silence as though he expected some objection, if not from the audience then from the groom. Jane studied Jasper out of the corner of her eye, wondering if he held any of the second thoughts he'd expressed to her the other day. But they were nowhere to be seen as he drew his lips to one side in a playful grin she matched.

Hearing no objections, Reverend Claire continued until it was time to exchange vows. With a seriousness to put her brother to shame, she faced Jasper, delighted to see him bring the same gravity to the solemn words. He'd already made one promise to her in private—

to always honour her. Today, he'd make a few more for everyone to hear.

Then it was her turn. So many times Jane had been selfish in her wants, but it was no longer about her any more. Jasper needed her as much as she needed him, not only to build his business but to rebuild the part of himself Savannah and the fever had damaged. She raised her eyes to his, determined he see how seriously she took her vows to him, too. He gently caressed one of her fingers with his as if hearing her silent promise.

Then Reverend Claire called for the rings. Giles handed Jasper a small box and Jane shifted on her feet, eager to see what he'd selected for her. She gasped when he opened it to reveal a diamond larger than the one in his cravat pin set in a thick gold band. He slipped it out of its case and on to her finger, the weight of it making her eye him with a sly smile.

He cocked a self-satisfied eyebrow at her and from the corner of her eyes she noticed all the women in the pews shifting to get a better look. She tried not to smile too wide in delight. Vanity was a sin, but she didn't care. She was wearing the biggest diamond in the church. Without waiting for Reverend Claire to tell her, she threw her arms around his neck and pulled him into their first married kiss.

Jasper escorted his new bride, who beamed like the morning sun, back to the Rathbone house and the wedding breakfast. A parade of revellers and well-wishers followed the new couple across the street and inside. Even Milton and his wife were there although they refrained from joining the receiving line.

Once the formalities were through, everyone went to the garden and the tables of food arranged among the rose bushes. A harpist played in the shade of the portico while hired footmen wove through the guests, offering champagne and headier spirits for the gentlemen. Jane was happily showing her ring to Justin and his wife Susanna when the clink of a spoon against a glass drew everyone's attention.

'To my son and his lovely wife.' Jasper's father's deep voice carried over the garden from where he stood on the portico with Giles and Jacob. His nose was red, his eyes heavy. Despite it being the middle of the day, he'd indulged in a generous amount of Mr Rathbone's fine Madeira. Jasper joined Jane as the entire crowd turned to admire them. 'I can't say I'm surprised to see you married, you two were as thick as thieves as children. One time, I caught them sneaking out of our house with a rope, threepence and a bottle of my best wine…'

'Henry, I'm sure no one wants to hear such stories today,' his wife gently reminded him, stopping him from finishing his tale of the morning he'd caught Jasper and Jane plotting to sell the wine and buy the pony Philip had refused to purchase for Jane.

'I suppose you're right.' Jasper's father rubbed his chin before he seemed to recall why he'd begun to speak. 'What I mean to say is, you two were meant to be together and I can't tell you how happy I am to see it happen at last. We worried about you, Jasper, when you were gone, feared you'd never make it home again, but you returned to us and to Jane.' He raised his glass to them. 'We love you both and wish you the greatest happiness.'

The guests raised their glasses in agreement. Jasper swept Jane's lips with a sweet kiss and the guests applauded.

'Well done, Jasper and Jane, well done.' His father clapped before hurrying to chase down a footman with a full tray of wine.

Jane entwined her arm with Jasper's. 'He's quite the orator, isn't he?'

'Indeed he is.' The speech reminded Jasper of the many his father had given during family dinners and Christmas mornings as a boy, the ones he'd missed while he'd been away. Across the garden, his father spoke with some associates, confident and sure of himself despite his having imbibed a little too much. If he ever learned what exactly Jasper had made of himself in Savannah, and London, he'd never toast him again.

Beneath the clear blue sky hanging over the garden, and with the guests laughing and chatting, it was difficult to take his worries seriously. With Jane working alongside him, they'd have the club founded in a matter of weeks and he could stop living two separate lives. He might retain a percentage of the hell, but he'd have nothing more to do with its nightly activities, no extending of credit or having a hand in how any of the clients decided to waste their livelihoods. His father would never find out exactly what he'd sent his son to and what kind of man it had made him.

'Jane, come with me.' Olivia, Jasper's eldest sister by ten years, hurried up to Jane and took her by the arm. 'Lily, Alice and I have some advice we're dying to give you.' She led Jane off to join his other two sisters near the fountain along the back wall, welcoming Jane into the circle of married ladies. Olivia, with their mother's fair complexion and lithe frame, talked the most, taking her role as eldest sister and potential marital mentor very seriously.

'Olivia wasn't so welcoming of Camille and Father wasn't so effusive with his congratulations at my wedding dinner.' Milton appeared at Jasper's side, intent on bringing shade to the sunny day. He'd always been the most serious of the three of them, fretting over the consequences of their plotted adventures. He'd become even more morose as an adult. 'But then you always did get the better deal.'

Jasper took a sip of his champagne to bite back the remark about it being his and his wife's own fault they hadn't received a warm wedding reception. This was not the time to start an argument. 'I think you got the better end of the deal. I've seen horrors you can't even imagine.'

A shadow seemed to pass over the garden until Jasper caught Jane's eye. She flashed him a proud smile to drive back the darkness encroaching on him and he raised his glass to her.

'There can't always have been death and disease. There must've been something more thrilling to have kept you there for so long.' It was the first sentence Milton had uttered to Jasper without each word dripping with condescension or jealousy.

Jasper studied Milton, seeing a hint of the brother he'd left and not the rival he'd become. 'There was at one time, but nothing, and especially no one, there who can compare to here.'

None of the women he'd been with in Savannah, not the jaded widows who gambled as hard as the men, nor the bored planters' wives who were eager to educate a man new to intimate nights, could match Jane. Her beauty was like deep water, not flashy or overdone, but steady, enhanced by her curves and the smooth fit of her dress. Her innocence called to him, as did her sharp wit and head for business.

'Of course, I haven't done too poorly.' The brief moment of fraternity vanished as Milton puffed out his chest in pride and lifted his champagne glass to his wife who stood in the corner. 'I've done well with Father, increasing his profits on more than one occasion, and I have a fine wife.'

Camille responded with a small smile before peering longingly at Jane and Jasper's sisters while they continued to talk. It gave Jasper a better understanding of why Milton had chosen her over Jane. His wife held back where Jane strode forward and she wasn't likely to show Milton up or reveal his weakness in business by exercising her strength. Milton might have avoided the challenges of a strong wife, but Jasper would welcome them, especially tonight. 'If you'll excuse me.'

Jasper wove his way through the guests to reach Jane, who stood now with Mr and Mrs Rathbone. Once beside her, he took her hand. He caught the slight intake of breath as he caressed her palm with his thumb.

'Tell me about your cotton-trading business in Savannah, Mr Charton,' Mrs Rathbone pressed. 'My father was a draper, and I used to help him in his shop. I once knew a great deal about southern cotton. I'm curious to see how much I remember.'

Jasper's thumbed stilled on Jane's palm and her fingers tightened around his. He knew as much about cotton as Uncle Patrick had, which was nothing. He hadn't expected Mrs Rathbone to be an expert. He racked his brain, trying to remember any of the conversations he used to overhear while pouring libations or slipping notes for more credit beneath the cotton-growers' pens. Nothing came to him.

'Don't pester him with work, Laura.' Jane batted her free hand at her sister-in-law. 'We're here to celebrate, not to be serious.'

'Marriage has changed you already, Jane. You rarely ever pass up a chance to discuss business.' Mr Rathbone regarded Jasper and Jane the way he used to when they were children and he caught them entering the house after being up to no good. Thankfully, Jasper's mother approached and drew the host and hostess away.

Jane brushed her forehead with the back of her hand. 'I see what you mean about lying to everyone.'

'Why didn't you tell me your sister-in-law knew about cotton?'

'Because I haven't heard her speak of it in years. I didn't think she'd bring it up today.'

'I might have to read up on the subject before our first family dinner,' he joked, working to set her, and himself, at ease.

* * *

Jane tried to share in Jasper's humour, but the brief interlude with Laura and Philip had left her shaken. Jane might have put Laura off the subject, but she'd noticed Philip scrutinising her and her husband.

My husband.

She stepped closer to him. Let Philip scrutinise them. She was a married woman now and he no longer had a say in her affairs.

It was dusk when the merry guests saw Jane and Jasper off in his landau. She could barely sit still beside him as the vehicle carried them from St Bride's Lane to Jasper's town house in Gough Square. In the privacy of the conveyance, she considered starting their marital relations early, but she didn't want to shock the driver when they arrived at their destination.

Instead, she enjoyed the weight of his arm on her shoulders and the solid muscle of his thigh beneath her palm while they laughed about Mr Jones having tried to outdrink Mr Charton and failing.

Once they reached his house, he introduced her to his few servants, then showed her around the recently painted and repaired narrow rooms filled with the same gaudy furniture as his office. Like the furniture in the warehouse, it had belonged to his uncle and had come with the house. They poked into this room and that, discussing the minor details of housekeeping while avoiding the most important one waiting for them above stairs. They'd been friends for years and shared some of the most private events of their lives. None of those would compare to what was about to pass between them.

At last, with darkness settling over the house, they lit the candles and followed the housekeeper, Mrs Hodgkin, upstairs. Jane's things were settled and away in Jasper's room, her life at last completely one with his, leaving only the melding of their bodies to accomplish. At thirteen, she'd dreamed of this night, but as she'd watched him from the back of Philip's landau as it pulled away from the Charton house, leaving him to his family and the ship that would carry him away, she'd never believed it possible. She held up her hand and the large diamond in her wedding band sparkled in the candlelight. He was hers and she was his.

'Do you like it?' he asked.

'I do. It's as overdone as the rest of your

things.' She motioned to the large, gilded four-poster bed from the warehouse, all but engulfing the room. It had been assembled and cleaned with a large mattress affixed to its sturdy frame.

'Redo the rest of the decor if you like, but I assure you, by tomorrow you will not want to part with this piece.' He slapped the post of the bed and it barely shivered, unlike her.

'You're so sure.' She swallowed hard, suddenly nervous.

'Incredibly so.' He slipped his arms about her waist and the room constricted even more.

'I hope you're right. After hearing so much about the deed, I'd hate to be disappointed.'

'You won't be.' He entangled his fingers in her hair, dislodging her curls from their pins as he brought his lips down to cover hers.

She gripped his shoulders and her knees began to fail. This was it, the moment they would at last become more than friends, but man and wife. She followed his lead, trying to match his moves as though they were engaged in a game of chess, but she soon gave up. All she could do was feel his breath against her cheeks, his hands gliding up her back and the anticipation engulfing her insides when he began to undo the buttons of her dress. Button by button he freed the silk from her shoulders until it dropped down over her hips to pool at her feet.

He leaned back to take in the curve of her waist beneath the stays and her breasts taut against the confining boning. Her skin tingled with the expectation of his touch, but instead he shrugged out of his coat and waistcoat before pulling his shirt over his head to reveal his captivating chest. He was all hers now and she was free to do anything with him. She touched his stomach lightly while he slid his hand up along the satin around her waist before reaching behind it to undo the laces of her stays. While he worked, he pressed light kisses to the tops of each breast, making her breath quicken before she inhaled sharply as her stays came loose and dropped to the floor.

The chemise billowed out around her as she stepped forward to caress the line of him, as curious about him as he was of her. Beneath his breeches she saw the evidence of his need and wanted to see more. She undid one button of his fall, waiting for him to stop her, but he watched with a crooked grin, his pupils as wide and dark as the next button she undid. At last the fall gaped open and she hooked her fingers inside the waist of his breeches. His chest expanded as her fingers brushed the smooth skin beneath while she pushed the buckskin down over his hips.

She followed them lower, coming face to face with his desire and wondering how she'd accommodate such a thing. She stood up fast, embarrassed for the first time this evening. He didn't leave her to suffer, but gripped the sides of her chemise and pulled it over her head. She stood before him naked, her breasts heavy beneath his admiring gaze, but she made no move to cover herself. She trusted him to guide her tonight.

He caught her by the waist and pulled her to him again. Her breasts flattened against his chest while his member pressed hot and full against her stomach. He clasped her buttocks as he brought his mouth down against hers, raw and hungry in his need. With small circles he traced the line of her neck. She arched back while he dipped lower and lower until his lips took in the tender point of her breast. She cried out, digging her hands into his hair as she braced herself against the sensation his caressing tongue created deep inside of her.

Aware of the ache he'd raised, he slid his fingers down her hips, trailed them across her stomach and then slipped them between her legs.

None of the books ever described this! She rose up on her toes, his caresses pushing her toward something just out of her reach. Then he withdrew and she moaned in frustration as she lowered herself, but he didn't allow it to last. He gathered her into his arms and carried her to the bed, continuing to tease her tongue with his.

The sheets were cold as he laid her on them and then covered her body with his. He gently nudged her legs apart with his knees and settled between them. She gasped as he pressed against her and she opened herself wider to him, ready to take him in. He didn't push forward but lingered there, painfully close and yet holding back.

She shifted her hips toward his, trying to draw him in, but he moved away again.

They'd been apart for too long, across too many years and so much sadness. She wanted to be one with him, to claim all of him as he was claiming all of her. She brought her lips to his ears. 'Please, don't draw away.'

He stilled in her arms. His heart beat against her chest and he rested his cheek against hers so she couldn't see his face. She didn't move, wondering if she'd made some mistake and if he'd slide off and leave her with the terrible, aching need in her body and her heart.

At last he rose up on his elbows. Sweat glistened on his forehead. 'Are you sure you truly want me?'

'I always have.'

He claimed her mouth with urgency, as if he could kiss her deep enough to erase their time apart. Then he brought his hips forward and in one smooth motion joined with her at last.

Jasper muffled her mouth with his, taking in her cries of pleasure as she took him into herself. He wrapped his arms tight around her, groaning as he claimed her innocence, selfish in his desire to have it and her. This was how it should have been years ago, with nothing between them, not her experiences or his, their lives intermingling in a way no one could interrupt. Her fingernails dug into his back as he stroked deeper into her, wanting to bring them so close they might never be apart. In the sweet entwining of her legs with his, he could feel her pulling him into her. She wanted all of him and he would find a way to give it to her, to be the man he'd promised he would be.

With her breath fast in his ear, her whimpers vibrating through his chest, he drove them toward a release greater than their bodies until at last their pleasure crested and they cried out together.

'Was it all you expected?' Jasper asked as she lay beside him, her hair spilling across the pillow and over her shoulder to cover the pink tips of her breasts.

'It was more divine than I could have imagined.' She stretched like a cat on her back beside him, making her full breasts arch and stoking the fire which still smouldered inside him. 'I probably shouldn't tell you so. It'll make you arrogant.'

He turned on his side to face her and laid a hot hand on her stomach, making small circles around her navel. 'Good, I take pride in my skills.'

The dolphin clock chimed ten times. Each knock of the tiny hammer against the bell stilled his hand and stole some of the calm he'd experienced during their lovemaking. In her arms he'd forgotten about the hell by the Thames and all the steps that had led him to it and everything it meant.

'What's wrong?' Jane asked.

'Nothing. I'm not used to being home at night. I'm usually at the hell.' It was a half-truth.

She rolled on her side and pressed her supple body against his, bringing her lips tantalisingly close to his. 'I'm sure Mr Bronson can do without you for one evening.'

'I'm sure he can.'

Chapter Seven

'Are you certain this is where the auction is being held?' Jasper asked as they ascended the stone stairs into the building in Somers Town.

'The paper was quite clear on the matter.' To Jane's amazement, he'd been incredibly solicitous in accompanying her here, despite her having woken him from a deep sleep this morning. Over the last two weeks, Jane and Jasper's lives had settled into a quiet routine. They spent afternoons and evenings in preparation for the opening of the club, then dined together before retiring upstairs for more intimate discussions. Afterwards, Jasper would go to the gaming room and remain there until dawn when he returned home to sleep while Jane rose.

'From what I remember of London, this

seems an odd place for a lady of, what did the advert say?'

'Fine breeding fallen on hard times.' Jane read from the cut-out advertisement for the auction to sell the goods of a genteel lady who'd recently died without heirs. Despite the very questionable neighbourhood, the quality things being sold to clear the deceased woman's debts included a fine set of china Jane hoped to purchase for the club. As a married woman with her husband by her side, she was free to travel here and to bid on anything she liked. It was a welcome change from the last auction she'd attended.

From an open upstairs window, the knock of the gavel against the wood and the auctioneer's booming voice announcing 'Sold' carried out over the noise of the street.

'Hurry, before we miss the best items.' She took Jasper's arm and pulled him inside, eager to reach the auction and get him away from the gaudily dressed woman across the street trying to catch his attention.

'I'm coming.' He bounded up the stairs past her, pulling her along. At the top, he tugged hard enough to make her skip over the last tread and land with a bounce in front of him on the landing. He caught her other hand and pulled her against him and away from the drop. The rumble of his laughter rose up to meet hers, the joy they'd taken in one another over the last weeks increasing. Whatever doubts she'd entertained about Jasper before the ceremony had long been destroyed by his constant humour and the hours they'd spent together. He wanted to be with her and they were revelling in their newfound freedom.

A balding businessman in a light coat mumbled his apologies while he passed them on his way out. His presence forced Jasper and Jane to assume a more professional air before they entered the room. It was a large one in the old house, a ballroom maybe, converted like the rest into a private apartment. True to its past it was embellished with chipped wainscoting, scrolled doors, tall windows hung with thick curtains and an abundance of gilt furnishings and knick-knacks.

'It looks like your office,' Jane whispered as they slipped behind the gathered crowd and gawked at the massive amount of baroque mirrors.

Jasper lowered his head to hers. 'Maybe this is who purchased all of my old things.'

'If you recognise anything, don't buy it back.'

'Why not? Aren't you eager to own a sofa with this much red brocade?' His breath tickled her ear while he motioned to the sofa behind them. 'Think how it would go with our bed and what we could do on it.'

'We could be quite wicked.' Jane slid him an enticing sideways look, almost ready to abandon the auction for home and more carnal pursuits when the auctioneer announced the next item.

'A large lot of French china in a classical pattern.' A man held up a plate and bowl. The china was the only thing of style and taste in the entire room.

'The set is perfect for the club and enough to get us started in the dining room.'

'Are you sure you want something from here?' Jasper fingered the tag of a very strange statue on the table beside them. The bronze couple was locked in an embrace worthy of the red sofa.

'I do.' The auction began, and only when she'd made the opening bid did she wonder at Jasper's question. 'Why shouldn't I?'

His eyes danced with mirth. 'No reason. Continue on.'

With the auction in progress, she couldn't pause to interrogate him. Winning the china proved easier than securing the Fleet Street property and it didn't come with a parcel of censorious looks from the other gentlemen crowded into the apartment. Whatever had enticed the other attendees here it didn't include a sizeable set of French porcelain. In a few bids, she'd won the lot at a price she couldn't wait to boast about the next time she dined with Philip.

'Congratulations, my dear. You've made quite an acquisition.' Jasper raised her hand to his lips and brushed it with a kiss. It sent a tingle down her arm and into places deeper down before the tight press of a restrained smile made her cock her head at him. He knew something she didn't and it was amusing him to no end.

'What are you thinking?'

'About the allure we'll offer to our clients. They can brag to their friends about eating beef off the notorious Mrs Greenwell's china.'

All Jane's plans to brag to Philip about her splendid purchase vanished. 'What?'

He pointed at the portrait of an almost-naked woman hanging on the wall behind them and surrounded by a number of other works to make her blush. Then it struck her why the address seemed so familiar. At one time, Jane and Mrs Hale had followed the famous courtesan's exploits in the papers, sniggering together at her boldness and quick to hide the stories whenever Laura or Philip had entered the room. It had been years since the woman's name had appeared in the gossip columns, but there was no forgetting her antics, including a dip in the Vauxhall Gardens lake in nothing but her chemise.

She whirled on Jasper, who continued to smile like a sly fox. 'Why didn't you say something sooner, or stop me?'

'Because I enjoyed watching you bid. You have a flare for auctions.'

'But think of the money we've wasted. If anyone finds out where we got the service they'll be horrified.'

'Or intrigued.' Jasper nudged her with his elbow. 'The china is the closest most men will ever come to a famous courtesan and we'll offer it to them. It'll make our club the talk of the Fleet.'

No, this was not at all as she'd imagined. It was better. 'You think so?'

'I do.'

'Then let's purchase the couch and really give them something to discuss.'

Jasper sat at his desk in the gambling hell, signing off on letters of credit. Through the wall behind him, a great cheer went up. *Someone must be doing well at the Hazard table.* He returned his pen to the gilded holder of a peacock with full plumage and reached for an equally ornate duster. He didn't wish the winner ill despite what it meant for the night's takings. After his day with Jane, it was difficult to be in a bad mood. Jane's joy at the auction, and the zeal with which she'd acquired a few more of the scandalous old woman's things, had been a delight to see. Afterwards, they'd spent the rest of the afternoon writing adverts for the club, the work drawing them closer together and hinting at a far better future than the one he'd imagined more than a week ago. With regret he'd left her to come here, eager to return to his bed and her arms come the sunrise.

A series of loud groans from the night's boisterous crowd began to puncture the quiet of Jasper's sanctuary. *The player's luck must have given out.*

Jasper reached for the grocer's bill when raised voices and an argument made him halt.

'Damn you, man, I'll do as I like. Spin the wheel.'

'Sir, please, listen to reason,' came a dealer's voice.

'Spin, you bastard.'

Mr Bronson rushed into the office. 'Captain Christiansen is playing too deep and losing and he isn't happy about it. I tried denying him credit, hoping it would be enough to discourage him, but he has his own money tonight, more than I've ever seen him bring here.'

'Where did he get it? He hasn't been to sea in months,' Jasper asked, rising from the desk.

'Don't know, but he won't have much of it if he keeps playing the way he is.'

Jasper traced the edge of the brass peacock's fan. 'All right, cut him off. Take Adam with you and escort Captain Christiansen downstairs as discreetly as possible.'

'That'll be hard. He's likely to make a fuss.'

'Then try to appeal to his gentlemanly sense of embarrassment and do what you can. I'll wait down there for you and tell him he's banned from playing here.'

'You sure you want to make yourself known?'

Jasper twisted his wedding band on his finger. 'This place will soon be yours. Better he have a grudge against me than you.' It would be Jasper's first steps out of the shadows, one of the many he'd have to take to leave this life behind.

Mr Bronson headed back into the game room to orchestrate the delicate removal of Captain Christiansen while Jasper made his way downstairs. He waited in the dim light of the warehouse. The scratch of a rat scurrying through the few crates stacked along the wall was barely audible over the laughter and voices drifting down through the ceiling. As much as he hated these encounters they were necessary. If he'd stepped in and taken similar action with Mr Robillard, and heaven knew how many others, so many things might be different now, including his view of himself.

He didn't need to wonder if Captain Christiansen was being disagreeable. His loud protests as Mr Bronson and Adam, the bulky footman, escorted Captain Christiansen to the ground floor were proof enough.

'How dare you treat me like a pickpocket?' Captain Christiansen wrenched out of Adam's firm grip. 'Do you know who I am?'

'The second son of Lord Fenton,' Jasper announced, stepping into the lantern light near the back door to meet the men.

'And who are you?' Captain Christiansen demanded. He was tall and round faced like his father the Earl, but with a higher forehead and more hair. His skin was tanned from his years at sea and would never lighten to a more aristocratically preferred pallid white.

'Mr Patrick, the owner of this establishment.' It was one thing for Captain Christiansen to meet him, but he wasn't ready for the man to spread his identity all over London. Jasper might be working to leave this life, but he still couldn't risk his family learning of it. 'I thank you for your patronage, but it cannot continue.'

'You think I don't have enough to play in your rotten room, but I have more money than you can imagine.' He poked one finger in the air at Jasper.

'I'm sure you do.' Jasper allowed the man his dignity in an effort to make him more compliant. 'But I don't permit men to ruin themselves here. I must insist you no longer frequent this establishment.'

'You can't ruin me. My brother is sick, the

wasting disease.' He seemed to relish his brother's impending demise.

'I'm sorry for his ill health.' Even with the lingering estrangement between Jasper and Milton, he'd never wish death on him, even if it meant Jasper and not Milton would inherit his parents' wealth and business. It made the need to be rid of Captain Christiansen all the stronger.

'My almighty father settled a great deal on me to make me resign my commission. I'm suddenly precious to him when before he didn't think twice about throwing me to the horrors of the Navy at thirteen.'

Jasper exchanged a wary look with Mr Bronson. Captain Christiansen hadn't been playing with his money, assuming he had any left, but his father's. In the last few days, Jasper had heard disturbing rumours about the Fenton family's mounting debts. He had no idea how much of Lord Fenton's already diminished wealth this man had lost.

Captain Christiansen mistook the silence. 'Already regretting kicking a future earl out of your filthy gaming room?' The captain was reaching far into the future and his lineage to try to assert dominance over Jasper—it didn't work. He'd lost his respect for nobility in America.

'I'm safeguarding the legacy your father has settled on you, the one you'll some day pass on to your son.' The Charton family might not have a manor house or a title, but his parents had always valued family and the business Milton would one day inherit, the one his father had inherited from Jasper's grandfather.

'There's your legacy.' Captain Christiansen spat at Jasper's feet. 'I could crush you and your little hell if I wanted to and I might just.'

He stormed past Jasper and out of the warehouse door into the thick fog blanketing the neighbourhood.

'I think that went well,' Mr Bronson said, his voice echoing in the dark room.

'As well as can be expected. Adam, please return to the gaming room.'

The footman hurried back upstairs.

Mr Bronson took his pipe and tobacco pouch out of his pocket, but did nothing with either. 'He can't ruin us. What we're doing isn't illegal.'

'I never thought you a legal scholar,' Jasper joked, trying to shake off the tight worry in his shoulders and Mr Bronson's words.

'I'm not, but I've been doing things like this long enough to make a habit out of knowing the local laws. Captain Christiansen can't do anything more than bluster.'

'No, but Lord Fenton could make things difficult for us, perhaps even see us closed. Earls have a way of wielding influence. Let's hope he doesn't take an interest in his son's evening activities.'

'How long do you think the son's been playing with his father's money?'

'I have no idea, but I'll have to find out.' He wasn't sure how he'd do so. He didn't know anyone in the Admiralty who could tell him when the captain had resigned his commission. Mr Rathbone might be on good terms with someone there, given his vast network of connections, but it would mean telling him about the club. Perhaps Jane could assist him, but he refused to drag her into the mire of his gambling affairs. He'd have to find a way to discover it on his own. 'How much did Captain Christiansen lose before you cut him off?'

'Two thousand. I was distracted by another matter and the Hazard man is new and didn't know to tell me.'

'Two thousand might be enough to catch

an earl's attention.' He rubbed his eyes with his fingers. As pleasurable as his mornings with Jane were, he was tired from missing a great deal of his usual sleep since the wedding. 'Uncle Patrick wouldn't have been this sloppy about managing clients.'

'He didn't exactly manage them as much as he fleeced them,' Mr Bronson snorted.

'You shouldn't speak ill of the dead.'

'I know.' He shoved the tobacco pouch back in his pocket and tapped the pipe bowl against his palm. 'What are we going to do about Captain Christiansen?'

'Nothing tonight.'

'Then go home and get some sleep.' Mr Bronson clapped him on the shoulder. 'You look like hell.'

Mr Bronson headed back upstairs, leaving Jasper alone in the warehouse. He didn't make for his carriage, but stared at the emptiness around him, broken only by the gaudy furniture in the corner. The furniture was some of the last tangible remnants of his life in Savannah, except for his uncle's ring on his finger, the one he'd won from a tobacco merchant. Jasper had no idea how much of the man's other goods and wealth his uncle had taken from him or how much of what Jasper had inherited had come from a similar source.

He twisted the ring on his finger. Jasper might have stopped Captain Christiansen from ruining himself, but he couldn't say how many other men had thrown their livelihoods away in Savannah without his knowing.

They chose to throw it away.

Even if he left the business it wouldn't stop men from chasing luck or betting on cards. Better they do it under the eye of a man who intervened rather than the many in London who'd bleed them dry. These were the tales Jasper had told himself, the ones he hoped Jane never discovered.

Chapter Eight

The Covent Garden Theatre glittered with the thousands of candles in the chandeliers hanging over the audience. Jane could barely sit still or concentrate on the performance on stage. She was too busy watching the audience from her place in the box Jasper had rented for the evening. She and Mrs Hale used to read about performances when she was younger, but Philip had deemed them improper for her to attend. Now she was a married woman, she could come here as much as she pleased and no one could disapprove or look askance at her because of it.

This was exactly how she'd expected married life to be.

'Are you enjoying yourself?' Jasper approved the bottle of champagne the footman held out to him and sent the man on his way.

'I could get used to doing this every night.' She sat back from the edge of the box where she'd been perched to watch the King carrying on with his mistress, Marchioness Conyngham, in a box across the way. Jane and Mrs Hale used to read about the woman in the papers. She never thought she'd be watching her and His Highness together before her and everyone. Between this spectacle and the glow of the last few nights of lovemaking, she felt very wicked and wanton. Philip was right to have kept her away from here.

'It can't be every night.' He wrapped a linen towel around the bottle and worked out the cork with a muffled pop. Then he poured some of the straw-coloured liquid into the two glasses on the narrow table between their chairs. Each turn of the bottle as he poured to avoiding spilling a drop whispered with his experience. This wasn't his first theatrical performance. 'I must work if I'm to keep you in style.'

Jasper took a deep drink of the champagne, barely tasting it as he examined his wife. She wore a rich purple gown embellished by a thin line of lace along the bodice where the tempt-

ing mounds of her breasts rose above the silk.
Maturity and poise hung in every elegant curl
tucked in the combs at the back of her head,
but her wide-eyed amazement and the ease of
manner between them were just as alluring.
Around her there was no pretending he was
someone else, no lies about slipping out to his
hell. They simply enjoyed their marriage and
all the delights it offered.

'Do you like your new earrings?' He caressed
the curve of her ear, following the delicate skin
down to where the gold-and-diamond bauble
shimmered with each of her movements.

She laughed as she pulled back, her joy as
effervescent as the champagne. 'I love them,
but you mustn't keep buying me things I don't
really need.' She twirled a gold bracelet on her
arm, another of his lavish gifts.

'It's the reason I bought them for you.' And
why he sent funds to Mrs Robillard. Spending money on them was the single penance he
could do to make up for his failings. 'You're
too sensible to spend my money so shame-
lessly.'

'You should be, too.'

'I don't buy anything I can't pay cash for right
away. You won't find a bill clinging to me.'

'Not even if I looked very, very, hard, over every inch of you?' She traced the line of his jaw with one gloved finger while balancing her champagne glass in the other hand.

He caught her fingers with his. 'Not even then.'

She bit one lip with her teeth with the same anticipation tightening his insides. 'We'll see tonight.'

The audience laughed and Jane whipped her attention back to the theatre. Jasper held her hand, enjoying her delight as she watched the spectacle in the audience as well as the one on stage. Her excitement reminded him of the thrill of seeing Savannah when he'd disembarked after the crossing and the morning his uncle had revealed his secret. It was the first time he'd thought well of the city and his years there instead of cursing it, and it was all thanks to Jane. It was hard to be around her and not view potential and possibility in everything instead of ruin.

I should have allowed her to wait for me, written to her and continued what she'd tried to start during our last night together. When she was old enough, she could have gone to him in Savannah, perhaps helped him see the pitfalls of his life and leave it, or at least been there with him through the darkest days.

She laughed with the rest of the audience, her eyes sparkling with her amusement, and he was glad she hadn't come to him. It would have killed him to see the hollowed-out disbelief mar her expression as it had everyone else's during the awful summer. He rested one ankle on his knee and settled back in his chair to enjoy the performance. He'd been at the hell the last few nights, but tonight he'd be home in bed with her. He squeezed her hand and she flashed him a smile to chase off his concerns.

Then Jasper glanced across the theatre. A few boxes below the King's he noticed Lady Fenton seated near the edge of her box with her noticeably wan eldest son. Jasper withdrew his hand from Jane's and took up his champagne flute to enjoy a bracing sip. There'd been no inkling Lord Fenton intended to involve himself in Captain Christiansen's debt, but it didn't mean either the Earl or his son weren't planning something. He wouldn't know until they sprung it on him. Until then he continued to search for someone in the Admiralty who could tell him when the captain had resigned his commission, but he'd found no one. It undermined the peace he found with Jane tonight, one to both settle and scare him. He'd been content in his life once before and Mr Robillard had stolen it. He wondered who might take it from him this time.

The curtain rustled behind him and the footman appeared again.

'Sir, this arrived for you.' He handed Jasper a note.

Jasper took the note, his enthusiasm for the evening dropping. It was from Mr Bronson telling him to come to the hell at once.

'What's wrong?' Jane asked.

He folded the paper and tucked it in his pocket. 'Mr Bronson needs me.'

'He can't handle whatever it is?'

'If he's asked me to intervene, it must be bad. I'll be home as soon as I can.' He rose and kissed her on the forehead, irritated to be pulled away, but the hell paid for every aspect of this evening and their life. No matter how much he wanted to stay here with Jane, he couldn't ignore business.

Lord Fenton stood across from Jasper in the warehouse. Mr Bronson had insisted he wait here instead of upstairs and Jasper was glad.

The less Lord Fenton knew about the Company Gaming Room, the better.

'To what do I owe the honour of this visit, Lord Fenton?' Jasper asked, even though he could guess.

'I wish to discuss my son's debts. I understand he lost a considerable sum here.'

'Not as much as he would have if I hadn't asked him to leave.'

'A gambling-hell owner with a heart, how quaint.' The aristocrat sniffed.

'A father coming to discuss his grown son's debts, what filial love,' Jasper shot back.

'Mind how you address me,' Lord Fenton sneered. 'The very existence of this lowly club hangs on my good graces. With a few words placed in the right ears I could see this establishment closed for good.'

Mr Bronson shot Jasper a wary look over the Earl's shoulders.

'With a few equally well-placed bribes I'm sure I could keep catering to a clientele far below the notice and interest of a lord. After all, I wouldn't want you to sully your hands dealing with mere merchants.' He might be preparing to leave the club, but he wouldn't see it closed and Mr Bronson and all the employees left without wages or employment. Let the man mortgage some property or do an honest day's work to meet his commitments.

'I won't have the Fenton name sullied by allowing some third-rate hell to take a substantial part of my son's settlement. I want the two thousand pounds he lost to you returned at once.'

Jasper imagined Lord Fenton wouldn't dare to march into a club in St James's and demand the return of money, but he had no compunction about doing it here.

'He understood the rules of wagers as well as you do, my lord, and he paid his debt like a true gentleman.'

'It wasn't his money to gamble with,' Lord Fenton continued as if it made a difference.

'That is a matter for you and him to discuss, I have no part in it.'

'You will give me back the money.' Lord Fenton banged his walking stick against the floor as if sheer will could move Jasper. It couldn't.

'Our discussion is now at an end. Good evening, Lord Fenton.'

Lord Fenton clasped the handle of his walking stick so hard Jasper thought he heard the wood crack. 'You will regret this.'

The man turned on the heel of his polished shoe and stormed out of the warehouse.

'What charm these lords have.' Mr Bronson pulled out his red handkerchief and wiped his brow.

'And an aversion to scandal and having their debts made public, especially when they have a wastrel son to marry off. It may keep him from troubling us further.'

'Seems a slim string to hang our peace of mind on.'

'It is, but it's the only one we've got.' Overhead, footsteps made the rafters rattle. Jasper looked up into the darkness. Everyone above him seemed so sure of their lives, but he understood how fast everything could fail. Disease wouldn't undo him in London, but his own mistakes and weaknesses might. He'd already lived through complete ruin once. He couldn't bear to endure it again.

The click of the bedroom door closing pulled Jane out of a deep sleep. She rolled over, confused about where she was until the gilding of the four-poster bed glimmering in the light from the grate caught her attention. With a contented sigh she turned to tempt Jasper into the exertion they'd been denied by his being summoned away from the theatre, but he wasn't beside her.

He stood by the window, staring out at the darkness just beyond it. The languid man who'd poured champagne was gone, replaced by the serious one who'd told her of Savannah in the carriage the other night.

She sat up. 'Jasper? Is everything all right?'

He turned his back to her as he undid his cravat. 'Yes, it's fine.'

'You don't appear as if everything is fine.'

'There were some things I had to deal with at the club.'

'What things?'

'Nothing you need to worry about.'

'Of course I worry about it, especially after you leave me at the theatre and then come home looking like the devil.'

He jerked the linen from around his beck. 'If I say it's nothing, then it is.'

She drew back a touch on the bed, wide-eyed with shock. He'd never snapped at her before.

He flung the linen over the back of a chair and scraped his hand through his hair, more contrite than irritated. 'I'm sorry, it was a difficult night. I had to deal with some issues I failed to face sooner because I've been distracted.'

By me. Once again she'd brought problems into a house, except this time it wasn't her parents', but her own. She wished she hadn't pestered him. It was another testament to how stubborn she could be when she wanted her way and the trouble it could cause. 'Then come to bed and let me help you forget about it.' She shrugged a little to make her chemise slide down over her shoulder to reveal the top of one full breast, wanting to be close to him and settle the unease inside her and him.

It didn't tempt him. Instead he turned his back to her to shrug out of his coat and waistcoat. 'It has been a long night. I need some sleep.'

Jane tugged the chemise back up to cover herself, as baffled as she was wounded. He hadn't hesitated to tell her about the Company Gaming Room, even treating his secret as though he'd killed a man, not backed a few card games. Tonight he was tight lipped about his troubles. It wasn't right, she wanted him to confide in her, but she couldn't force him to do it. Insisting had never made her reveal anything. She doubted it would work with Jasper.

She settled back down in the bed while he continued to undress, the whisper of his clothes the only conversation between them. She was tired and so was he. The last few nights had been pleasurable but long. They both needed rest and afterwards he might be more willing to talk to her.

At last, he slid into bed beside her, but didn't reach out to hold her or laugh with her like he normally did when he returned early in the morning from his hell.

'Goodnight.' He kissed her on the forehead, not with affection but with dismissal before rolling on his side, his back to her.

She turned on her side, too, careful to stay as far away from him as she could. How dare he dismiss her like some maid! She had no idea why he'd done it. The new earrings lying in a crystal dish on the table beside the bed caught her eye and a bolt of fear made her stiffen.

Maybe it's me. Maybe he regrets our marriage. The old nagging feeling she wasn't worthy of affection covered her like the early morning darkness before she pushed it back. Nothing in what he'd said or done since the ceremony had hinted at such a thing, until he'd all but shoved her away tonight.

She stared at the far wall turned orange by the smouldering coals, determined to be sensible and not fall prey to late-night worries, but it was difficult. Eventually, he was sure to explain, but patience wasn't one of her stronger virtues.

She closed her eyes, ignoring how cold the bed was when he didn't hold her. The uneasy sense this wouldn't be the last time Jasper might not turn to her for comfort continued to nag until the rising sun lit up the room and, unable to remain still any longer, she rose to begin her day.

Chapter Nine

Jane sat at the burled-wood-and-gilded writing desk in the sitting room to review receipts and the correspondence she'd collected in regards to the building. The new furniture would be delivered in a few days, an elegant and sizeable amount commissioned by a London merchant who had been sunk by the sudden drop in coffee prices. Jane had snatched up the unpaid goods at a splendid price and they would soon be installed at the club.

Jasper had yet to rise and, if it hadn't been for Mrs Hodgkin interrupting her more than once to discuss the dinner menus, she would have been quite alone this morning. After the delight of the theatre, this wasn't exactly how she'd pictured spending today.

Johnson, the butler, entered with a few letters. 'Would you like me to leave these here or take them up to Mr Charton?'

'You can leave them here. They're enquiries into services. We needn't bother Mr Charton with them.'

Johnson placed the letters on the table beside her then left, his wan face not betraying whatever he thought about his employer sleeping so late. Jasper had mostly been at his parents' house since coming home and all the servants in this one were new. They knew as much about his affairs as they did about his gaming hell, which was nothing. They were kept in the dark about it to make sure they didn't inadvertently mention it in front of his family. They thought he went to a club for gentlemen merchants every night.

Jane set down her pen and rose. She wandered to the window and pushed aside a curtain to take in Gough Square. A nurse and her young charges were out in the centre, enjoying their daily walk, and there was no one else to be seen. The clerks and shop owners who filled the houses in the square were up and hard at work, including her, while her husband slept.

She turned away from the window and

leaned against it, biting the nail of her thumb. Jasper couldn't have built a successful gaming hell if he was a layabout.

Maybe I should be glad he's still in bed. Once he was up they'd have to face each other and the lingering questions and awkwardness of last night. He hadn't been pleased to see her then—she wasn't sure he'd be any more excited by her presence now.

It left a sour taste in her mouth as she sat down to read a note from the painters about progress on the Fleet Street property's walls and she tried her best to forget it. Hopefully, his distance and reluctance to talk to her was nothing more than a fluke. Years ago, there'd been times when Philip, after seizing collateral in the middle of the night to keep a debtor from making off with it, had been up, too agitated to sleep. She'd come downstairs to sit with him and talk. Unlike Jasper, Philip had welcomed her company.

Enough of this. It had taken a while for Laura and Philip to come together nine years ago. It hadn't been easy and they'd struggled during their first few months of marriage to become acquainted with one another after wedding as strangers. Jane had the advantage of a long history with Jasper and their entire lives together, but it didn't mean the adjustment to their new situation wouldn't be difficult. This was only a setback and setbacks were to be expected. She would be sensible about this and not act like a flustered lover or dwell on the incident and make it worse.

She began a reply to the painters when the sound of the front knocker made her pause. It was loud and she hoped it didn't wake Jasper. She twisted the new gold bracelet on her arm as she listened to the butler open the door. She expected to hear the butcher she'd summoned to give her a price on his goods. Instead, a gaggle of female voices filled the house.

Jasper's sisters.

Before the butler could announce them, they spilled into the sitting room in a wave of chatter and greetings.

'I hope you don't mind us intruding.' Olivia tossed her reticule in a chair to announce she didn't care whether she was intruding or not, she intended to stay.

'We were shopping nearby and wanted to see how you were getting on,' Alice added.

'Oh, I adore the way you've rearranged the furniture.' Lily peered about the room, adjusting her dark curls after removing her bonnet. She flung it down on top of the pile of reticules and pelisses rapidly mounting on the chair.

'I assume Jasper is at the club today?' Alice asked while she removed her gloves.

'Yes, he's usually there during the day. I sometimes go with him, but I had to stay behind to see to some other matters.' Jane glanced out of the sitting-room door and at the empty stairway just beyond it. She hoped Jasper didn't wake up and come downstairs. If he did, he should hear his sisters and know better than to reveal his presence. She was sure neither of them wanted to make excuses for why he was home or for his sisters to think he didn't work as hard as their husbands, or that there was some reason Jane had lied to them about where he'd been. She didn't like lying, but it was necessary. He did work as hard as their husbands, but not at a business they would approve of, at least not yet. It almost made her wish the sisters would leave so she could return to the organising of the club. The sooner it opened, the sooner Jasper might leave the hell and whatever had made him so aloof this morning.

'Make sure he doesn't work too hard,' Lily

admonished as she sat down at the small tea table near the window. 'He always comes to Mother and Father's appearing exhausted. I've seen smaller bags at the coaching inn than beneath Jasper's eyes.'

'Perhaps it isn't work keeping him up...' Olivia suggested.

The sisters threw back their heads in laughter. Jane smiled, not as amused. In the past, with them being so much older than her, they'd rarely paid her much mind. Today, they treated her like their equal, not a young naive girl to be instructed or ignored, and she was repaying their respect with fibs and falsehoods. Jasper was right, it wasn't easy deceiving everyone they knew.

'Johnson, tea,' Olivia called as she joined her sisters at the tea table. 'Oh, I'm sorry, Jane. Forgive me for forgetting my place, this is your home now.'

'I don't mind.' But she did mind them calling unannounced. It would be difficult to hide Jasper sleeping in the mornings if his sisters decided to make a regular habit of it.

'When will Jasper be back? I want to chide him for making you work at all,' Lily enquired. They'd always chipped at each other more than the other siblings, because she, being closest in age to Jasper, had felt it her place to boss him around. It appeared she still did.

'I don't know,' Jane mumbled as she took hold of the back of the chair to pull it out and sit down. She didn't want to give them a time and have them lingering here waiting for him to return and then catch him coming from up-stairs.

Alice grabbed Jane's wrist and held it up, letting out a long whistle as she admired the new gold bracelet. 'How beautiful. Did Jasper give it to you?'

'He did.'

'Tristan never gives me such elaborate gifts,' Alice complained as she took the chair beside Jane's.

Lily eyed the bracelet with her mother's scrutiny. 'Uncle Patrick must have left Jasper more money than he told us about for him to be able to afford such things.'

'Yes, he did.' Thank goodness she wasn't wearing the earrings. She didn't need to raise any additional questions about Jasper's income, ones she had no intention of answering.

'Oh, Lily, stop being so practical and allow them to enjoy themselves,' Olivia scolded before turning to Jane. 'Is all going well with the club? We expect it will open soon?'

They all leaned in to hear Jane's answer.

'Soon.' Jane smiled a little too wide, not liking this topic any better than the one about money or Jasper's whereabouts. 'There's no end of details to deal with.'

'Oh, don't we know.' They all shook their heads in agreement, each of them active in their respective husbands' businesses, as well as minding the children and running the households. The reminder of their own responsibilities turned the conversation from Jane and Jasper's affairs to the sisters' second-favourite topic besides gossip: family. All during tea they discussed their husbands and children, sparing Jane from any more awkward questions, but not relieving her worry Jasper might appear and raise more. If he did, she hoped he had a good reason for why he was upstairs when Jane had said he was out, for she didn't.

After an hour of tea and conversation, the Charton sisters rose to take their leave.

Olivia dug into her reticule and withdrew a note for Jane. 'I almost forgot. Mother and Father have decided to hold their first dinner for you the evening after next. Say you can make it.'

'We can.' Jane fingered the invitation, pretending once again to be elated. She'd spent the better part of the morning deceiving the sisters about her and Jasper's income and habits. She didn't relish further sullying her conscience by making up more tales during an entire evening with Jasper's parents, except there was no avoiding it.

'I remember my first dinner after Daniel and I married,' Lily mused, then pursed her lips in displeasure. 'Jacob drank so much he made himself sick.'

'If Alice hadn't smuggled him so many glasses of port it never would have happened.' Olivia laughed, too much like their father to mind.

'I did no such thing,' Alice protested as the sisters made their way out of the house and to their waiting carriage.

Johnson closed the door behind the chatting sisters, then held out a letter to Jane. 'Mrs Charton, this arrived while you were with the ladies.'

Jane took the missive, turning the cheap and wrinkled paper over to read Jasper's name and address written in a round and flowing hand, a woman's hand.

Jane swallowed hard until she noticed the postmark. Savannah. Whoever this was, she was safely on the other side of the ocean.

And still writing to Jasper.

Jane turned the letter over a few times, wondering if she should open it. She wasn't a jealous person, but the strange way he'd behaved this morning, and the distance between them as they'd lain together in bed, gripped her. She wondered if this woman had something to do with his change in attitude.

His business being hers, she saw no reason to leave it sealed except for fear. Inside the tattered missive might be a truth about Jasper she didn't wish to discover. She wasn't sure she could bear the humiliation of learning she didn't have Jasper's real affection and never would.

Stop this! She didn't want to cower beneath her fears and worries.

'I'll take it up to him.' She might keep their business from his sisters, but she would not countenance secrets between them. Whatever this was, she would face it and deal with it.

Jane marched upstairs and into Jasper's

room. She threw open the curtains and a wash of sunlight lit up the bed.

'What are you doing?' Jasper grumbled from where he lay in a tangle of white sheets and pillows. He sat up, blinking at her, his hair mussed, a slight stubble along his jaw. In the open collar of his shirt she caught the sheen of perspiration. Her interest in the mysterious letter began to ebb at the sight of him and she fingered the curtain, her skin warmed by more than the sun on her back. She longed to linger with him in bed, but it wasn't her habit to be so wanton during the day, especially when there were issues to address.

'It's time for you to get up.' She let go of the curtain and perched beside him on the bed, flicking the letter with the edge of one nail, reluctant to bring it up despite her former determination. 'Your sisters were here. They said you need more sleep.'

'Do they now?' Like all younger brothers he didn't think much of their wisdom. 'Apparently, you don't agree with them.'

She ignored his comment. 'And they want more nieces and nephews.'

'It'll be difficult to do both at the same time, but I'm certainly willing to try.' He took her arm and pulled her against his chest, the merriment of the theatre enveloping them again. The strange man from before dawn was gone and her old friend was with her once more. He was warm against her bare arms, his skin moist from the spring air filling the room. It contrasted with the coolness of the sheets in the part of the bed where he hadn't been lying. She slid closer to him, allowing his kiss to make her forget all the worries and concerns of this morning and the letter.

He laid her down against the sheets, covering her body with the delicious weight of his. She hooked one leg around his, her dress sliding up to reveal her thigh, and he clasped it with one hot hand, meeting her urgency. He slid his hand beneath the muslin of her skirt and traced the line of the ribbon holding up the top of her silk stockings.

The letter in her hand crinkled, reminding her why she'd come up here. She flung it away and surrendered to his need and hers. He was her Jasper again, tender and attentive, his body as familiar to her as her own. He belonged to her, despite his past and hers, and the distance between them from before dawn was forgotten as they melded together.

* * *

Jasper lay against the sweat-dampened sheets, the anxiety of last night and this morning driven off by Jane's sweet caresses. He smoothed her hair and she turned to look up at him, her chin on his chest and her firm breasts pressed against his stomach. A wariness their lovemaking had banished returned to draw her lips tight. It was the same look she'd greeted him with when she'd first marched in here. It unsettled him and he reached for her to drive away her censure or uncertainty with his caresses.

He tucked one slender lock behind her ear, then cupped her cheek with his hand. He shouldn't have pushed her away this morning. He should have confided in her, told her about Lord Fenton's threat and allowed her sweet voice and curving arms to soothe him. But there was no reason to undermine her peace of mind by suggesting the hell and the money he made from it might be in danger. Without his income, her dream of the club and a fine life beside him, the one she'd envisioned when she'd first proposed they marry, would end. Let her be a happy wife for as long as possible, the two of them enjoying each other and the

pleasures of life, not mired in all its troubles
and confusions. Jasper had tasted enough bitterness in Savannah. He didn't need it here.
'What's wrong?'

'A letter arrived while you were sleeping.'

'Not bad news, I hope?'

'I don't know. I didn't open it. It's for you.'
She leaned over and snatched it off the floor,
curving her back and tempting him with the
roundness of her bare buttocks. Before he
could do more than caress the firm flesh, she
sat up, her hair falling down her shoulders to
cover her breasts, the delight in her eyes dim-
ming as she held out the paper. 'It's from Savannah.'

All his passion crashed to the floor.

He took the envelope. The weeks it had
taken for the letter to cross the Atlantic in the
musty hold of a ship had left it watermarked
and wrinkled along the corners, but it hadn't
obscured the handwriting. He recognised it
at once.

'Who's it from?' she asked.

The distance he'd kept from her this morning returned to slap him again. He sat up and
swung his legs over the side of the bed. Moments ago, they'd been open and vulnerable

with one another—now he intended to close off a part of himself again. 'Maybe a land developer or merchant needs me to sign a paper. In the rush to settle my affairs, I probably forgot something.'

'It's in a woman's hand.'

'With so many dead, often widows are the only ones left to do business with.' It was a partial truth and the best he could offer her.

'I see.' Her shoulders eased, but not the anxiety making her bite her bottom lip.

He slipped his hand behind her neck and drew her to him. 'Don't worry, there's no woman in my life except you, not in London or anywhere else.'

'You promise?'

'I do.' He swept her lips with an honest and tender kiss, then rose, despising himself and all his lies. 'Now, I must dress. There's a solicitor I plan to visit, one recommended by Mr Steed, who might be interested in our offer of retaining his services for our clients.'

'Good.' There was no enthusiasm in her word, just suspicion and wariness and it faded the glow from their lovemaking.

He tugged one finely pressed and folded shirt out of the wardrobe and pulled it on. 'I thought we might visit the Royal Theatre tomorrow night since we've already seen Drury Lane. I've never been there. Would you like that?'

'Yes, it would be grand.' She didn't sound elated.

He turned to his mirror to tie his cravat, aware of her watching him, the room shrinking and tightening under her scrutiny and his own unease. He couldn't open the letter in front of her. There would be too many questions and answers he refused to give. He wished he had a private space of his own. With the exception of his office at the hell there wasn't one so he endured the present tension. He had no choice.

He shrugged on his coat, eager to be free of her questioning glances and the hesitation marring her natural spontaneity. It was too much like the way his parents used to regard him whenever he left the house after dinner while tossing lies at them about where he was going. He hadn't expected or wanted it to be like this with Jane and it hadn't been, until today. He sat down to pull on his boots, struggling to remain cheerful and light under the weight of her presence. 'I saw a necklace at the jeweller's yesterday. It would go well with your earrings. Would you like it?'

'If you want to buy it for me.' She shrugged, her breasts rising and falling to tempt him to stay, to take her in his arms and touch the connection they'd enjoyed when they'd come together, but he didn't. The letter and everything it meant was a wall between them and at this moment he could not overcome it. 'Lily already thinks you're being too extravagant and your inheritance must be larger than you've told everyone. I said it was. I misled them about a number of things this morning.'

'I told you it wouldn't be easy.' Jasper brushed her cheek with the back of his fingers, leaving his hand to linger by her face, wanting to drive away the strife clouding her eyes, but he couldn't.

He was causing her distress, but he refused to discuss his concerns about Captain Christiansen or the reason for the letter from Savannah. It pained him to keep so many things from her, but she'd already been forced to lie to her brother and sister-in-law at the wedding breakfast, and to his sisters, and he'd noticed the anxiety it caused her. He couldn't ask her to carry any more of his secrets than he already had.

'And I accepted it so I have no one to blame but myself,' she replied with a bravery her sad eyes betrayed. She did blame him because she'd guessed he wasn't telling her everything, especially about the letter.

He tucked the missive in his coat pocket, hiding it away like he hid the story behind it. Every day they were together, he danced closer and closer to telling her the truth. He was deceiving her like he was everyone else and it hurt more than any of the other times he'd done it. He'd vowed to make her the most important person in his life and he could keep the promise. However, he hadn't vowed to reveal his whole self to her, both the good and the dark so tortured he shuddered to think of it. He wouldn't have her spit on him the way Mrs Robillard had. 'It'll change soon.'

'Will it?' It was the first hint of doubt since before the wedding and it increased his own.

'Of course. Now I must go before I lose what's left of the day.'

Jane watched Jasper all but sprint from the room, and her. They'd been so close when they'd made love. Then she'd shown him the letter. He might have smiled and chatted as though all were well, but it wasn't and once again he'd balked at telling her why. All she could surmise was that it had to do with the hell, and Savannah, and it wasn't as simple as a forgotten signature or missed transaction.

She picked up her discarded clothes and began to dress, at a loss for what to do. It wasn't in her nature not to insist on having her way, but she couldn't chase Jasper down and demand he speak with her. She didn't want to drive him off more than she already had and risk losing the warmth of his touch or the joy of his company. Assuming it wasn't fading already, or perhaps something she'd never really possessed.

She clutched her chemise to her chest, Mrs Fairley's words about her not really knowing him coming back to her. The modiste was right—after nine years apart, there were aspects of Jasper still hidden from her, including his full life in Savannah. He might have come home, but it didn't mean his heart wasn't with someone there. He'd done nothing before to make her suspect another woman, but catching cheaters wasn't her strength.

She shimmied into her stays, reached around behind her and began to lace them up, pulling so hard on the laces she feared they might snap. She refused to be left alone and forgotten by the one man who'd pledged before their family and friends to cherish her, but if his heart lay elsewhere, there was little she could do to secure it. If she pestered him too much for affection and confidences he didn't want to give, then one day she might awake to discover him gone, the way his brother had disappeared to Scotland.

She let go of the laces and slumped down on the edge of the bed. They might be married, but it didn't mean he couldn't leave her. Not even a ring or a ceremony could bind him to her if he didn't want to be bound. He must still have friends in America. He could go back and make a new life for himself while leaving her here to wonder when and if he might ever return. Being abandoned would be a bigger embarrassment than never having married.

She rose and jerked on her dress. *Let him leave me.* The marriage gave her the freedom to engage in trade without censure. Except it was no longer an occupation she wanted without Jasper. He did care about her, he always had. His kiss had been as honest as his caresses, but something had changed between them over the last couple of days and she wasn't sure what it was or why.

Sadly, she had no idea how to cross this new barrier or bring out the man she'd met at the altar, and there was no one she could discuss it with. He'd sworn her to secrecy about their life together so she could hardly have tea with Laura and ask for advice. She'd have to figure this out on her own. She rose to finish dressing, trying to keep her chin and her spirits up. She would be sensible about this. They were married and would be together every day. She'd find a way to pry his troubles from him and banish them so they never came between them again, despite the sickening feeling this was darker and deeper than she was prepared to face. Give her contracts or loans any day. She could handle those, but things like emotions and marital relations left her baffled.

Hearty laughter drifted in from the gaming room, making Jasper look up from signing debts. Jasper couldn't share in his clients' joy, not with his missteps with Jane and the unopened letter staring at him. After he'd left her, he'd paid a call on the solicitor, treating the man to a fine dinner while enticing him to work for the club. When Jasper had ordered a second bottle of wine, he'd tried to convince himself it was to woo the man, but it wasn't the real reason he'd chosen to dine out. It was to avoid Jane.

Facing her before dawn after Lord Fenton's visit had been difficult. He hadn't meant to be short with her, but he'd needed peace and a chance to ponder things. It was difficult to do with her so close and insistent on asking him what was wrong. Better she remain ignorant of the workings of the hell in case real trouble descended on them.

Then, when all had been well this afternoon, and he'd held her in his arms thinking their early morning troubles were over, the letter had reared its ugly head. He should've been more cordial in addressing her concerns, but his mind had turn to brick when she'd handed him the letter. The more sleep he lost, the harder it was for him to maintain control, the way it had been impossible for Uncle Patrick to remain calm when Jasper had demanded he do right by Mr Robillard.

Jasper closed his eyes, still able to see Uncle Patrick standing across from him in the old

Savannah gaming room, his full face as red
as his ruby ring.

'*You're choosing that spineless planter over
me after everything I've done for you?*'

'*What you're doing isn't right and you know
it.*'

'*Now you're the moralist? You didn't mind
taking his money before and spending it on
your fancy house and fine things, did you?*'

The anguish of facing the man he'd once
admired, his image of him warped like a bad
mirror by his experiences, still burned. Everything he'd believed and cultivated about himself and his life in Savannah had died in that
moment.

He opened his eyes. The letter sat before
him on the blotter. He couldn't ignore it any
longer.

He tore it open and unfolded the paper to
read Mrs Robillard's words.

Dear Mr Charton,
I am writing to inform you my eldest son,
Jackson, has decided to apprentice with
a doctor in Boston. As you might imag-
ine, the cost is beyond what I am able to
afford.

I am grateful for the assistance you continue to provide to me and my children. I appeal to you to forward these additional funds to allow Jackson to set himself up in the world, as you are the one who helped pull his father down. I have included the amount and where it should be sent.

I look forward to your prompt reply.
Mrs Robillard

Jasper set the missive on the blotter. Despite everything Jasper had done for her and her children, her hate showed in every word. Unlike his uncle, he recognised how much he deserved it.

He wrote a note to Mr Steed to send the requested money and a little more for Jackson's living expenses. It was the right thing to do, even if no amount could ever undo the damage he and Uncle Patrick had wrought or the way it still haunted him.

Mr Bronson knocked once, then entered, less jovial than usual. 'Not a very lucrative night for us.'

Jasper's pen stilled over the paper. He glanced at the paintings adorning the walls.

They weren't reproductions, his uncle having acquired most of them in payment for debts. They were a safeguard against too many losses. Most men might come here for business connections instead of cards, but it didn't mean Jasper's fortunes couldn't change the same way Mr Robillard's had. He'd made rules against how much a client could lose, but not the amount they could win. 'Anything I should be concerned about?'

'No, just Mr Portland enjoying a good run of luck. They never last. I don't expect his to.'

'Let's hope not.' Jasper sealed the note to his solicitor, not as cavalier about Mr Portland's winning streak as Mr Bronson, especially when a cheer rattled the paintings behind him. Part of him hoped Mr Portland's good fortune held. If he won enough to bankrupt this place it might be a godsend, forcing Jasper out of this life and all contact with it for good. Except without the income from the hell he couldn't pay for Jackson Robillard's future, his employees' or Jane's.

'Something wrong?' Mr Bronson asked.

'I received a letter from Mrs Robillard.'

Mr Bronson nodded, needing no explanation. He'd been there and seen everything.

Jasper sat back and laced his hands over his stomach. 'Tell me, if the quarantine hadn't been imposed and Uncle Patrick hadn't fallen ill, could I have convinced him to return Mr Robillard's plantation?'

Mr Bronson took his pipe out of his pocket and tapped the bowl against his palm. 'I like to think regaining your good opinion meant more to him than being king of the manor, but it's hard to say. He could be a good man to those he cared about, but he had a nasty streak, too. He tried to keep it from you because he used to say if someone like you admired him then he couldn't be all bad, then Mr Robillard came along. It was the first time you got a glimpse of what a grasping bastard Patrick could be. It's why he got mad at you. Realised he couldn't fool you any longer.'

This wasn't anything Jasper hadn't mulled over during the countless hours alone in his house in Savannah during the quarantine while he'd listened to the cannons being fired to clean the air, his body hollowed out with hunger and the stench of death all around him. There'd been warnings before Mr Robillard: a debtor beaten up here, a man thrown out there, furniture and goods appearing in the middle of the night with no explanation asked and none offered. Jasper had chosen to ignore these, too enamoured of Uncle Patrick to see the truth until Mr Robillard had forced it on him.

He twisted the ruby ring on his finger, his uncle's ring, the one he'd removed from his hand before the men had come to take his body away. Jasper hid the truth about his past from Jane, the way Uncle Patrick had hidden his from Jasper. It wasn't right, but if he snatched away her illusions the way Mr Robillard had stolen his, she might despise him as much as Jasper had his uncle. He couldn't bear to see her admiration for him turn to disgust. Without her, he might never be more than the damaged and deceitful man who climbed the warehouse stairs each night. He wanted to be more, even if he wasn't sure if it was possible. He would do all he could to shield Jane from the destruction of her dreams, but the letter's arrival reminded him of how many things were out of his control.

Jasper rose and handed Mr Bronson the signed debts, returning to business. Things had happened and no amount of 'what ifs' could undo them. He must move forward, no matter how much the past still hung on him. Too many people relied on him for him to succumb to his doubts, though they seemed to increase every day.

Chapter Ten

'I can't wait for you to see what I've done.' Jane's voice carried over the clack of the horses' hooves as the carriage carried them towards the building on Fleet Street.

Jasper had awakened out of a deep sleep at noon to find Jane standing over him and he'd braced himself for another round of questions. They hadn't spoken since he'd left her yesterday, but instead of pressing him about the letter and the hell, she'd pulled him from bed, explaining her ideas for the club in rapid sentences and excited words, pretending, like him, all was well between them.

She continued to speak and Jasper watched her more than he listened. This was what he wanted her to be, a thrilled young wife instead of a strained worried one, the woman who still believed in him and their future. 'I'm sure your improvements are brilliant,' he complimented.

She touched her finger to her chin and looked up at the carriage roof. 'There is a noticeable lack of cherubs in the new decor so you may not care for it.'

'Then I insist on one or two gilded pieces, for nostalgia's sake. The dolphin clock from our bedroom, perhaps?'

'I'd indulge your request except I don't want prospective clients clasping their cravats in horror.'

Jasper threw back his head and laughed, the lightness he'd always enjoyed with her returning. 'No, I don't want to drive our clients away.'

The carriage came to a halt in front of the Fleet Street club.

'We're here.' The carriage door banged against the side as she flung it open and dashed out. The ribbons of her blue bonnet fluttered behind her as she weaved through the people cluttering the pavement. At the door to the building she stopped and waved one fawn-coloured glove at him to follow, her smile bright like the sun off the windows.

He slowly approached her, admiring the dark lustre of her hair and the joy she found in his company. She was like a flower growing through the cracks of the pavement, something beautiful in the midst of the ugliness of his life. When he was with Jane, he could believe he wasn't so awful or beyond saving. He wondered who would arise to make Jane see the truth about him, to make her despise him as much as he'd come to despise Uncle Patrick.

He jerked to a halt at the foot of the three stairs leading into the building, his heart racing in panic. *I can't lose her.*

'Come on, what are you waiting for? You must see it.' She grabbed his hand and tugged him through the doorway.

'What do you think?' She threw out her arms where she stood in the centre of the entry.

Jasper turned slowly, taking it all in. Before, it had been difficult to imagine the building as more than a former tobacconist's shop and house. Legitimacy and respectability whispered in the green-and-red paint on the walls in various rooms and the furniture with simple lines decorating them. In one, comfortable chairs were arranged in sets of twos and threes in corners, near the window and in front of the fireplace, encouraging men to come in, sit down and discuss trade and contracts. Under Jane's guidance, it had been transformed into something he'd dreamed about since coming home and maybe even before. 'Amazing.'

'As you can see, I found a place for our purchase.' She pointed to the red couch in the high-ceilinged entrance hall, stately against the far wall, its gaudiness muted by the staid surroundings. 'It's the first thing men will see when they enter.' She stepped closer to him and slid him a saucy glance, making the curls by her temples whisper against her cheeks. 'If you could let it slip where it came from, and embellish the story to say this was where Mrs Greenwood entertained the King, it'll draw more men in here.'

'Too bad we didn't buy the painting of Mrs Greenwood to hang over it.'

Her full lips formed into a plotting, and enticing O. 'I wonder if we could still get it.'

'We could make some discreet enquiries.' He trailed his fingers across her shoulder to tickle her neck, her enthusiasm as irresistible as her soft skin.

She playfully batted his hand away. 'No enquiry into a famous courtesan's portrait can be discreet. Besides, I don't want to be too obvious about our efforts to attract patrons.' She sauntered to the staircase to inspect the repairs to the banister.

He strode into the dining room where tables of various sizes stood with tasteful dining chairs encircling them. The newly acquired china sat in neat sets at each place ready to be marvelled at by clients. He ran his hand along the flat line of the back of a chair. In the daylight it was stunning, in contrast to the Company Gaming Room which showed its tired tackiness in the sunlight. This establishment breathed potential. The very real possibility he might at last break with his disreputable life and remake himself, to be able to walk into his parents' house and face them and Jane with a clear conscience, to stride down the streets with his head held high, openly greeting the men who gathered here, filled him with hope.

The heels of Jane's boots clicked across the wood floor as she came to join him. 'Isn't it wonderful?'

'It is.' He wrapped his arms around her waist and held her tight, more grateful than passionate. He'd been fighting alone for so long, thinking it was up to him to heave himself out of the muck. All the while she'd been working and striving to help him. Perhaps he should tell her everything. Maybe she'd find a way to free him from his past and present troubles the same way she had worked so hard to free him from the hell. It tempted him as much as her hand sliding beneath his waistcoat and her fingers twining in his hair to bring his mouth down to hers.

He was about to take her to the couch and add another story to its lore when a cough made him stop. They let go of one another, straightening their clothes as a lanky youth entered the dining room from the hallway leading to the back of the building. 'Miss Rathbone—I mean Mrs Charton. I didn't expect you today.'

'Good morning, Mark.' Jane shifted effortlessly between seductive wife and practical businesswoman. 'Jasper, Mark is the son of one of Philip's men who guard the warehouse. I hired him to keep an eye on things when the workers aren't here. We don't need thieves pinching our new furnishings.' She turned to the young man, wagging a finger at him like a schoolmarm. 'However, if we were thieves we could've been out of here with half the fixtures before you came in on us.'

The boy lowered his bushy red head. 'I'm sorry, Mrs Charton, I was in the back seeing to a delivery from the draper.'

'Good, the new curtains have arrived. Did the plasterer call again?'

'No, but another man came here this morning. Says he knows Mr Charton and wished to see him.'

The entire building shifted around Jasper before he forced it to still. 'Who was it?'

'Wouldn't give his name, but he was thin with nice clothes, if a bit tattered about the edges.'

It didn't sound like anyone Jasper knew, but it didn't mean Lord Fenton or Captain Christiansen hadn't learned who he really was and sent someone to harass him. Whether they meant to do more than threaten to shut down the club he didn't know. He'd seen bankrupt gamblers in Savannah take out their frustration on dealers and hell owners in dark alleys. It wasn't difficult to imagine it happening here, though somehow an earl would remain blameless while Jasper and Jane suffered. 'If he calls again, inform me immediately. I want to meet him.'

'Should I send him to your house, sir?'

'No!' Jasper coughed, aware of the surprise in Jane and Mark's wide eyes. He cleared his throat and spoke again, careful to keep his voice as even as if he were giving instruction for the baker. 'Tell him to wait for me here, then summon me at once.'

'Yes, sir.'

'That will be all, Mark,' Jane dismissed him and the boy shuffled back to wherever he'd been before they'd arrived.

She turned to Jasper, a wrinkle of concern marring her forehead. 'Who do you think the stranger is? Someone from Savannah who might out us?'

'There aren't enough people left in Savannah to out us.' Her willingness to include herself in the fraud of the Company Gaming Room touched him, except it wasn't right. He was the one with secrets, not her, and the desire to be alone gripped him once more. He wanted space to think without having to pretend he wasn't troubled, but he wouldn't have it while she stood here watching him. 'Most likely someone I used to know. Father told everyone I was back once the moratorium was lifted.'

She eyed him like her brother used to, but

much less subtle in her suspicions. 'Then why the need to keep him from our house?'

Tell her. She had a right to know the potential danger the stranger represented, but still he held back. Each night she went to bed believing she was safe. He couldn't shatter her peace of mind, especially over something that might turn out to be nothing. The man could be anyone, maybe an old acquaintance or even the former owner of the shop. There was no reason to frighten her. 'I'm sure your brother taught you it doesn't hurt to be cautious.'

'He did.'

'Good, then let's not worry about it unless we must. There are, after all, other more pleasurable matters to dwell on.' He pulled her into a kiss. It whispered with a deeper affection, one he was hesitant to name or bring out into the light. It wasn't fair to allow her to believe he was a strong man of integrity, but he couldn't endure losing the faith in her blue eyes. She still believed in good and bad and the strength of love. He didn't wish to steal these things from her the way they'd been ripped from him. He needed her belief in him and their future to help support his. He allowed the tender kiss to come to a sweet end and drew back to study her beautiful face. In her embrace he was Jasper Charton again, not the wounded man who'd returned in his place. 'Shall we try the couch or should we venture home?'

'As the curtains are not hung and Mark is still about, I think we should go home.'

Jane clung to Jasper during the carriage ride home, made weak by the play of his fingers beneath her skirts, the heaviness of his hands on her breasts through her bodice, and the raking of his teeth against her neck. The demands of his desire and hers muted the noise of the streets but not her suspicions about the stranger, or Jasper. Her decision to ignore the events of yesterday and continue on had made things well between them for a while, but the moment Mark had mentioned the stranger, she'd felt Jasper pulling away from her. Even now when he held her, it wasn't only to make love but to distract them both. Again, something was wrong and he refused to tell her what.

Their spirited sprint up the front stairs of the house once they reached home didn't contain the lightness of the auction in Somers Town or their night at the theatre. Even once they were in bed with her skirt hiked up about her waist and his jacket discarded on the floor, his mind was somewhere not even her caresses could touch. The hesitation which had settled over him didn't come off as easily as his waist-coat, despite how hard he worked to make her believe otherwise. Even while she undid the knot of his cravat and traced the hollow of his neck beneath with her tongue, the quickness of his kisses and the steady pace of his fingers were almost mechanical. He was here, yet he wasn't as free with her as he'd been before. She considered holding back a part of herself, too, but she couldn't. Whatever was bothering him, he was, in his own way, turning to her instead of pushing her away and she cared too much about him to deny him the comfort of her embrace. She fumbled with the buttons of his waistcoat, wanting nothing to come between his body and hers. Despite her suspicions about him, in his arms, she felt beautiful, and special and loved.

Love.

She pulled back, her hands stilling on his shirt, unsure if it was really love. She hadn't bargained for anything but friendship when they'd negotiated their betrothal and she hesitated to assume there might be more. At times, their shared humour drove away his brief flashes of darkness, and his confidence in her abilities kept her doubts about herself at bay. He was so much more to her than a friend and the fire in his eyes tempted her to defy her fear and say it aloud, but she couldn't. She wasn't sure he'd say it back or appreciate her trying to drag him into affection he wasn't willing or prepared to give. She took his face in her hands and kissed him hard, meeting his furious passion with her own, wanting, like him, to lose herself in their coming together, to forget her worries and simply be one with him.

They lay together hours after the sun had set and the trays of dinner brought to their room had been discarded on a table near the door. Jasper held Jane while she slept, his body content from their lovemaking, if not his mind. In the Fleet Street building today, he'd begun to believe he could finally leave the gambling life. Like Mrs Robillard's letter, the stranger had reminded him how tight a hold it still had over him.

He pressed a kiss to Jane's temple and inhaled her sweet perfume, searching for the calm she offered, but he failed to find it. During their first few minutes in bed when her eyes had held his, more than friendship had passed between them. Remorse had stopped him from reaching out to seize it. If he'd never gone to America, if he'd rejected Uncle Peter's vices instead of embracing them, then he'd be worthy of Jane's heart.

He closed his eyes and tried to sleep, but the clock beside him chimed twelve times and exhaustion made his thoughts spin faster. She was doing everything she could to free him of this life while he was clinging to it, and risking her peace of mind and her safety in the process. He took a deep breath, concentrating on Jane's steady breaths and the softness of her cheek against his arm to try to settle himself. In his mind he pictured her beneath him, crying out in pleasure at his touch, laughing with him at jokes and sharing his troubles. It settled him for a while, but the later it grew, the more the agitation inside him continued to build. He should stay here tonight with her, but he wanted to go to the hell. If Lord Fenton or Captain Christiansen had connected him to the club, then they might confront him tonight, allowing him to deal with them instead of worrying about what they might do.

Jasper slid his arm out from underneath her. She murmured in her sleep and he paused, waiting to see if she would awaken, but she rolled over and went back to sleep. He lingered bedside the bed and watched her sleep, a peace he craved decorating her pretty face. He wanted to caress her soft cheek, to crawl in beside her and hold her, to see if she could push back the shadows tonight like she had in the carriage, but the demons were too strong. With regret, he took his clothes off the back of a nearby chair and left the room.

'Jasper Charton, I've been waiting for you.' Chester Stilton stepped out from the shadows near the warehouse door, his cravat as dishevelled as his hair.

Jasper paused beside his carriage, careful to keep his panic under control. 'What are you doing skulking about warehouse doorways in the middle of the night?'

'I went to your building in Fleet Street, but you weren't there. I'm glad you decided to come here tonight to play. I must speak with you.'

So Chester was the one Mark spoke to.
What he wanted remained to be seen, but as
long as Chester believed Jasper was another
gambler, it lessened the risk of him seeing him
here. Jasper could think up a thousand ways
to explain his presence to his parents if need
be, more lies, more deceit. It came too easily
to him, even if it still stung his heart like a
punch. 'There's no reason for us to speak. We
aren't associates or friends.'

'I know we've had our differences, but I
need your help.'

'You insulted my fiancée.'

Chester shrugged, trying to appear humble, but it further distorted his already rodent-
like appearance. 'A lapse in judgement on my
part, but you didn't catch me at my best. I
must play tonight. You said you were connected here. Perhaps you can speak with the
owner. I need to win before my creditors force
me abroad.'

The fever lighting up his small eyes made
Jasper take a step back. He'd seen this look
in a hundred other men's eyes before they'd
lost everything. That moment was when Jasper
should have stepped in to stop them, to save
them from being consumed by their habits. As

much as he disliked Chester, he wouldn't give him the chance to ruin himself.

'No, I won't help you. Go home and speak with your father about work, tell him about your debts and find an honourable way to pay them before it's too late.' He was a desperate man which explained why he'd approached him. Desperate men were capable of anything, except walking away from the cards.

Chester's greed turned to hate and he clutched Jasper by the lapel. 'You think you can look down on me because your father refused to give me a loan?'

Jasper knocked his hands away and pushed him back, ready to pummel the man if it drove him from here and saved him for the mistakes so many, including Mr Robillard, had made. 'I don't care who my father extends money to or not. His business isn't mine and if you're smart, you won't rely on luck to save you. Only hard work and legitimate effort can do that.'

Chester pulled back in disgust as if Jasper had suggested he accept the King's shilling and enlist to escape his debts.

Then the door to the warehouse opened and Mr Bronson stepped through it, a number of credit notes in one hand. He failed to notice Chester. 'Jasper, good you're here. I need you to sign for Mr Portland's credit. He isn't so lucky tonight.'

Jasper flicked his glance to Chester and Mr Bronson caught his mistake too late.

Chester was all triumphant smiles while he glanced back and forth between the two men. It made Jasper wish he had struck him.

'No wonder you knew about my debts,' Chester hissed with gloating realisation. 'This is your place, isn't it? It certainly explains the clientele and all the expensive things you can afford.' He jerked his thumb at Jasper's carriage.

'What are you doing here? You were told not to come back,' Mr Bronson growled with an authority to help cover his mistake, but both he and Jasper were acutely aware of it.

The cheesemonger's son tugged at his collar before he regained his nerve. He turned his beady eyes on Jasper. 'I'm glad I did. It seems tonight will be more lucrative than I originally imagined. What will you pay to keep me from telling everyone what you're up to here, especially your sanctimonious father? Imagine how he'll feel when he learns his progeny runs a gambling hell, especially after giving me a lecture on the evils of cards? He'll be the laughingstock of the Fleet.'

'I won't give you a farthing.' This wasn't the first time someone had tried to blackmail him. He'd learned from Uncle Patrick long ago never to give in. If he did, Chester would own him and every night it would be a new and larger demand until he ruined him, then eventually told his secret anyway. He was already a slave to the hell, his past and all his lies. He wouldn't become one to this fool. 'Say what you like to who you like, it makes no difference to me.'

Chester's smug smile dropped like his jaw. Jasper brushed past him, Mr Bronson falling in step beside him as they headed inside.

'You'll regret not paying me,' Chester yelled after them before the door swung shut, leaving him outside in the mist.

Jasper stopped in the darkness, pressed his fists to his hips and took a deep breath.

'I'm sorry,' Mr Bronson offered, his voice as tense as Jasper's insides.

'It's not your fault.' *It's mine.* Try as he might to avoid complications, they seemed to be seeking him out.

'What are you going to do about him?'

'I don't know. With any luck, he'll flee abroad before his desire for revenge outpaces his good sense.'

'We could handle it the way Patrick used to,' Mr Branson suggested.

'No.' He was too much like his uncle already without sinking to the level of common street thug. 'We'll leave it be for now.'

Jasper rubbed his chin, his many mistakes piling up on him, along with those of his uncle. Uncle Patrick no longer had to face them, but Jasper did, every day. He had a sickening sense that his carefully constructed world was about to come crashing down around him. There was nowhere else for him to go if things fell apart here and this time so many more people would suffer.

The bark of a dog on the street outside startled Jane out of sleep. Her back was cold and she turned over to find Jasper missing, again.

He must have gone to the gambling room. She pulled the coverlet up to her chin and snuggled into the soft mattress, but the sound of a bird outside announcing the coming dawn, and the front door opening and closing downstairs, made her sit up. She listened for the fall of Jasper's boots on the stairs, but heard nothing except a slight noise in the sitting room beneath their bedroom. It wasn't like him to linger downstairs when he came home.

She twisted the sheets between her fingers, wondering if she should go down or leave him alone. He hadn't come up for a reason and she feared her questions would revive the awkwardness of their previous early morning encounter. However, if he was suffering she didn't want to leave him alone. In the weeks after Philip's first wife had died, Jane had caught Philip up at night many times. The helplessness Philip had experienced over his wife's death had haunted him and robbed him of sleep. He hadn't been any more forthcoming about his reasons for being up than Jasper had been the other morning, but she'd guessed. Then Laura had come into Philip's life and helped him to open his heart and leave the tragedy of his wife's death behind. It had brought them closer together and uncovered the love developing beneath their marriage of convenience. Jane wanted to do the same for Jasper and be to him what Laura was to Philip.

Unless it wasn't Savannah keeping him up, but guilt. She turned the diamond wedding ring on her finger, hesitant to risk rejection again, but she didn't want to sit here in the darkness with so many questions about the letter and his sudden reserve torturing her either.

She rose, tugged on her robe and left the room.

The wood of the stairs was cold against her bare feet. Outside, a few voices of men making their way along the street carried in through the closed windows. In another hour or so light would fill the sky and more people would join them to begin their long day.

Once downstairs, she crept up on the sitting room, pausing outside to listen to the steady fall of Jasper's feet as he paced inside, her courage wavering. It was clear he craved solitude and she didn't relish another fight, but she couldn't leave him in pain either. Jane braced herself and stepped into the room. 'Jasper, what's wrong?'

He whirled on her, his pale skin reddening at the interruption. Embarrassment brought a faint flush to his cheeks before it vanished, replaced by the testy irritation of a lack of sleep combined with being startled.

'Nothing, go back to bed.' He flicked his hand at her.

'No.' He was mistaken if he thought he could dismiss her like a child.

'Don't be so stubborn.'

His accusation rattled her more than it should have. Milton used to call her stubborn, so did Philip, Justin and, on a few occasions, Mrs Hale. It had turned people off her so many times, but she had never thought it would happen with Jasper. It bit into her determination, but still she continued on. 'I want to know what's wrong and don't lie to me about it not concerning our venture or some other such nonsense. I want the truth about whatever is going on at the hell and the letter you received today.'

His eyes flashed with irritation. 'I needn't explain myself to you or anyone.'

Jane stepped back, stunned but not cowed. 'If you think you can hide things from me, you're mistaken.'

'I'm not hiding anything.'

'You wouldn't behave like this if you weren't. Tell me what it is.'

'I said there's nothing.' The tightening of the lines at the corners of his eyes betrayed him. She'd cornered him, but it was a hollow victory.

'Liar.'

'Don't chastise me like you've never had troubles you've kept from everyone.'

The image of her mother's sickroom and her on her knees beside the bed almost startled the argument out of her. She hadn't told him about her guilt. She'd never told anyone. With him all but scoffing at her, she wasn't about to reveal her greatest failing. 'This isn't about me. I've seen how this kind of thing eats at people and the damage it can do. Philip worked so hard to hold back from Laura, even after her uncle tried to kill her. It changed him and almost drove a wedge between them until Laura overcame it.' *With love,* she wanted to say, but this wasn't the time to say it and put him off the idea for good.

Jasper studied her with a sadness to make her ache. 'You must accept there are things you can't know about me.'

Like who the woman who wrote the letter is. Fear began to overwhelm her but she held it at bay. If she allowed it to engulf her, she'd lose this argument for sure. 'So you say, but what happens when there are children? With the way we've been carrying on there are sure to be. Will you be there for them at night like your parents were for you or will you be too busy handling your private affairs to care about their welfare or mine?'

'You wouldn't say such things if you had any idea what I'm dealing with to ensure your and our future children's welfare.'

She marched up to him. 'Then tell me everything you're facing, no matter what it is, and we'll find a way to deal with and overcome it together.'

His expression went blank and she held her breath, thinking he might at last confide in her. A coal popped in the grate and outside two men called to one another before their voices faded off down the street. 'I don't need your help. I need my privacy.'

'Fine. Pace a hole in the floorboards for all I care, but don't wake me when you finally decide to come to bed.'

Jane fled the room, her hands shaking at her sides. This wasn't the Jasper who'd kissed her so tenderly and laughed with her during the day. He was a stranger she loathed and she didn't know what had brought about the change.

Perhaps Mr Bronson knows what's wrong.

She considered paying a visit to the hell and asking him, but she hated to garner information about Jasper in such an underhanded way. She didn't know how he would react if she did and he discovered it.

She paused in the upstairs hallway, catching the faint reflection of herself in the black-speckled mirror. She was no longer sure this was a fluke and not some indication of how their future together might be. Jasper, her oldest friend, her husband, was, like everyone else, pulling away from her. In the darkness, the image of her six-year-old self being chased out of her mother's sickroom by the cranky old nurse reflected back at her.

'You've done enough damage already, child, now get out.'

'But I want to see my mother. I need to see her and say I'm sorry.'

'Your apologies won't help her. You should have listened when she told you not to sneak out to the fair instead of insisting on having your way, you naughty child.'

Jane screwed her eyes shut against the image and the stinging tears. The nurse had had no right to be so cruel and dismissive, and neither had Jasper. *I was only trying to help him, like I wanted to help Mother.*

Her father and mother had been the first ones to leave her.

He won't leave me. He can't. He needs me. She dashed into their room and slammed the door shut. She snatched up the poker and knocked the coals with it, trying to elicit some warmth from the fading fire and making the flue ring with the racket. Without her, Jasper would never have his club, assuming he really wanted it. She'd heard nothing more about any plans to turn the hell over to Mr Bronson but she also hadn't asked. After tonight, she wondered if she'd be able to question him about anything without it getting his hackles up.

She dropped down on the hearthrug, tossed the poker aside and pulled her knees to her chest, barely touched by the warmth emanating from the grate. The chill creeping through her was too severe and it made her teeth chatter. She wondered if the man she'd faced tonight was the real Jasper, the one she'd caught more than once hovering in the shadows just behind the carefree man. Perhaps she hadn't noticed it before because she'd been too eager to marry to see the truth.

Tears slid down her cheeks. She'd wanted a life for herself and in marrying Jasper she'd thought she'd achieved it. She'd also wanted to be the most important person to someone and she wasn't. Whatever he was hiding or trying to accomplish by keeping their spheres so separate was the most important thing to him. She came in a distant second and it stabbed at her because for all her hesitations about saying the word while they'd been intimate yesterday, she did love him. She always had and it hadn't stopped during their time apart. She'd tried to convince herself she didn't need his heart and could exist in a marriage without love, but like so many other aspects of her present situation it was a lie. She wanted him as much now as the night she'd tried to secure his heart nine years ago, to be his true wife in a real marriage, and he was pushing her away this morning like he had then. It made the sting of it even more severe.

This wasn't at all how she'd expected marriage to be.

Jasper slouched in the chair with a view of the window. He stared at the brightening sky and the single star visible over the building across the way. He needed sleep, but he didn't go upstairs. Jane had left him an hour ago and other than the clank of a poker echoing through the chimney, he hadn't heard anything from the floor above since. If she was asleep, he could slip in beside her and rest. If she was awake, he wasn't sure he could endure another spat. If she did rail at him, then he deserved it. She'd come down to find him because she cared and he'd shoved her away, as careless of her feelings as Uncle Patrick had been of Mrs Robillard's plight. He hadn't meant to be short with her, but during the day it was easy to be close to Jane, to laugh and tease with her. Not even her tender touch could drive back the ghosts at night.

He tapped the arm of the leather chair. The charade required to maintain his life was starting to crack around the edges and he wondered how much longer he could hold it together before something slipped and he revealed more than he was willing to explain. The effort of having to conceal his troubles, to sneak past her and then add more lies to the ones he already maintained when caught made it more difficult to control. He needed space to wrestle his past into submission and there was only one way to achieve it. She wouldn't like it, but it must be done if he hoped to find a way to defeat his demons and be the kind of husband Jane deserved.

Chapter Eleven

Jane climbed the stairs to their room in search of Jasper, her feet dragging with her exhaustion. It had taken ages to fall asleep after the row with him this morning. When she had, it'd been a light sleep only. Near sunrise he'd climbed in beside her, careful not to touch her. She'd pretended to be asleep to avoid another argument, but she'd remained wide awake, sure he did, too. Around six, when he'd at last fallen into a deep sleep, she'd risen, unable to lie there any longer.

She'd gone downstairs and thrown herself into business for the club before paying a visit to the furniture maker to arrange for the sale of the remaining things in the warehouse and to purchase more sedate items for the private conversation rooms. She was back home now and there was no more avoiding him today, not when she needed to discuss the transfer of goods from the warehouse to the furniture maker. Jasper had granted her a free hand to make contracts or buy and sell items, but some matters still required his assistance.

The sight in their bedroom stopped her short.

Mrs Hodgkin and the scullery maid were carrying Jasper's things out of their room and into the adjoining one.

Fear slammed into her chest. *He doesn't want to be with me any more.*

'What are you doing?' she asked the housekeeper, hating the way her voice shook.

Mrs Hodgkin stopped, surprised by the question. 'Setting his things in the other room as Mr Charton requested.'

'But *this* is his room.'

'I thought you'd be more comfortable if you had this one to yourself.' Jasper's voice carried from behind Jane. Mrs Hodgkin and the scullery maid slipped away to finish their task as Jane faced her husband. 'I don't want to disturb you as I come and go at night, nor can I be disturbed when I'm sleeping in the mornings.'

He made it seem as if it was for her benefit

when in reality it was for his. She refused to allow it to stand. 'And you thought to inform the servants before you told me?'

'You've been gone for some time,' he stated as if it was reason enough to take action behind her back. It made her wonder what else he was doing and not telling her about, like the letter and the woman who'd written it.

'And you were so eager to be out of my room you couldn't wait?' She might not have wanted to hurt him at the auction, but she wouldn't mind doing so now. All she could see was her having to face Philip, her friends, all of the Fleet while they sneered at her for not having been able to keep a husband. 'How long until you decide to leave this house as well?'

He had the nerve to balk at the question. 'Never.'

'Then am I to go?'

He hesitated before answering in a measured voice, 'Jane, this changes nothing between us except where I sleep. Most married couples don't share a room and it will only be until I give up the hell and return to normal hours.'

'And when will that be? Have you spoken to Mr Bronson about it, made any arrangement, or were you too busy packing up your things to see to your own affairs?'

He pressed his lips tightly together and she knew she was right. It terrified her because it meant she might be right about his leaving, too. It was the man from the sitting room this morning appearing again. It frightened her as much as seeing his things piled on the bed in the adjoining room.

'This isn't right, Jasper, and you know it, and nothing you say will convince me otherwise.'

His face softened, as if he sensed his decision had hurt her and he wanted to soothe the sting. He slipped his arm around her waist and tried to pull her close. 'Having separate rooms doesn't mean you'll always be sleeping alone.'

She went stiff in his arms, waiting for him to apologise to her and explain what had happened last night at the hell and promise her things between them would be fine again, but he didn't. Instead he brushed her cheek and temple with his lips.

The stubborn woman inside her wanted to push him away, but the one who craved his affection made her languid in his arms. Maybe this was his way of apologising and making things right between them, the way last night had been his means of seeking comfort. He made a trail of kisses across her cheek and down to her jaw and caressed the hollow of her neck with his tongue.

She tilted back her head and closed her eyes, savouring the sweep of moisture and the sweet tickle of his breath. She forgot all of her arguments for or against the plan as he began to undo the small laces at the back of her dress. It wasn't an attempt to keep them apart. He wanted her—it was apparent in the quickness of his breath in her ear and the eagerness of his fingers against her skin. She was his wife and this arrangement wouldn't be for ever.

Then she turned her head and noticed his things laid out on the bed in the adjoining room. It was no coincidence Jasper had thought of this arrangement after she'd confronted him and refused to leave him be. With his kisses he was trying to pretend everything from this morning hadn't happened and all was resolved between them, but it wasn't.

She wrested out of his embrace. 'Don't try to placate me. The next time you attempt to make love to me, be sure it's because you want me, not because you want your way.'

She stormed out of the room and down the hall, refusing to be humoured like a child or made to come or go according to his whims. She'd hold out on him until he finally told her something or decided he wanted separate rooms to become separate lives.

She came to a halt at the top of the stairs, all her early morning worries rushing back to her. *I should march in there and confront him, refuse to allow whatever it is he is trying to do,* but her usual stubbornness failed her and she didn't move. She was wary of what else he might do if she did insist on them sharing a room. She didn't want to make demands, drive him away, or lose the warmth of his touch or the joy of his company. *Maybe I was too fast to anger and walk out.* If she'd held him tighter, been more complacent instead of haranguing, she wondered if she might have changed his mind.

She went downstairs to the sitting room and began to pace, confused and lost about what to do. His embrace last night before their fight, and their time at the club, had contradicted everything he was saying and doing today, but he was withdrawing from her and she must stop it, even if she didn't know how. She wished there was someone she could speak with, but if she dared broach the subject with one of Jasper's sisters, the story would spread through the family like a fire and probably jump to the Rathbone household. Heaven knew what Philip would say. It eliminated Laura as a confidant, too, especially since Laura and Philip had no secrets between them. Though he kept his business separate from his family, he was at home in his office during the day, taking as much interest in Laura's life as she did in his. She could speak with Mrs Fairley, but the modiste was in Salisbury visiting her sister and not expected back for another week.

For all the change in her situation and surname, she might as well be a spinster again.

She stared at the bookshelf across the room, noting how her old novels mingled effortlessly with the ones Jasper had inherited from his uncle. If only she knew how to make her and Jasper's hearts and lives fit together so neatly. She could balance ledgers and negotiate contracts but she couldn't win her husband's love or his confidence.

Then one green-leather spine with gold-embossed letters caught her notice. She slipped it out from among the others.

Glenarvon.

She smiled as she traced the shiny title. It had been one of the first books Mrs Hale had secreted for her years ago. The two of them had read it, sneaking off to the garden to discuss the scandalous tome away from Philip's hearing and his disapproval.

Mrs Hale!

She clutched the book to her chest. Speaking to Mrs Hale would mean breaking her promise to Jasper but she had to do it. He was already going back on his vow to honour her and this wasn't how she wanted to live. She needed advice and help and she was sure Mrs Hale would keep her secret. Heaven knew she'd kept some before, even colluding with Jane to create a few. With this being Mrs Hale's second marriage, she must know something about husbands.

'He's running an illegal gambling hell at night,' Jane blurted out to Mrs Hale as they sat together in the small morning room of Dr Hale's house. Through the wall she heard Dr Hale speaking with a patient, his voice low and steady. Years ago, she'd come here numerous times when Philip had been courting Arabella, his first wife and Dr Hale's daughter.

'A gambling establishment. How exciting!' Mrs Hale drank in the news as she did every other scandal the two of them had ever shared.

'It isn't exciting, it's awful.' Guilt pressed on her as much as anxiety. She'd promised Jasper she wouldn't tell anyone, but he'd also promised to make her his primary concern and he hadn't. 'He's away from me all night and sleeps all morning. I hardly see him except for afternoons and evenings when we, well, you know.'

'I do.' She poured tea in Jane's cup, eyeing her through the steam. 'Is that why you're here?'

'No.' She rose and went to Dr Hale's bookshelf to straighten a few books. She'd rather be here about a possible baby instead of this worry. She turned and took in the familiar room. After Arabella had passed, Jane used to sit here with Dr Hale, trying to help him in a way she hadn't been able to do with Philip. In his grief her brother had retreated into a more severe stoicism than before, while Dr Hale had appeared lost. Later, when Thomas was old enough, Jane used to bring her nephew here to see his grandfather. The visits had helped ease Dr Hale out of his mourning and it had made a great difference to them both. In the cosy sitting room, Jane hoped to garner a little of the comfort she'd been able to offer during that difficult time. 'The gambling hell isn't the worst of it. There's something serious tormenting Jasper, something he won't tell me about, and I think it might be another woman.'

Mrs Hale motioned for Jane to return to her seat at the table. Jane sat across from her and told her about the letter from Savannah and Jasper coming home from the hell in the mornings, troubled but unwilling to discuss it with her. 'I love him and I want this to be a real marriage, but I'm not sure he wants the same.'

Mrs Hale reached across the table and squeezed her hand. 'I think he does and I suspect it's the reason he changed his mind about marrying you. Deep down, he realised you can help him face whatever he's dealing with and you must, or things will never be right between you.'

'But the woman in Savannah?'

'Perhaps she is just a widow he's done business with.'

'And if she's not?'

Mrs Hale let go of her hand and sat back. 'Jane, if there is one thing I've learned after two marriages, it's the need to trust your spouse and to give him the benefit of the doubt. Until you learn otherwise, don't worry yourself into a panic about a woman an ocean away. If you're patient, I'm sure the truth will eventually come out and it will probably be nothing like what you're imagining.'

'It wasn't with Milton.'

'And you must stop allowing your experience with him to guide you in this. Jasper is not his brother and you worrying about what might be, instead of what is, won't help you.'

Jane threw out her arms in frustration. 'I don't even know what is and what isn't. He won't tell me and it's coming between us and I have no idea what to do.'

Mrs Hale picked up her spoon and stirred her tea a moment before she tapped it on the side of the cup and laid it in the saucer. 'I think, deep down, you do know what to do.'

'I don't, it's why I'm here,' she blurted through clenched teeth. This wasn't at all what she'd expected from her old mentor. Jane's outburst didn't rattle Mrs Hale who sat calmly across from her, hands folded in her lap just as she always had when Jane had come to her fuming about one thing or another. Jane rolled her shoulders and calmed herself, not wanting to drive away Mrs Hale like she was driving away Jasper. 'If I did, then I would do it and things wouldn't be as bad as they are.'

'I know you like to take action, to get to the meat of the matter, but Jasper isn't an obstacle to overcome or a problem with a neat solution. If he's holding on to his secrets as you say, he'll fight like a wounded badger if you try to wrest them from him.'

'Are you saying I was wrong to try to force him to talk?'

'Not at all. Sometimes, you have to try something before you know it won't work. Now it's time to try something else, something only you as his wife can do. You were his closest friend for a very long time, the one person he chose to entrust his secret to and then to wed. You know him better than possibly anyone else and what it will take to reach him and gain his confidence.'

'But—'

Mrs Hale held up one hand to silence her. 'There is nothing to stop you from doing this except your doubt in yourself and your value to him.' She reached over and cupped Jane's face with her hands. 'You're a very strong young lady and, while it hasn't always worked in your favour, it is an advantage and not a weakness, and you must learn to see it as such.'

'How can I when all anyone has ever done is chide me for it?'

Mrs Hale tilted her head at her in amused disbelief. 'And have you ever listened to all those people in other matters, such as purchasing buildings?'

'No.'

'Then why take their word for it this time?'

Because over the years she'd come to realise they were right. She wasn't a strong person, just a stubborn one whose desire to always have her way had killed her parents and now was driving her husband away. Jane took a deep breath and shoved her doubts down deep inside her. She'd always pretended to be strong so others would think she was solid against those who wanted to pull her down and so she might believe it, too. The last few days had shown her how weak she really was. If she dared to speak about it with Mrs Hale, then the woman who held so much faith in her might at last see it, too.

Mrs Hale smoothed a strand of hair off her forehead. 'Trust in yourself, Jane, and in Jasper's concern for you, and I promise all will be well.'

* * *

Jane returned from Mrs Hale's, pondering everything she'd told her. She didn't share her friend's belief in her strength or her ability to find a way out of her present troubles. If she could, she would have done it by now, but everything seemed to be growing steadily worse. She shuddered to think how it all might end.

She was not two feet in the door when Johnson approached her. 'Mr Steed is here to see you, Mrs Charton. He's waiting in the sitting room.'

'Thank you.' Jane reluctantly made for the sitting room, in no mood to deal with anyone today. 'Mr Steed, I hope this unexpected visit is good news.'

She needed a little good fortune to lift her spirits.

Mr Steed rose from where he'd been sitting and bowed to her. They'd met before when Jasper had taken her to his office to arrange for her to manage his accounts once they were wed. He was tall with sandy hair and the charm of Jasper, but more sedate in his application of it. 'It's neither good nor bad, Mrs Charton, only necessary. Since Mr Charton has given you power to handle his affairs, I thought you could approve this bank draft. He instructed me to send it at once and there's a ship leaving for America in the morning. He promised to deliver it to me yesterday, but it must have slipped his mind. I'm eager to send this with the captain. It will prevent any unnecessary delay.'

He removed a paper from the fine leather satchel he carried and held out the draft. Jane took it and swallowed hard, determined not to fly into a panic. 'Who is Mrs Robillard and why is Jasper sending her this much money?'

'He's been sending money to her since he first engaged me after coming home. As for why, that is something you will have to discuss with him. He offered me no reason and it isn't my habit to ask. If you'd like, I can wait on the draft and speak to him myself.' He reached for the paper, recognising his mistake in bringing it to her. The pity on his face reminded her of the way the elder Mr and Mrs Charton had looked the morning they'd come to tell her about Milton. It was exactly what she hadn't wanted to experience in marriage, what Jasper had promised her wouldn't happen and yet here it was. What other secrets of his were waiting to rise up and humiliate her?

The possibility added to the disquiet surrounding her since leaving Mrs Hale's.

'No, he told me the other day he received a note from Georgia about some unfinished business. This must have something to do with it.' She'd bet her eye teeth it wasn't the sort of commercial interest Jasper had alluded to, but it allowed her to save face with the solicitor. She refused to stand here and have him think her a betrayed wife who'd inadvertently discovered her husband's infidelity. 'I'll sign the draft and speak to Jasper about it later.'

'Of course.'

Jane took the paper to the writing table and signed the document, her fingers tight on the pen to keep it from shaking as she wrote her name. Then she handed it to Mr Steed, who tucked it back in his valise.

'Thank you, Mrs Charton. I hope I haven't inadvertently caused you any distress or concern,' he apologised while Jane escorted him to the front door.

'Of course not.' She smiled brightly, trying to shake off his embarrassment as well as hers. 'Good day, Mr Steed.'

He slipped on his hat and darted down the walk to his waiting carriage.

With as much composure as Jane could manage she returned to the study while Johnson closed the door. She stopped in the centre of the narrow room, fighting back the wave of distress crashing over her.

Jane slumped into the gilded chair by the desk. Maybe this was the real reason he'd been reluctant to marry her. He'd hoped his paramour from Savannah might join him. Except Mrs Robillard was married. No wonder Jasper had changed his mind. Better to wed a free woman in London who could help him with his club then pine for a married one in Savannah. *Except he isn't pining. He's sending her money.*

If he were upstairs sleeping, she would march up there directly and ask Jasper about this mysterious woman. But she didn't know where he'd gone while she'd been out. She would have to wait until he returned to escort her to his parents' house for dinner.

His parents.

It was bad enough she intended to enter their home while lying about Jasper's true occupation and income, but to be forced to play the role of the happy newlywed while she worried about his fidelity was more than she wished to bear. Perhaps she could plead a headache and not go, except it would probably have his sisters flooding in here wondering if she were with child, since she never took ill. There was nothing to do but go and face his family, guilty conscience or not. She'd taken on Jasper's lies when she'd married him and she must endure them and whatever troubles they caused her as she'd sworn to do at the altar. It didn't mean she wouldn't discover the truth, but it wouldn't be tonight. She couldn't hope to maintain any sense of composure if Jasper confirmed her suspicions. She must keep her concerns from everyone, including Jasper, until she could find a moment and a way to face him and discover at last what was going on. It made her feel more alone and isolated than when she'd lived with Philip.

This wasn't the way her marriage was supposed to be.

Chapter Twelve

Jasper sat across from Jane in the coach as it carried them to his parents' house and the dinner party awaiting them. He hadn't seen Jane since their encounter in their bedroom. Even after he'd come home from the jeweller's to dress, she'd been so occupied with Mrs Hodgkin there hadn't been a moment for them to talk. He'd been secretly relieved, in no mood for a fight before they left for his parents' house. When at last he could no longer put off facing her, he'd braced himself and come down from dressing to find her waiting for him in the sitting room. She'd been polite and sweet, peppering him with innocuous questions about his day and allowing him to escort her to the carriage, her small hand on his arm, her copper-coloured evening dress whispering against his legs as they walked. Yet for all her pretence to everything being well, the stiffness of her gait and the shallowness of her smile told him it wasn't and, like him, she was doing her best to hide it.

It was time for him to make amends and bring the light back into her expression.

'I have something for you.' He removed a long, slender velvet box from his coat pocket and held it out to her.

She eyed it and him with suspicion. 'What is it?'

'Open it and see.' He perched on the edge of the squab, eager for the smile his gift would bring to her red lips. He needed her good humour. He didn't have enough of his own.

She pushed back the lid, her eyebrows rising at the gold-and-diamond necklace inside. 'It's stunning.'

Her response wasn't. There were no effusive thanks, no squeal of delight or the throwing of her curving arms around his neck like she'd done before their visit to the theatre. With his gift he'd tried to recapture the joy of their first week together, just as he'd strived to maintain the connection between them this afternoon when he'd kissed her. He hadn't been manipulating her into agreeing to his plan for separate rooms, only searching for the connection which had bound them together over the last few weeks, the one he'd severed with his foolishness. He should have known better than to think he could do it with jewellery.

She lifted out the necklace and the diamonds flashed in the carriage lantern light as she held it out to him. 'Will you put it on me?'

'Of course.'

She turned her back to him and he took both ends of the cool metal and slipped it around her neck. Her perfume encircled him like the gold did her neck, the arch of it tantalising beneath his fingertips. He wanted to press his lips to the tender skin, to make her sigh and tilt her head back to rest on his shoulder, to draw her closer and banish the discomfort between them. He fastened the clasp, then rested his hands on her shoulders. Her skin was soft and warm and as familiar as his own. When he slept in the mornings, he would miss the heat of her beside him and the ease of laying his palm on her firm thigh. The nights would be colder, too, without her in his bed. He thought he'd needed space, but he was fast learning what he needed was her. He was about to admit he'd been a fool to leave her room when the carriage rocked to a halt.

She turned her head, her eyes catching his, the uncertainty in their blue depths as strong as in the pit of his stomach. If he'd never gone to America, if he'd rejected Uncle Peter's vices instead of embracing them, if he'd kept his promise to redeem himself, he'd be worthy of Jane's heart.

Let her help you and make everything right again. He couldn't, not when they were moments away from facing his family.

He removed his hands from her shoulders and she slipped back across the carriage to take her seat and wait for the driver to open the door and hand her down.

Jane held Jasper's arm as they climbed the wide staircase to reach the sitting room and the party waiting for them. The necklace sat heavy around her neck. She wanted Jasper's whole heart and the respect he'd promised her, not expensive gifts. She wasn't as convinced as Mrs Hale of her ability to draw him out, and feared the distance between them would continue to grow until it could never be overcome. One day, she might walk into the Charton home alone the way she had after her failed engagement. She never wanted to face such humiliation again.

Voices and the melodious notes of Lily's piano playing drifted out of the upstairs sitting room, adding a warm cheeriness to the house which could not penetrate her and Jasper. She'd been here a thousand times, but this would be her first as a wife trying to pretend everything with her marriage was well when it wasn't.

They reached the sitting room, and Jasper's sisters surrounded her in a flutter of oohs and ahhs over her new necklace. A week ago Jane would have tossed back her head to display her gift and revel in their admiration. Tonight, she wanted to hide it and herself. She should be grateful he'd thought of her and wanted to make her happy, but it was all on the surface, as false as the sets on the Covent Garden Theatre stage. Beneath the sparkle of the gems were so many questions and troubles she had no idea how to untangle. There'd been no time in the carriage, even during the moment when, with his hands on her shoulders, she'd wanted to reach out to him and ask if he still cherished and cared for her as he'd promised he would.

While Jane spoke with the Charton sisters, Jasper remained beside her as stiff as a horse-hair cushion. He did what was expected of him, greeting his twin brothers with his usual charming smiles and jokes, his clothes impeccable as always, but she caught the tension around his eyes, the subtle avoiding of her questioning glances. It made it difficult for Jane to hold her smile and pretend, like him, everything was splendid.

She believed she was fooling everyone until Mrs Charton approached them, studying them with motherly regard. 'Jasper, Jane, you both look so pale. Tomorrow night you must come with us to Vauxhall Gardens. The distraction will help you both.'

'I think it would be lovely,' Jane lied, adding another to the many already accumulated. Jasper was right, it ate at her like the distance between them did.

'Perhaps another evening, I have some business to attend to,' Jasper refused his mother with an apologetic smile, but it did nothing to ease the tiredness in his eyes. Apparently, she wasn't the only one being worn down by this charade. How he'd managed it for so long while living in his parents' house she couldn't imagine.

'Jasper, come here. Giles wants to talk to you about something called a railway.' Mr Charton drew Jasper away, while Mrs Charton occupied herself with her grandchildren.

Jane was left to the sisters who dragged her to the arrangement of sofas in front of the fireplace, sat her down and peppered her with questions about how she and Jasper were getting on. Jane twisted herself into knots making up the imaginary life she lived with Jasper, the one they should be enjoying instead of this half-marriage.

Camille, Milton's wife, sat across from her, listening intently and saying very little. More than once she caught Jane's eye with a solemnity to make Jane wonder if the woman suspected Jane's unease or if it was lingering discomfort over what had happened between them. For the first time Jane didn't care about the past or Milton or Camille. All she cared about was Jasper and how there seemed to be more than the distance of the room between them.

She watched him while he spoke with his father. He didn't notice her at first, but then his eyes met hers and the regret darkening them made her want to rush to him. Instead, she was forced to remain on the sofa pretending happiness for the benefit of his family. It made her feel more like a trained monkey than a married woman.

When the sisters at last lost interest in discussing Jane's married life, Olivia stood to suggest a new amusement. 'Who'd like to join me in a game of whist?'

A noticeable quiet drifted over the room.

Mr Charton thumped his hand on the table beside him, making a statue of a shepherdess rattle on her porcelain base. 'Not in my house you won't.'

'Risking a pence or two among family isn't going to land anyone in debtors' prison, Father,' Olivia scoffed. 'After all, it's not as if I'm suggesting we establish a gambling den in the sitting room!'

Jane exchanged a wary glance with Jasper, wondering if Olivia suspected them. She didn't believe so. Olivia had always been the most rebellious and outspoken of the three sisters and much more like Jasper than any of the other girls.

Mr Charlton levelled a warning finger at his daughter. 'If you'd seen the many men who've wasted my loans and their livelihoods on cards, you wouldn't think it so funny.'

'Everyone understands your feelings on the matter, Henry,' Mrs Charton gently chided from where she held court near the window, surrounded by her grandchildren. She wore her favourite red-silk gown with a matching turban her daughters called old-fashioned, but which she adored. She was still lithe, despite having borne seven children.

The subject would have been dropped if Milton hadn't decided to step in. 'It's a disgusting habit and, like Father, I'd be ashamed of anyone in this family who ever resorted to such a lowly way of life.'

'Says the man who's proven his talent at sneaking around,' Jasper hissed.

The room went silent—even the grandchildren stopped talking. Across from Jane, Camille lowered her eyes and her cheeks turned bright red.

'I think you've been away too long and forgotten how things are done in this family,' Milton hissed back. Beside him, Alice allowed Jacob a drink from her glass. Jacob started to hand it to Giles when a warning look from Mrs Charton made him hand it back to his sister.

'We can chastise a man for his sins, but once they're done they're finished. Now on to better topics,' Mrs Charton insisted, bringing the matter to a close. But it didn't smooth Jasper or Milton's ruffled feathers, or ease Jane's guilt. The family had accepted her even after the debacle with Milton and here she was, sitting in their midst, as two-faced as Milton.

'Let's play musical chairs instead,' Alice suggested. Chairs scraped over the floor as the siblings and their husbands dragged them into place and Lily struck a chord on the piano to begin the game.

Olivia participated, but appeared more bored than amused. It was clear she and her brewery-owner husband didn't mind small amounts of gambling. Jane wondered if she'd side with her and Jasper if their secret ever came out. She didn't know Olivia well enough to be sure.

While the elder sisters and their husbands laughed and raced around to find open chairs, Milton sulked in the corner with Giles, who rolled his eyes at having been cornered by his complaining elder brother. When he finally managed to slip away and join Jasper and Mr Charton, Milton's wife fawned over her spouse, trying to bring him out of his sulkiness to join the game. When Milton rebuffed her to help himself to the brandy in the corner, his wife remained by the wall, ill at ease among all the laughter.

Jane felt sorry for her. It wasn't an emotion she expected to encounter, but there it was. She had more experience than she cared to admit with a husband pushing her away.

The brewer raced around the chairs behind Olivia who reached the open one first. The activity distracted Jane from noticing Jasper's absence. She had no idea when or where he'd gone. No one else was missing.

Did he leave without me?

She shifted nervously on her feet. She used to read in the papers about husbands sneaking out never to be seen again. There was a ship leaving for America tomorrow. She was about to ask Mrs Charton where Jasper had gone when the rustle of skirts beside her made her turn. Camille approached, as pale as always, but there was a hint of determination in her mouse-like eyes. Jane forced herself not to scurry away from her like some startled elephant.

'Good evening, Jane. I haven't had a chance to speak with you the last two times we've been at events, but I wished to congratulate you on your wedding.'

'Thank you.' Jane did her best to be gracious. She and Camille had never been more than passing acquaintances, her father and mother moving in the same circles as the Rathbones and the Chartons. When they were young, they'd seen one another at birthday parties and teas, but they'd never been close. Other than having stolen Jane's fiancé, Camille had never done or said an ill thing to Jane.

The laughter of the other married siblings rang through the room. It covered the quiet conversation between the ladies, although Jane couldn't help but notice Mrs Charton regarding them before she turned back to her youngest grandson.

'I also want to apologise for what happened,' Camille stated without hesitation.

Jane gaped at Camille. She hadn't expected this. She'd prefer it to be Milton, but she'd take it from the wife.

'I'm quite over it, as you can see.' She would have motioned to Jasper, but he was nowhere to be found. The same awkwardness she'd experienced the first time she'd attended a party after the unexpected elopement, when everyone had cast sympathetic looks her way, draped her again. 'We needn't speak of it.'

'But we must. You see, I didn't mean to hurt you, but Milton and I were so in love we couldn't help ourselves.' Camille said it in such a way Jane knew it wasn't boasting. It stabbed at her because no such driving passion had met her and Jasper's union. It had been a bargain, a negotiation, with little promise of more. 'He also told me you'd already broken with him.'

He would, the lying rat. 'Then why the secrecy and the elopement?'

'My father doesn't share my good opinion of Milton.'

Few did, but Jane didn't want to cast aspersions on the love of Camille's life.

'I would have spoken to you about it sooner, but there's never been a good time. Since we're sure to be together at many gatherings in the future, I don't want any bad blood between us and I'm eager to see Milton and Jasper reconciled, too.'

The woman was a fiancé-stealing saint. 'I'm afraid it isn't up to us.'

She couldn't settle the current tension between her and Jasper, much less work a miracle between the two brothers.

'We can certainly help. If you'll agree to do it, so will I.'

She held out her hand to seal the pact with a shake. Jane stared at the ivory-satin glove covering it before she took it, Camille's honesty and concern melting Jane's grudge, but not her doubts about a reconciliation. It would be even harder to settle things between the brothers if Jasper turned his back on her for good, choosing his American woman over her. Her chest tightened as she imagined the looks and whispering she'd have to endure then.

'I knew I could count on you. You're so clever and quick. I've always admired you because of it.' It wasn't flattery and it left Jane speechless. Milton didn't deserve his kind wife. 'If you ever need someone to discuss things with, I'd be honoured to keep your confidences. I know how difficult it can be in this family.'

'Yes, it can.' Even if Jane wasn't ready to spill her heart to the woman who whispered across the pillow to Milton, it was a comfort to think someone recognised a little of what she was facing, even if they didn't know the true extent. It bolstered her confidence. If Camille could face her after what she and Milton had done, then Jane could be as courageous when it came to facing Jasper. She didn't care if they were at his parents' house. She wouldn't run away from her fears any more, or try to act as if they didn't exist or as if everything was fine. She'd knowingly gone along with his schemes, allowed him to set the tone for this marriage, afraid if she didn't he would never give her all of himself, but it hadn't worked. It had exhausted her and she couldn't allow it to continue. She'd have a true husband and a real marriage.

'If you'll excuse me, I must find my husband.'

She had no idea where he'd gone, but she knew the Charton house well. She'd spent hours here with Jasper and Milton as a child, going up and down the servants' passage to steal sweets from the cook while doing her best to avoid the dancing lessons Mrs Charton had imposed on her and her older girls. Dancing hadn't interested her and she'd stolen away to find the brothers after the first quadrille. Mrs Charton, seeing the futility of pressing any more lessons on her, had never chased after her or demanded she act like a proper young lady. No one had. She missed the freedom of those old days, especially in regard to Jasper. Her relationship with him had been so simple and straightforward back then without all the complications of secrets, the past and the involvement of her heart.

She headed for Mr Charton's study, remembering how she'd found Jasper there the night of his going-away party. He'd been contemplating the atlas on the stand near the desk, measuring again and again the distance between London and Savannah, the distance between himself and his family, and her. She'd tried to bolster his spirits, realising then how unlikely it was they would ever see each other again. Storms took ships all the time, as did sickness. Yet he had survived it all. He'd come back to her and made her his wife. She wouldn't allow the past or another woman or whatever tormented him do what the entire Atlantic had failed to do—separate them for good.

She peered inside the study, relieved to find him here and not on his way to catch a ship to America. He stood before the fireplace, staring at the portrait of Mrs Charton's siblings from five decades ago. The girls wore the fuller skirts then in fashion, their hair powdered and piled high on their heads. Mrs Charton, her round face fuller but her lively eyes unmistakable, stood holding the hand of her young brother, Patrick, while her elder brother and sister lounged on a nearby *chaise*.

Jane slipped up beside Jasper, the questions about Mrs Robillard and their future together begging to be spoken, but she held back. She was risking being hurt again and for the pain of abandonment to crush her, but she refused to be left alone and forgotten by the one man who'd pledged before their family and friends to cherish her. Mrs Hale was right, she shouldn't doubt herself, but being open with anyone about her fears had never been her strong suit, except with Jasper. It was time to put some faith in herself and her old friend again.

'I had the most interesting conversation with Camille,' she stated, refraining for once from being blunt and jumping right in. She wanted to avoid startling him or setting him on his guard.

This garnered his attention at last. 'Camille?'

She nodded. 'She apologised to me.'

Jasper's eyes widened. 'Wonders never cease.'

'She also wants to help end the trouble between you and Milton.'

Jasper opened and closed his hands where

he held them behind his back. 'If she can manage it, then she's quite the miracle worker.'

'I said I'd help her.'

The faint humour in Jasper's eyes faded as he studied the carpet beneath his feet. 'That's very generous of you.'

'I'm not doing it for her, but for you, although I'm not sure I should.' She trembled as she met his eyes. Once she broached the subject, there would be no going back. She would face the truth, no matter the consequences, and live honestly with herself and Jasper at last. 'Who is Mrs Robillard and why are you sending her money?'

Jasper's neck tightened, her question striking him as hard as the news about Mr Robillard's death. Shame welled inside him, fuelled by his family's censure and the widening gulf between him and Jane. He studied her, a thousand excuses and ways to put her off colliding inside him, along with the temptation to answer her questions. He'd tried to keep his past from her, but she'd discovered something of it and, unlike her concern about the hell, he couldn't shrug her off or avoid answering her very direct question. The challenge for him to be honest with her at last tinged her steady gaze, along with numerous unspoken accusations.

He rubbed the back of his neck, for the first time understanding why Mr Robillard had done what he had. The shame of facing his mistakes had left him with little choice. Jasper forced his hand down to his side. No, Mr Robillard had been a coward, taking the easy way out and leaving others to deal with the consequences. Jasper wasn't so cruel or weak. Where Mr Robillard had thrown away all chance to redeem himself, Jasper could reclaim the trust he'd damaged, but in doing so he'd have to show her the darkest parts of himself, the ones even he shied from viewing.

She shifted on her feet and the diamonds around her neck sparkled in the candlelight. They reminded him of her bright eyes the night he'd showed her the hell and her willingness to join with him in all his ventures, good and bad. He'd shown her the basest parts of himself then and she hadn't run from him. It was time to trust she wouldn't again and remove at least one of the obstacles he'd put between them.

He turned to the portrait and his uncle's childish smile. 'Mr Robillard was a plantation

owner who used to gamble at the Savannah
hell. A week before the yellow fever really took
hold, he lost everything at the tables. The next
day, he shot himself, leaving behind a widow
with three children and no means of support.'

He could feel her ease beside him as she
took in what he said. 'So you send her money
to help her?'

'It's the least I can do.' He reached out and
took hold of the mantel, leaning hard against
his hand, hesitant to go on, but he had to.
Maybe if she could forgive him he could at
last forgive himself. 'I was there the night Mr
Robillard lost everything. I was the one who
extended him credit, allowing him to continue playing, deeper and deeper until there
was nothing left. I'm the one who drove him
to ruin and to kill himself.'

She slipped her hand in his free one, squeezing it gently instead of offering him useless
condolences or trying to convince him the
planter's death wasn't his fault. Her silent patience allowed him to continue.

'After Mr Robillard killed himself, I tried to
convince Uncle Patrick to return the plantation
to Mrs Robillard, but he wanted to be Lord of
the Manor and he wasn't going to let right or

wrong get in the way of his dream. It was the first time I realised how cold he really was. Afterwards, I stormed out of his house, ready to be through with him because he wasn't who I wanted to be and it wasn't how I wanted to live. I didn't see him again until a few weeks later when the fever was destroying the town and his maid came to tell me he was ill. I went back to his house to take care of him, expecting to find him more humble and repentant.'

'But he wasn't.'

Jasper shook his head. 'He blamed me for his illness. Said I could have made sure there was food in the house before there was none to be had, paid the nurse and the maid more money to stay, taken care of him the way he'd taken care of me during my illness the year before.'

'And still you stayed to see to him.'

He let go of her hand and tugged off the ruby ring. 'I couldn't let him die like a lonely dog, even if he did it while cursing me for betraying him and everything he'd ever done for me.' He turned the ring between his thumb and forefinger. 'After the quarantine ended, I returned the plantation to Mrs Robillard, but with everyone dead there was no one to work it and the land couldn't support her or her children. By helping her I'm trying to make up for what Uncle Patrick did to them and convince myself I'm nothing like him.'

She cupped his chin and turned his face to hers. 'You are nothing like him.'

'Aren't I?' He pulled away from her and pinched the ring between his fingers, pressing on it so hard he hoped the metal would bend and the stone would shatter. 'All the years I was with Uncle Patrick, I did everything I could to emulate him, wilfully refusing to see what he was or what it made me. Then, when I had the chance to walk away from it, I came home and went right back to being a hell owner.'

'Then give it up, now, tonight.' She laid a settling hand on his shoulder. 'Turn it all over to Mr Bronson and walk away. Stop allowing it to destroy you and us.'

He slid the ring back on his finger as a different fear smothered him. The image of a narrow and dark bedroom stinking with sickness and the thick southern air rose up to blot out Jane, while the weakness of hunger and the uncertainty of survival ripped at his gut once more. 'I can't.'

She plucked her hand off of him. 'What do you mean you can't? If it's tormenting you this much, you must.'

He glanced at the study door, remembering where they were and who might stumble in on him. He dropped his voice and stepped closer to her. 'You don't know what it is like to go without, Jane, to be starving and not be able to buy food, not to be able to escape the death and poverty around you. If I give up the hell and the club fails, we could lose everything.'

'It would never be so dire. We have our families to help us.'

'Not if they find out who I really am.' Chester Stilton's threat echoed in the silence. Uncle Patrick had concealed his real rottenness for years, but it hadn't lasted, and neither had the glamour and gain of the gambling room, or even Jasper's secrets. He touched her cheek, tracing the delicate line of it. 'I won't see you suffer the way I saw so many others suffer in Savannah.'

She covered his hand with hers. 'We're stronger than this, Jasper, strong enough to face anything thrown at us, but only if we do it together. The hell is pulling you away from me and it will continue to do so unless you give it up.'

'If we lose the money from the hell, we'd be poor in months.'

'We can live off my inheritance.'

'I won't ruin you.'

'It's worth the risk if it helps you.' She brushed a few strands of his hair off his forehead. 'Besides, I don't need fancy jewellery. I only need you.'

He stroked the line of her jaw with his thumb. She was offering him a real chance to be a better man and it increased his guilt. He should have confided in her sooner, drawn her closer instead of trying to keep her away. She was an exceptional woman who deserved respect and love.

Love.

He didn't say it, but it was there in his eyes as he gazed at her. He did love her and she loved him, but it wasn't enough. Not even the bonds of family had been able to stop Jasper and Uncle Patrick from falling out, especially when things had turned dire. If he and Jane lost everything, she'd blame him for their misfortune the way Uncle Patrick had blamed him for his. 'Don't you understand? I'm doing this for you.'

Jane lowered her hand and stepped back, a loss of hope to remind him of Mrs Robillard filling her eyes. 'You're choosing the hell and all the lies and troubles it entails over me and our marriage.'

'No, Jane, you're wrong.' He reached for her hand, but she jerked it back.

'I'm not. I've done all I can to establish the club, but in your mind it's already sunk before we've even opened it.'

'I didn't say that. I want out of the hell, but I can't see the men I employ plunged back into poverty, or risk losing my ability to help Mrs Robillard and her children, and I refuse to place our security or our futures in jeopardy.'

'And what future would that be? I've spent most of this evening fooling your family about our livelihood and about us, and you've gone days doing the same to me. You think I don't know you're keeping things about the hell from me, things that are bad enough to make you lose sleep and to ask for separate rooms?'

'I'm doing it to protect you.'

She raised a finger at him. 'Lie to yourself as much as you wish, but I told you the day we were betrothed I didn't want you to conceal things from me, or embarrass me the way Milton did with your secrets and deception, and yet that's all you've done. Do you know what it was like to stand before Mr Steed and sign the draft, not knowing if I was giving him permission to send money to your lover? I don't want to sit around wondering where the next unpleasant surprise will come from or when I'll be humiliated by you again. The Jasper I used to adore never would have done this to me.'

'You're right. He wouldn't have, but that Jasper is gone. He died in Savannah.' At one time, he'd wondered who would appear to destroy her faith in him and in the end it hadn't been anyone but himself. He'd been a fool to think he could return here and redeem himself, and now Jane saw him for the ruined and blighted man he really was. He waited for her to curse him, to rail against him, but she simply stared, as lost today as the morning of her parents' funeral. He'd comforted her then; he couldn't do it tonight because he was the one making her grieve.

The fast fall of footsteps in the hall punctuated the silence between them before Giles burst into the room. 'Jasper, we need you in the sitting room. It's an emergency.'

Without a word to Jane, Jasper followed Giles out of the room, cursing the interruption. The moment to draw Jane back to him, to find a way out of this mess, had slipped away, taking with it so many things. 'What's happening?'

'Someone Father refused for a loan is here. He's not happy and he won't leave.'

'Why aren't Father's men removing him?'

'Jacob went to fetch them.'

They turned down the hall and made for the sitting room. This wasn't the first time an irate man with a parcel of debts hanging over him had stormed into the house. It had been years and it made Jasper realise Jane was right about his father's lax security. He'd have to make sure it was changed. He wouldn't have his family threatened by anyone.

Then he and Giles turned the corner and Jasper stopped dead on the threshold. Across the sitting room stood Chester Stilton, his bloodshot eyes wider and more frantic than when he'd approached Jasper the other night. His clothes were wrinkled and the aroma of cheap wine hung about him.

'Ah, here's your prodigal son now.' Chester threw out his arms to Jasper, wavering on his feet. 'He can tell you I'm right. He can confirm everything I've told you.'

It was then Jasper noticed the deathly still

in the room. The secret he'd feared coming out for so long had been revealed. The evidence was in the faces of his family as they stared at him, especially his father. The disappointment bending his shoulders cut Jasper like a sabre. His mother stared at the rug under her feet, as stunned as the rest of the family by what she'd heard. Everything great and wonderful they'd believed about their son had crumbled and there was nothing Jasper could say or do to defend himself or build back what Chester had torn down.

'He runs a gambling hell in a warehouse near the Thames, enriching himself by ruining honest men, teasing and tempting them with the promise of riches while he plucks them dry,' Chester sneered.

Jasper's father's men, led by Jacob, pushed past him and Giles as they hustled into the room. Chester writhed against them as they grabbed him by the arms, his voice growing higher and more frantic when they dragged him toward the door. 'If you don't believe me, ask his little wife why her husband isn't warming her bed at night. She'll tell you I'm right.'

Jasper turned to discover Jane beside him, her humiliation as palpable as his father's. She didn't come close to him as she had in the study or slip her hand in his and offer her silent support. Instead she moved away and he didn't fault her for it. All she'd ever asked for was his care and friendship, and all he'd done was heap her with scorn and shame and drag her down with him in his family's eyes.

'Get him out of here,' his father commanded his men.

They pulled Chester to the door, bringing him close to Jasper.

'I told you I'd ruin you,' Chester spat out while he continued to fight the men, his feet dragging over the wood when they pulled him into the hallway. Chester's curses faded down the stairs and outside as the men dragged him away. Silence engulfed the room. Not even the coals dared to crackle as Chester's revelation continued to echo off the walls.

'Is it true?' A purple rage tinted his father's face as he fixed on Jasper.

The time for lies was over. It was time for the truth. Deep down in the places he hid from everyone except himself he was glad. 'It is.'

His sisters gasped along with their mother. Only Milton seemed to be enjoying the spectacle, grinning like a covetous player watching the Hazard wheel spin. Jasper ignored him and examined the rest of the family, some of whom, like Lily and Giles, avoided his gaze. Whatever esteem they'd held for him and everything they'd thought or imagined about him had been destroyed, just like he'd torn himself down in Jane's eyes.

'Did you know about this?' his father flung at Jane.

'I did.'

Jasper stepped between his father and Jane, trying to shield her from his mistakes the way he'd failed to do before. 'I made her promise not to tell you. I'm to blame for everything, not her.'

His father's fury whipped back to Jasper. 'How could you? How could you live in this house and deceive us like you did? We loved you, took care of you and all the while you were sneaking behind our backs to betray every value we hold dear.'

Jasper closed his eyes, hearing his uncle's accusations in his father's, except here he deserved them. All the things his father and Jane blamed him for doing, he'd done. He opened his eyes and faced him, ready to confess to everything, even if it destroyed for good their love and concern for him. He refused to hide his real self any longer. 'I didn't come home and do it. I did it in Savannah, too. This is what Uncle Patrick taught me, not the cotton trade. How to lure men into his gambling house and use their weaknesses to enrich myself. He hid it from you and taught me to do it, too.'

His father's jaw slackened and for the first time ever he seemed at a loss for words. His siblings exchanged surprised looks, but his mother's fallen face as she stared at the rug hit Jasper the hardest. Like her son, everything she'd believed about her favourite brother was being ruined. He didn't want to tear his family apart or cause any of them more hurt than he'd already inflicted, but he was done with lying. This was who he was and this was his past, and they must finally see it.

'If we'd known what we were truly sending you to, we never would have done it,' his mother offered in a soft voice, struggling like the others to take in the news.

'I don't blame you or Uncle Patrick. I blame myself. I could have written to you and come home when he told me his secret, but I didn't. I chose my path in Savannah and I chose it here.' He turned to Jane who nervously spun

the bracelet on her arm, as uncertain now
as she'd been the morning he'd almost broken their engagement. 'If I could go back and
change it all I would. I never wanted to hurt
anyone. I only wanted to ensure those I love,
especially you, were secure in a way that I
wasn't at the end in Savannah and I did it the
only way I knew how.'

Jane's fingers stilled on the bracelet, but she
said nothing. This wasn't how he'd wanted to
reveal his heart to her, but she had to know
he loved her. He always had. Maybe it would
help her not to regret so many things the way
he did. If he could undo it all he would, but it
was no longer possible.

Jasper shifted on his feet, eager to leave.
He couldn't stay here, not with everyone staring at him as though he were some ugly thing
masquerading as a husband and son. He'd vio-
lated the beliefs they held sacred and passed
himself off as an imposter. It was time for
him to go.

Jane stared at the empty doorway to the sitting room, avoiding the accusing and censorious looks of the Charton family. She couldn't
face them, especially Milton and the sneer

he tossed at her or the disappointment in Mr Charton's eyes. After all their years as friends of her family, everything they'd done for her, she'd rewarded their affection by betraying their trust. She deserved every bit of the shame covering her. Except it wasn't only her own actions garnering their condemnation, but Jasper's, too, and he was no longer here, having left her to face his family alone. He had said he loved her before he'd gone, but it didn't matter if he wasn't willing to remain beside her. Once again someone she loved had left her and she wasn't sure he would ever return.

Unable to stand the silence any longer, she held her head high and walked slowly out of the room. Tears blurred her vision and she hung on tight to the banister to stop from tripping down the stairs. In less than an hour her world had fallen to pieces and she was more alone than the morning the nurse had shooed her from her mother's sickroom.

She reached the bottom of the stairs and crossed the entry hall, wiping her eyes in an attempt to pull herself together in front of Alton, who waited beside the open door. The tears wouldn't stop and no matter how tall she stood, the old butler she used to accept peppermints from continued to watch her with a mixture of pity and disapproval, and it tore at her.

Outside, she wrapped her arms around her against the chill, unwilling to go back inside for her wrap. She approached the carriage with slow steps, hesitant to go home and sit alone while all of her and Jasper's mistakes haunted her. She was tired of being alone and wouldn't do it any more. There was only one place she could go, to the one person who'd never walked away from her, even when she'd done her best to push him away.

Chapter Thirteen

'Jane?' Philip stood behind the butler as Jane stepped through his door, the front of her dress spotted with tears. 'What's wrong?'

'Jasper's gone,' she choked out. 'And everything is a mess.'

Philip opened his arms and she flung herself into them and began to weep into his coat. He rubbed her back while he led her across the foyer and into the sitting room where Laura joined them, offering her embraces along with Philip's. They didn't press her to speak, but waited patiently while she cried until Laura had to excuse herself to see to the children.

Then at last Jane sat back and dried her eyes with Philip's handkerchief and told him what had happened. Philip didn't shake his head in disappointment or greet her confessions with the heartbroken disbelief Mr Charton had offered. He simply listened while she explained about the hell, their fights, her visit to Mrs Hale and Chester Stilton's scene at the Chartons, and how Jasper had left them afterwards.

'He isn't going to come back to me, I'm sure of it. He's going to leave me like so many others have, like I deserve for what I did to Mother and Father.'

Philip frowned, perplexed. 'What did you do?'

'I brought the fever into the house by disobeying them.' Jane hiccupped. 'If I hadn't, they might still be alive.'

Philip shifted on the sofa to face her. 'You don't believe it's your fault they died, do you?'

The dark secret she'd carried for years demanded she remain silent, but she was tired of acting like one person to shield the other wounded one beneath, or pretending like Jasper to be someone she was not. 'I was the one who went to the fair with Jasper and Milton because I wanted to see the elephant, despite Mother telling me not to go. I was the one who brought the fever into the house and gave it to her and Father. I'm the one who caused them to die. I'm sure everything I've had to endure these last few years is a punishment for what I did.'

Tears welled in her eyes again and the years of blame pressing down on her were made worse by tonight and the heartache of losing Jasper.

Philip laid his hands on her shoulders and met her eyes. 'It wasn't you who got them sick. It was Father. He'd been in St Giles to collect a debt, but the man who owed him was suffering with a fever. A number of the people in his building were, but no one had said anything for fear the authorities would send them to the pest house or quarantine their homes. As soon as Father realised how sick the man was, he forgave the debt and left. His charity wasn't enough to stop him from contacting the illness, or giving it to Mother.'

'But my cold?'

'It was an unfortunate coincidence you were sick around the same time.'

Jane stared at the vines in the carpet beneath her feat, stunned by what she was hearing. Her disobedience hadn't killed her parents, it had been something far beyond her control. It didn't seem possible and yet it was. 'I never knew.'

'I never thought to tell you because I didn't realise you blamed yourself for what happened.'

'I never told you or anyone because I was too ashamed, as I was too ashamed to admit the troubles between Jasper and me.'

'Laura and I guessed as much.'

Of course he did, but for the first time it didn't anger her. 'You knew about Jasper's gaming hell, too, didn't you?'

'Yes,' he answered without hesitation or apology. 'I've vetted every man who's ever come to me for a loan, I did doubly so for the one who wanted your hand. I discovered it then.'

'Yet you still let me marry him. Why?'

Philip rested his hands on his knees. 'Do you remember how, after Mother and Father died, you wouldn't leave my side?'

She nodded. 'I was afraid I'd lose you, too.'

'I feared the same thing.'

'You?' She gaped up at him. 'You're never afraid!'

'I am, more than I'm sometimes willing to admit.' He placed his arm around her and drew her into the crook of his shoulder. 'You were so precious to me. You always have been, since I first saw you wrapped in Mother's white shawl when I was sixteen. When they left us, I was terrified of failing you as a guardian.'

She slipped her arms around her brother's waist and held him tight. 'You've never failed me.'

He hugged her closer. 'Do you remember, in the weeks after the funeral, how Jasper used to come here every day asking you to play with him?'

'I do.'

'One day, he came by when you were asleep on the sofa in my office. When I met him on the portico, he asked again if you could come out. I explained how it might be some time before you'd be ready to play and it would be best if he didn't return until then. Do you know what he said to me?'

'No.' She sat back, amazed. She'd never heard this story.

'He said he knew you were sad and afraid, but he was still going to come every day because he didn't want you to be lonely. He wanted you to know he was here for you and would be until you were ready to meet him again. I admired how, at eight years old, he possessed enough insight into what you were facing to be so persistent, and was grateful he kept coming back until the day you were finally ready to leave my side. It's why I let the two of you get away with half the things you did when you were younger. I was confident he'd watch out for you and keep you safe.'

Tears slipped down Jane's face as she remembered the morning Jasper had come here again and she'd finally been able to meet him in the garden, to smile and play for the first time in weeks.

'He reminded me of our conversation the day you two were betrothed,' Philip continued. 'He told me you were lonely again and needed him, and if I didn't agree to the betrothal, he'd come back every day until I did. I realised then, despite his secret activities, and whatever he was facing from Savannah, together the two of you could handle them all.'

Jane wiped the tears off her face. 'But we haven't.'

'You will.' Philip took her hands in his. 'You'll find a way.'

Jane studied her brother's long fingers entwined with hers, struggling to take in everything he'd said. For all these years she'd been mistaken about so many things, including herself. If she'd had the courage to speak about it sooner, she might have viewed the events of her life, herself and even Jasper differently. She let go of his hands and stared at the large diamond in her ring, turning it back and forth to catch the rainbows inside the stone.

Philip was right, Jasper had always cared for her as she'd cared for him. His refusal to give up the hell hadn't been about choosing it over her, but his desire to look out for her as he'd always done and to see to the welfare of his employees and the widow he felt he'd wronged. Even when they'd faced his family he'd done all he could to protect her, to step between her and them and take the blame for what was happening. Then he'd said he loved her and still walked away. It left her as confused about what to do as the day she'd visited Mrs Hale.

Mrs Hale.

'She was right,' Jane murmured.

'Who was right?'

'Mrs Hale. She said I knew best how to help Jasper and I do. He's the one hurting this time and he needs me to come back for him as often as it takes to make him see he is a good man.' Like Jane, Jasper believed he wasn't worthy of love because of his past. It was time to prove he was wrong.

* * *

Jasper climbed up the stairs of the warehouse, his hand shaking as he reached into his pocket to fish out the keys to his office. He stopped in the darkness, not wanting to fumble for the metal like some drunk off his liquor. He pressed his hands against the rough wood of the wall. He'd walked the streets for hours, trying to settle himself before he'd come here, reluctant to face that this was all he had left and all he was. For a while he'd begun to believe he might be more than ruined men, cards and bets. Jane had helped him imagine it, but not even her love had been enough to overcome his past or his flaws. They'd flooded over him like a storm wave and he hadn't been able to stop it.

The memory of his father's disgust when the truth had come out made him screw his eyes shut. The family who'd rushed to embrace him when he'd stepped out of the carriage from Portsmouth, gaunt and stinking of fever, had recoiled from him tonight. It was like the morning he'd set sail for America when he'd believed he'd been banished from everyone he'd ever loved, flung out of the family like some unwanted coat. They'd been right to send him away, to distance themselves from the weakness inside him. It had consumed everything good and wonderful in his life, including Jane.

I should go back to her and try to make things right. He dropped down one step, ready to leave the darkness of the gaming house for the light she offered, then stopped. After the way he'd treated her, he couldn't hope to regain her heart. He'd chosen this over her and didn't deserve her forgiveness or her love.

A strange quiet met him as he trudged down the hallway. The click of chips and the clink of the ball in the Hazard wheel were gone along with the cadence of voices punctuated by laughter. The door to the gambling room stood open.

Jasper stared inside the room in disbelief. It was empty except for Mr Bronson, who sat at a table turning a chip over and over in his fingers. Jasper hadn't seen him this dejected since word had reached him from outside the city of his father's passing. Around him, cards lay scattered on the baize, chips discarded and chairs at haphazard angles to the tables.

'What happened?' Jasper's question broke

the silence and halted the steady turning of the chip in Mr Bronson's fingers.

Mr Bronson tossed the chip aside and rose, surveying the empty room. 'Lord Fenton came barging in here with the constable. Demanded we shut down. I challenged him to show me where in the statute it said what we're doing is illegal. When neither his lordship nor the constable could cite the bill, they left. But so did all of our clients. None of them wanted to find himself in gaol or in the newspapers. After the dust up, they aren't likely to return.'

Jasper rested his hands on the back of a chair and leaned hard on his arms. Months of striving to bring this together, to create something for himself, while balancing all of the many lies he'd created to allow it to flourish, had all been ruined. Along with it went the livelihoods of his dealers and footmen and the future support for Mrs Robillard, and especially Jane. He'd come here because he'd believed this was all he had left and even this had been ripped from him.

'I'll open the club as soon as I can and I'll employ the dealers and footmen there. You'll have a place there, too.' He'd already wounded his own family. He wouldn't see others suffer or children starve because of him.

'I can't. These merchants of yours will recognise me from here and they'll avoid me and anything connected with me like the plague. Luckily for you, few people can connect you to this place.'

Jasper dropped into a chair, his belief in the club helping him or anyone else fading. 'They will soon enough.'

Jasper told him what had happened at his parents' house, his voice echoing off the wooden walls and through the empty room. 'In less than one night I've managed to lose everything.'

'You still have your wife and the two of you are clever enough to come out of this some way.'

'She isn't likely to help me, not after what I've done.' He tapped the green baize as he looked around at the messy room.

Mr Bronson hauled himself up, and dropped a wide hand on Jasper's shoulder. 'She didn't look down on me when we met, or scold me for leading you astray. She took me for who I am and didn't judge me for it. Over the last few weeks, I've seen you come here with more enthusiasm for being rid of this place than you ever had for owning it. She helped bring about this change in you. She can help you, if you let her.'

Mr Bronson patted his shoulder, then wandered out of the room, leaving Jasper alone.

Jasper studied the paintings in their gilded frames, his insurance against ruin, but they meant little. It was all money and nothing more, as worthless to his soul as it had been to buying food in Savannah. Jane had been the one thing of value he'd possessed and he'd lost her.

'Jasper?'

Jasper stood and whirled to find Jane standing in the gaming room doorway, as welcome a sight as the ship bobbing in the harbour in Savannah ready to take him to England. 'Jane, what are you doing here?'

'I came to see you. You're my husband and if you think I'm going to allow you to push me out of your life, then you are very much mistaken.' She wound through the tables to reach him, as tenacious as on the afternoon she'd slipped into his bedroom. This was the Jane he remembered and had first fallen in love with, not the wounded one in his parents' house, the one he'd never wanted to hurt. 'It's time for all the guilt and blame to end, for both of us.'

'There is no both of us, just me and what I did.'

'No, for years I believed everything terrible that happened to me was because I deserved it for making my parents sick. It tore me up inside until I was convinced I wasn't worthy of love. I was wrong about it and so are you.'

'I have done bad things.'

'And they end tonight.'

'It doesn't change my past or my breaking my promise to you. You wanted to be cherished and not to be humiliated, and I failed to do both.'

'I forgive you, Jasper. Now it's time to forgive yourself.' She shifted closer to him, her scent pushing aside the stale odour of pipes and wine. She laid her hands on his shoulders, her touch light and powerful all at once. 'I love you, Jasper, I always have and I always will, no matter what.'

He didn't move back or try to silence her. Every lie he'd ever told, each failing he'd endured had been revealed and still Jane wanted him. Nothing, not his own mistakes or anyone's wickedness, had stolen her from him. He'd been searching for evidence of his goodness and it had been here before him all along in her. He encircled her waist with his arms, bringing her as close to his body as she was to his soul. 'I love you, Jane, and I have for years.'

'I know.' She rose up on her toes and pressed her lips to his.

In the circle of her embrace the fear of discovery and ruin he'd carried for so long at last lost their hold over him and nothing remained except the mutual love between them. Nothing could take this away. He was worthy of her and her heart and all the happiness it entailed. The warehouse could be burning down around them and he wouldn't care. The elation inside him was too great. She was peace and he had her.

He broke from her kiss and pressed his forehead to hers. They stood in silence together, their breaths mingling like their hearts. Only one dark spot remained. 'What will we do about our exile from the Charton family?'

'I think it will be a temporary one.' Jane playfully fingered the buttonhole of his coat, beaming brighter than she had at the altar.

'You think so?'

'If they forgave your brother, I'm sure they can forgive you.'

'Even my father?'

'Haven't you realised by now, where his children are concerned, he's all bluster and no bite? Your mother will bring him around. She always does.'

It might be a while before they were invited to dinner again, but with Jane in his arms, he could believe the invitation would eventually come. Until then, he would do all he could to make himself an honest man worthy of their affection and Jane's.

'Perhaps another addition to the Charton clan would help ease the way,' he enticed, nuzzling Jane's neck, her skin as luscious as his first taste of food after the quarantine had ended.

'Are you sure it's wise, given the uncertainty of our income?'

'I don't care. I won't ever put off anything again because I'm concerned or worried.'

She tilted back her head, her eyes wide with her passion for him. 'Then I'm certainly willing to employ such a persuasive a tactic.'

'Then we will start at once.' He pressed his

lips to hers and she wrapped her arms around his neck. He had her heart, her life and her future and they were the only things he needed.

Chapter Fourteen

Johnson opened the door and to Jasper's surprise his mother entered. He braced himself, not having expected to see her so soon. In the three days since the notorious dinner party he'd heard from no other Charton, not even Jacob or Giles, who he'd expected to sneak over here in search of details about the hell and Jasper's formerly seedy existence. Instead, it had been Jasper and Jane alone in the house with no visitors, spending every day and even more pleasurable nights together, rebuilding the intimacy they'd almost lost.

Behind him on the stairs, Jane stopped, sliding her hand in his as his mother approached them.

'We must speak.' She marched into the sitting room, expecting them to follow.

Jasper exchanged a wary look with Jane, then they strode into the sitting room together, ready to face whatever his mother had in store for them.

She sat down in a wide bergère chair and motioned for them to take the facing claw-footed sofa. They sat down together side by side, exchanging sly looks and trying not to smile like naughty children who'd been caught out.

'To what do we owe the pleasure of this visit, Mother?' Jasper asked through a restrained smile.

It was then his mother's stern expression cracked a little about the eyes, and a twitch of amusement lifted one side of her mouth. 'I wish to discuss with you the events of the other night.'

Jasper squeezed Jane's hand tight, humility replacing his humour. 'I'm sorry for what I did. I never meant to hurt anyone, or deceive you, or change your views of Uncle Patrick.'

'Yes, well, that was a shock. But I already knew about the hell.' His mother shifted her shoulders with, if he was not mistaken, a touch of guilt. 'I didn't think your father would find out about it in such a dramatic fashion.'

'You knew?' He and Jane gaped at each other. It wasn't possible.

'Of course I did. I didn't raise seven children, four of whom are boys, and not learn to detect when something suspicious is taking place. It's how I saved most of my china from being broken when you were younger.'

'How did you find out?' His mother wasn't one to frequent questionable establishments.

'After your first month home, when you began to look better, I started questioning your tall tales about where you went at night, so I had Giles and Jacob follow you to see where you went and learn what was going on.'

'They knew, too?' Jane gasped.

'Yes.' She touched one finger to her chin and peered up at the ceiling. 'Jasper's father and Milton might have been the only ones who didn't know, which surprises me given how poorly everyone in this family holds on to secrets.'

It explained Olivia's boldness about whist at the dinner. 'Mother, I never took you to be so clever.'

'Where do you think you got your talent from?' She settled her wrap around her arm with a sniff of pride.

'Apparently.'

'But I'm here to discuss your future. How soon until your club is ready to be opened?'

'My wife knows best.' Jasper motioned to Jane. 'She's the one who's been managing it.'

'In a day or two if we want,' Jane answered, her pride evident in the quickness of her response and her raised chin.

'Good, then you must open it at once.'

Jasper tapped his boots against the floor. 'Men aren't likely to patronise it if they discover I was the hell owner and I'm sure Chester Stilton has told everyone he knows by now.'

The problem was one of the many things he and Jane had discussed over the last three days, but so far they'd reached no solution. They still owned the building and everything in it, and they had to find a way to make it turn a profit, and employ Mr Bronson, as well as all the old footmen and dealers.

'No one will find out,' his mother proclaimed, quite pleased with herself. 'I met with Mr Rathbone, who spoke to the elder Mr Stilton and explained the risk to his business if you do not maintain your contract with him due to his son's unfortunate outburst. Mr Stilton is sending Chester to the Continent, mostly to escape his creditors since he refuses to pay his boy's debt. The truth about the hell's ownership will go with him. Even if people whisper about it, I think it will help you as much as Mrs Greenwood's couch and china.'

Jasper stared at his mother in disbelief. He'd expected his entire family to shun him, but instead they were doing all they could to help him. 'Is there anything about our lives you aren't aware of?' Jasper laughed.

'Heavens, dear, do you think I sit at home embroidering all day?'

'I'm glad to learn you don't.' He'd have to employ his mother to recruit clients. She was a master of organisation.

'What about Mr Charton?' Jane hazarded, fingering her wedding ring. 'He can't be happy with us.'

'He wasn't, but I brought him around by reminding him of how we forgave Milton and by pointing out if he doesn't forgive and help Jasper, then Jasper might return to gambling.'

'I never would,' Jasper stated with force and his mother nodded.

'I imagined as much, but the threat was enough to convince your father. Your brother might take a little more time, but I imagine as soon as your club is successful and he sees more to gain in being your brother again instead of your rival, things between you will be much better.'

'I hope so.' He and Milton would never be as close as they'd been as children, but that wasn't entirely Jasper's fault. Jasper took Jane's hand again, remembering her desire to help him and Milton reach some reconciliation. If anyone could find a way to make it happen, it was her.

'I never realised your mother was so cunning,' Jane said with a laugh once the door was closed and Mrs Charton was on her way home. 'I wonder if she's aware of the gilded bed upstairs and how long it will be before your sisters barge in here to view it, then go home and demand ones of their own.'

'There isn't another like it.' He slipped his arm around her waist and pulled her close. She pressed her hands to his chest, his heart beating beneath her palms in time to hers. 'It's an original, like you.'

Jane tilted her head back and savoured Jasper lips on hers. She loved him and he loved her, and all their plans for the club and their life together would unfold just as they'd dreamed.

This was exactly how she'd imagined marriage would be.

* * * * *

*If you enjoyed this book
make sure you read these linked stories
by Georgie Lee, featuring characters who
appear in THE SECRET MARRIAGE PACT*

*A DEBT PAID IN MARRIAGE
A TOO CONVENIENT MARRIAGE*

*And don't miss these other great reads
by the same author:*

*THE CINDERELLA GOVERNESS
MISS MARIANNE'S DISGRACE
THE CAPTAIN'S FROZEN DREAM*

MILLS & BOON®
are delighted to support
World Book Night

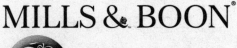

MILLS & BOON®

AWAKEN THE ROMANCE OF THE PAST

A sneak peek at next month's titles...

In stores from 1st June 2017:

- **The Debutante's Daring Proposal** – Annie Burrows
- **The Convenient Felstone Marriage** – Jenni Fletcher
- **An Unexpected Countess** – Laurie Benson
- **Claiming His Highland Bride** – Terri Brisbin
- **Marrying the Rebellious Miss** – Bronwyn Scott

0517/04

MILLS & BOON®

EXCLUSIVE EXTRACT

Desperation forces Georgiana Wickford to
propose to her estranged childhood friend.
The Earl of Ashenden swore he'd never wed,
but the unconventional debutante soon tempts
him in ways he never expected!

Read on for a sneak preview of
THE DEBUTANTE'S DARING PROPOSAL

Georgiana couldn't really believe that his attitude could
still hurt so much. Not after all the times he'd pretended
he couldn't even see her, when she'd been standing
practically under his nose. She really ought to be immune
to his disdain by now.

'Did you have something in particular to ask me,'
Edmund asked in a bored tone, 'or should I take my
dog, and return to Fontenay Court?'

'You know very well I have something of great importance to ask you,' she retorted, finally reaching the end
of her tether as she straightened up, 'or I wouldn't have
sent you that note.'

'And are you going to tell me what it is anytime
soon?' He pulled his watch from his waistcoat pocket
and looked down at it. 'Only, I have a great many
pressing matters to attend to.'

She sucked in a deep breath. 'I do beg your pardon,
my lord,' she said, dipping into the best curtsey she

could manage with a dog squirming round her ankles and her riding habit still looped over one arm. 'Thank you so much for sparing me a few minutes of your valuable time,' she added, through gritted teeth.

'Not at all.' He made one of those graceful, languid gestures with his hand that indicated *noblesse oblige*. 'Though I should, of course, appreciate it if you would make it quick.'

Make it quick? Make it quick! Four days she'd been waiting for him to show up, four days he'd kept her in an agony of suspense, and now he was here, he was making it clear he wanted the meeting to be as brief as possible so he could get back to where he belonged. In his stuffy house, with his stuffy servants, and his stuffy lifestyle.

Just once, she'd like to shake him out of that horrid, contemptuous, self-satisfied attitude of his towards the rest of the world. And make him experience a genuine, human emotion. No matter what.

'Very well.' She'd say what she'd come to say, without preamble. Which would at least give her the pleasure of shocking him almost as much as if she really were to throw her boot at him.

'If you must know, I want you to marry me.'